"When I finished reading the tenth page of Heart of Earth I knew the novel was going to take me on a sci-fi adventure I would remember and talk about... I highly recommend this novel for anyone who is looking to satisfy their cravings for good sci-fi or just plain good reading. Five Stars!"

— Sherrod M. Wall (Author, *From Heaven to Earth*) (on *Heart of Earth*)

"It's infused with subtle humor.... I actually got a clutch in my throat towards the end.... Really good, stand-alone YA sci-fi with potential for sequels. Recommended!"

— K. A. Krisko (Author, *Stolen*) (on *Heart of Earth*)

THE CHANGING HEARTS OF IXDAHAN DAHEREK

BOOK TWO

HEART OF MYSTERY

Mark Laporta

MARK LAPORTA

THE CHANGING HEARTS OF IXDAHAN DAHEREK

BOOK TWO

HEART OF MYSTERY

MARK LAPORTA, author of *HEART OF EARTH*, the first book in Ixdahan's saga, looks forward to a time when the values of friendship and social responsibility are the first things that come to mind when we say "success." With his feet in the stars and his head on the ground, he has learned to see an upside-down world as normal. A fan of the creative and performing arts, language, science and utterly stupid puns, he knows all roads lead to roam.

THE CHANGING HEARTS OF IXDAHAN DAHEREK

Book Two

Heart of Mystery

Chickadee Prince Books
New York

For Janet and Alex

CHAPTER 1

"I'm *telling* you," said an insistent voice, "they developed it on their own!"

"Do you hear yourself?" asked an irritable voice. "The Vrukaari. Acquired. Magclad Tech. Without. Stealing It."

"Saw the prototype myself," said the insistent voice. "Made the blast from a particle rifle fan out like the tailfins of a Cahlneera blowfish."

"No need for vulgarity," said the irritable voice, with a slight tremor.

"You think that's gross," the insistent voice continued, "how about this? The cladding was dense enough to act as the hull of a starspanner."

"You saw *that*?" asked the irritable voice, which belonged to Chaldraheen Ishialdrol, Group Leader, Intergalactic Security, Khaltreaballoorn Sector.

And so the excited mentallic conversation continued, across the 4.25 light years separating Snaldrialoor and Vrukaar Prime, until the insistent voice of FieldOp 2nd Class Ixdahan Daherek faded out into the emptiness of space-time.

Ixdahan shook his head. It was almost a year since his return from exile on Earth. Here he had defeated Lieutenant Colonel Relsheesharb Yarrow, and he still had to fight hard to be heard. Really. His victory *should* have been enough to commute his sentence for treason. Did the classified files he sold Ambassador Ghaar lead straight to the invasion of Earth? Totally beside the point.

Ixdahan ground his teeth.

"Ungrateful *pilaarni*," he mumbled. For it was only the influence of Pertahru, Ixdahan's father and Snaldrialoor's most distinguished diplomat, that had earned him this sliver of mercy: No jail time, in exchange for service in the Snaldrialooran Security Agency, referred to across the Seven Known Galaxies as the SSA.

Good thing no one on the Homeworld believed the "Earth creatures" had helped him stop the Vrukaari invasion, he realized. The more he captured the world's imagination as a hero acting alone, the higher his standing might rise. That is, if he could ever live down betraying his people.

Of course, cousin Jalgren Altrollinhar, Professor of Transgenomics at Lohaar University, also deserved some credit. He'd outlined the attack strategy Ixdahan had launched with his human friends, Lena, Vance and Callie Ann. But the last thing cousin Jalgren needed was a reputation for aiding intergalactic criminals.

And knocking down Ixdahan's heroic myth another notch was the last minute assist he'd received from Captain Dahaleen Altriavahn, the decorated commander of the Snaldrialooran starspanner, *Kryldria Valaarn.*

Those limitations aside, he knew he'd still been given a rare gift: The chance to show the universe he was just as brave as he was stupid, an opportunity most people would kill for.

"So glad that's over," said Ixdahan.

A wave of relief washed over him as he stepped out onto the gaudy main plaza of Gitraarinahol, the capital city of Vrukaar Prime. That era of his life had passed and it was time now to make his rounds, undercover, as a Deputy Building Inspector.

It was also time to admit, as he had every day since emerging from the transmog chamber on an SSA starspanner, how disgusting it was to inhabit a Vrukaari body. Between its blobby torso, stubby limbs and saggy, slimy skin, Ixdahan's transmogged body was more unbearable than any prison cell he could imagine.

"Like living inside a rotting double-cheese pizza," he said to his robot assistant, 17/Chaarnactral.

The AI's composite surface glinted slightly in the pale red light of Vrukaar Prime's dwarf star.

"So you have told me," said 17/Chaarnactral. "Though I find no mention of *pizza* or *cheese* on the Galactic Array."

"Skip it," said Ixdahan. "Just tell me where-to next."

It hardly mattered: His building inspections were as routine as they were futile. The Vrukaari real estate industry was so corrupt, he could cite a property owner with 100 major violations and no action would be taken — with the possible exception of bribery.

Besides, his real job was being the eyes and ears of the SSA in this sector of the city. His mission? To sniff out irregularities and alert Group Leader Ishialdrol to any unusual activity.

Up until last night, Ixdahan's posting had been as uneventful as the life cycle of a Jubthorian mud worm. He'd kept his senses open, filed his field reports and even made an effort to take part in Vrukaari society.

He'd made friends, turned up at the holotheaters and made a point of being seen out on the town with, occasionally, a female on his arm.

Of course, the thought of making out, as one slab of rotting double cheese pizza to another, didn't exactly thrill him. But after nearly a year of living each day as a Vrukaari, with Vrukaari senses and a Vrukaari set of appetites, he sometime found the prospect somewhat … mandatory.

"You're doing it again," said 17/Chaarnactral.

"Doing what?" asked Ixdahan. As they exited the plaza and turned right onto Ghaltraxaan Boulevard, Ixdahan looked at the robot out of the corner of his eye.

"Shuddering," said 17/Chaarnactral. "This is not a high probability behavior among your adopted people and will make you stand out."

Ixdahan gazed up at the squat, brassy, ovoid buildings that passed for office towers in this city.

"I'll keep that in mind," he grunted. "Are we almost there?"

Lena. Lena Gabrilowicz, the Earth girl who had helped him take down the Vrukaari strike force leader: Ixdahan knew she would understand.

She knew what a double cheese pizza was. *She* also knew what the expression "totally gross" meant, in a way neither his haughty Snaldrialooran countrymen nor the slime-drooling idiots he dealt with on Vrukaar Prime could grasp.

She was, in fact, the one person who understood *anything* about him. That was why, naturally, she lived thousands of parsecs away on a planet in the Remote Regions.

Still, his feelings were mixed on the subject of where he'd rather be.

As unpleasant as his life was on Vrukaar Prime, at least he was dealing with a mentallic people who were aware of the larger universe. Like it or not, it was easier to be himself in this galaxy, simply because the dominant cultures were way more similar to the world he'd grown up with. And yet, on Earth, he'd found....

But, OK, this was no time to relive the past. If he were ever to return to a normal life on the Homeworld, he'd have to *deliver*. And that's why he'd been so excited to tell Group Leader Ishialdrol about the demonstration he'd seen last night at Shelsgriadahr University.

It was also why he was now so depressed that his report generated no enthusiasm.

"We'll look into it, FieldOp Daherek," Ishialdrol had said. "Good work, nice initiative. But we at the Bureau don't have the luxury of jumping to conclusions. Besides, none of our other operatives in Vrukaari space have reported anything similar.

"But…." Ixdahan sputtered.

"They're good people, Son, with a lot more field experience than you, and they can't corroborate your story. So it's possible your reading of the data is … imprecise. See my problem here? But go ahead, gather more evidence and we'll see where it leads."

At that rate, Ixdahan knew, the Vrukaari could develop The Ultimate Weapon before "the Bureau" so much as raised an eyebrow. Not that any of the blue-gray, eight-tentacled, liquid- methane-breathing Snaldrialooran security operatives actually had eyebrows.

"Raising an eyebrow," was an Earth expression from one of its many languages, an expression like countless others that had permanently altered his view of the universe.

"This way," said 17/Chaarnactral. "You're on."

And so Ixdahan proceeded through the lobby of a large metropolitan hotel, smack in the middle of town. In spite of himself, his six eyes snapped up to hotel's glittering, high-vaulted ceiling. There he saw thousands of brightly lit, solid crystal facets, suspended from an intricate latticework of chrome-plated steel.

All the while, glimmering reflections from the ceiling splashed onto the top of the lobby's walls, which were faced in pure white Ybitrian marble and draped in long, sweeping arcs by the satiny sheen of thick lavender bunting. Yet when Ixdahan's exhausted eyes turned away from the ceiling, they found no rest in the hypnotic patterns of gold thread woven into the lobby's blood red carpeting.

Ironically, with so many distractions, he nearly missed the iridescent royal blue banners — which announced the vast intergalactic trade show already underway in the hotel's main conference rooms:

TECHNOLOGY FRONTIERS:
THE GREAT LEAP FORWARD 7615

"Have to see this," he told himself. There'd never be a better opportunity to prove how fast the Vrukaari were advancing.

"Give me a minute," he told the robot. "Why don't you start the inspection without me?"

"You know that's against protocol," said 17/Chaarnactral. "You also know what happened the last time you ordered me to violate it."

"Right," said Ixdahan. His mind filled with a vivid memory of the robot's recent breakdown, a sight too pathetic to be witnessed ever again. Who would have thought an AI could wet itself?

Resigned to patience, Ixdahan made a show of inspecting the hotel's heating and fluid systems. He cited a series of violations and recommended cost-effective ways to bring the massive hotel complex into compliance with local, regional, planetary and interstellar code.

"I see the Deputy Inspector is an optimist," said the hotel's concierge to the dour building manager, who stood a few feet to the left of her desk.

"An endearing trait in the young, don't you agree?" she asked. But if the building manager agreed, it didn't show up in her scowl.

"We'll appeal these outrageous allegations, you realize," she said.

Ixdahan struggled to keep from laughing as the spiteful female flared the nostrils on all five of her noses.

"As you wish," he said. One thing the Group Leader had stressed throughout his training was the need to avoid conflict.

"Whatever you do," Ishialdrol had warned, "don't stand out."

"A little young to be issuing orders, aren't you?" snarled the building manager.

"Orders?" said Ixdahan. "No, no ... merely suggestions. Everything's open to interpretation. What I see as a violation, the Review Board may see as the highest level of compliance with the law. Wiser minds than mine will make the final ruling."

The building manager glanced at the concierge, snarled again and hustled out of the concierge's office without a hint of goodbye.

"Nice work," said the concierge. "You obviously did a little research before coming over."

Ixdahan squinted at the slightly stooped female.

"What do you mean?" he asked.

"Oh, come on," the concierge snickered. "Like anybody from the Inspector's office would be so agreeable to a building manager who *wasn't* the beloved daughter of Aalthrashrintorb Leek."

"Oh that," said Ixdahan. "That's ... common knowledge."

"Whatever," said the concierge. "All I know is, it usually takes a full half hour to shut her up. For that, I'm grateful."

Ixdahan felt his temperature rise.

"Grateful enough to give me a pass to the technology trade show?" he asked.

"That and a free dinner at the Neutrino Lounge," said the concierge. "You a big eater?"

Ixdahan nodded to 17/Chaarnactral to retrieve his ticket and the dinner coupon, backed away from the concierge's desk and headed for the entrance to the trade show. 17/Chaarnactral rolled after him.

"What about your other appointments?" it asked.

"Reschedule them," said Ixdahan. "It's not as if anyone's dying to see me. Now come on, I'll need you in full recording mode."

The burnt-orange robot stopped short.

"You don't have to say that," it said.

"What?" said Ixdahan.

"You don't have to *constantly* issue commands that are 100 percent congruent with standard protocol," said the AI. And with that, it collapsed to the floor like a 5-year-old on its way to a major meltdown.

"But," said Ixdahan.

"I'm a fully functional, 17-class, artificial intelligence!" the robot shrieked. "You don't need to talk to me like I was the ... the ... navigation system on a Ybitrian garbage scow."

"*Sacred Mentality of the Dark Voids,*" thought Ixdahan, "it's happening again." Ixdahan put his right hand on the robot's left shoulder. He knew he had to act fast, before 17/Chaarnactral's erratic behavior got them kicked out of the hotel,

"Reboot," said Ixdahan, "and then I'll buy you a nice, new energy cube at the shopping mall."

17/Chaarnactral looked up into Ixdahan's eyes like a cocker spaniel begging for a Milk Bone.

"The one with the memory upgrade?" it said.

"Yes," said Ixdahan. "Ready to reboot now?"

Ixdahan sighed as 17/Chaarnactral began cycling through its reboot process. Over a period of 10 Earth minutes, more indicator lights than he could count blinked on and off in a dizzying pattern.

"Rebooting," said Ixdahan to a pair of overly curious passersby. This, he had to say, hardly qualified as Not Standing Out. But what was he supposed to do when Headquarters continually denied his request for a replacement? Moons of Dahltriala'ahn! They refused to send a repair tech.

"Too conspicuous," the Group Leader had said. "And don't take it to a local technician. This is supposed to be a Vrukaari model. One look at its insides and anyone worth their crafts worker's license will know it's Snaldrialooran. Besides, how bad could it be?"

"This bad," said Ixdahan under his breath.

At last, his robotic assistant regained whatever passed for consciousness in an artificial intelligence. His soul weary, he patted the advanced-design carbon nano-tube construct on the back.

"Come on," he said, "Let's go get you that battery, OK?"

"Not necessary," said 17/Chaarnactral. "Sensors indicate current energy pods at full capacity. Ready to proceed as per protocol."

It was always this way after a reboot. Every acquired personality nexus had been wiped away. For the next few hours, the robot would operate strictly within the narrow limits of its original programming. At the moment, Ixdahan could expect nothing from his sidekick but objective assessment and rational process.

The problems would emerge later, due to the robot's faulty firewall, Ixdahan assumed. During the course of the day, shreds of the personality nexus from every other AI it interacted with got spliced together at random until a new, erratic personality emerged. The result was a mentality as emotionally unpredictable as the high school kids Ixdahan had met on Earth.

Come to think of it, Ixdahan wondered, could his own vivid memories of Earth be seeping into the mind of the AI, subtly warping its metadigital pathways until…? Well, he had to admit it was possible. But the funny thing was, despite everything, he also missed the AI's quirky side, nano warts and all.

As he neared the entrance to the trade show, with 17/Chaarnactral's meltdown behind him, Ixdahan still couldn't shake a sense of impending danger, which seemed to come out of nowhere. Because if the Vrukaari had upped their technology game, it was still reasonable to assume they were a generation or more behind Snaldrialoor's rapid tech development.

And yet, no sooner had he and 17/Chaarnactral entered the main room than he saw how far off a "reasonable" train of thought could be.

CHAPTER 2

Trillions of kilometers away from Ixdahan's soon-to-be-shocked central nervous system, another sentient life form was enjoying the most fascinating summer of her life. Off the southeastern coast of Alaska, suited up in scuba gear like the rest of the research team, Lena Gabrilowicz relished the undulating flutter of her swim fins in the water.

At a depth of 60 feet, the ocean opened up before her and took her breath away. Or at least it would have, if she didn't have a breather stuffed snug in her mouth as her instructor had told her over and over again.

"Breathe normally," she'd said, "but most important, *remember* to breathe."

It was the first summer in five years she hadn't spent in Harmony Beach with her dad and, so far, she was only a little bit nostalgic. After all, it was so exciting to study humpback whales with a professor from Oregon State University. So why obsess about the past?

Especially, that is, the recent past, like last month's break up with Silvano. She definitely didn't want to think about that ... again.

Trouble was, there wasn't a lot left of her past she *did* want to think about. What? She should mull over last year's crazy alien visitation, the one that almost reduced the entire human population to bubbling globs of slime? That was a kind of excitement she could do without, even if she did get the chance to meet strange little Derek Dixon — whose real name was something seriously weird, like, Ixdahan Daherek.

What was it about him that had drawn her in?

Probably, Lena decided, the quality of his mind and, the longer he lived on Earth, the way he cared about the people around him. Nevertheless, he'd been the indirect cause of the terrible danger that enveloped her, her family, her friends ... and everyone else.

"The whole planet almost crashed and burned," she thought, as she fought the urge to mumble into her breather. Her suit, she reminded herself, was equipped with a radio transmitter. The last thing she needed was for Professor Cray to hear her rambling on about her life-threatening encounter with the son of a Snaldrialooran diplomat.

Come to think of it, the professor was on the radio now, pointing out a pair of humpback whales that had just come into view about 20 yards ahead.

"Well, that's something I haven't seen too often," said Professor Cray. "Look at the way they're facing each other, head to head, kind of like two gossipy neighbors."

Stranger still, it wasn't a moment later before a second pair, and a third, swam up. Lena watched as the six of them arranged themselves in a circle.

"More like group therapy now," said Lena.

In a flash, she remembered the few sessions she'd attended … five years ago … while she was still trying to cope with the loss of her mom. It hadn't gotten any easier, but maybe right now, this summer, was the time to move on.

"Don't sulk," she told herself. Instead, she swam in as close as she dared. How beautiful the whales were, in their own way, with their broad fins, ridged bellies and knobby snouts!

The professor was speaking again, but now a distinct quaver had entered his voice.

"Come on, let's surface," said the professor. "I want to see if Jocelyn has any new readings."

Jocelyn Cray was the professor's daughter, a graduate student who'd already logged many hours of diving time and published an article about humpback behavior patterns.

"Cetaceans," she called them, a scientific term she wore like a badge of honor.

Lena couldn't say she liked Jocelyn, or disliked her either. There was something too … emotionless … about her, as if marine biology were the only thing in the universe she could care two clam shells about. Was it Asperger's syndrome or was it … no, it couldn't be….

Lena broke the surface and swam the remaining few feet to the *Whales B Cray*, the 22-foot twin vee ocean cat research vessel she'd arrived in. Though she hardly noticed anymore, the boat was decked out in the university's colors: forest green, trimmed with lemon yellow.

No way there are any aliens left, she thought. *No way. Not after Derek's people cleaned up the place.*

She was, in fact, the one person left on Earth to remember the Vrukaari invasion, including those chattering mutant mailboxes, the horrible Mr. Yarrow and what Yarrow did to … to poor Blade Northrop. The Snaldrialoorans had taken care to adjust the memories of everyone on the planet, except Lena, whom Derek argued had earned the right to have her mind left untouched.

Lena pulled herself up over the side of the boat and followed the lead of the other student on the team, whom she barely knew. She carefully removed and stowed her tanks, and made sure the breather and mask didn't get tangled or squashed.

"The cameras definitely picked up unusual social behavior down there," she heard Jocelyn telling her father. "You actually saw this, the circle?"

Cray scratched the sandy-gray chin whiskers of his moth-eaten beard.

"And *not* the first time, come to think of it," he said. "But the circle was better defined just now and looked more … intentional."

The cameras Jocelyn referred to were part of a discrete network of sensing equipment the Marine Biology Department had set up, right before the start of the summer session. The idea was to capture every scrap of new data before the humpbacks took off for Hawaii to have their babies.

"Any song events?" asked the professor, as he slipped the air tanks off his back.

According to Jocelyn, unusual song events were becoming more common. Instead of the long, sustained tones rolled out over tens and hundreds of kilometers she was used to, these humpbacks were producing short bursts of sound.

"Kind of like, you know, a conversation or an argument, even," said Jocelyn.

"When did that start?" asked Toffel de Graaf, a tall Dutch transfer student Lena barely knew.

Professor Cray looked out at the wide ocean and shielded his eyes against the glare. The irregularities, he explained, had started a week after an unexplained energy surge rocked the entire area from Prince William Sound to the Kenai Fjords.

Lena didn't like the sound of that. The last time a blast of energy from an unknown source had ripped into the Earth, she'd ended up in the hospital for a week, her hands coated in a deadly Vrukaari fungus. The same one, in fact, that destroyed Blade Northrup.

"It is like the cetaceans are … what is the English word … transmogrifying," said Toffel.

At that, the hairs stood up on the back of Lena's neck. She hadn't heard that word since Derek … since he….

Jocelyn rolled her eyes.

"Oh, please," she said. "There has to be a rational explanation. There's no way that species evolution can occur on such a scale or at such speeds. Besides, I'm sure this can be attributed to a passing viral infection — something else this planet's great polluting corporations will have to answer for."

"Stop it, both of you," said Professor Cray. "This is not how we do science on my boat. We need hard data, and a dependable way to test a hypothesis under controlled conditions. Right Lena?"

"Yes, Professor Cray," said Lena. But though she wanted to take comfort from his stern words, she knew too well what-kind-of "virus" could do what-kind-of damage to Earth creatures. She bit her lip. That it could be happening again was too horrible to think about.

Lucky for her, a rain storm began blustering in the distance above the open water.

"OK, let's motor back to the lab," said Cray. "We can't gather data to support *any* theory at this point."

Before long, the *Whales B. Cray* was tied up at the University outpost's marina and Lena was heading back to her dorm.

Toffel ran up beside her.

"Pretty weird, no?" he asked.

"Weird, yes," said Lena. "I'm not sure about the pretty part. Have you ever heard of whales carrying on like that?"

"Never," said Toffel, as he rubbed his left hand over his close-cropped blond hair. "It is like they were under some external influence, but that is rather insane, no?"

"Totally," said Lena, and gave him a friendly wave before jogging off in the direction of her dorm.

"Totally," she said, under her breath. She threw open her door, flopped down on her bed and was relieved to see that her roommate, Dorothea Bradley, was still out foraging for boys.

Boys.

Ever since Silvano, that was one topic of "scientific inquiry" she had soured on. For now, Lena Gabrilowicz was all business.

And it was just as well, now that she had tons of new information to absorb. For one thing, the number of parallels to last year's experience were mounting up fast. She grabbed her laptop, and was determined to sort this out by making a table, so she could correlate….

But between the excitement of her first research expedition with Professor Cray and her first extended trip with the scuba gear, she could barely keep her eyes open. As she plopped down onto her bright yellow sheets, she gave in to the heaviness of her eyelids as her back and shoulder muscles followed the example set by her tired feet and legs, relaxing, easing into....

Blaahroohl! Ahaahlbrooda ulaahyaa ... a voice echoed in her mind, which sounded exactly like the songs of the humpback ... except ... these were more like individual words.

Gaheeraahn rarhlkoal sussulaahaon.

Was that the same voice, or was a second voice chiming in with agreement or dissent? One thing was certain, this wasn't Derek. It had to be the humpbacks, no matter how scary a thought that was.

Worse, while she had no idea what the voices were saying, she couldn't mistake the fear they dredged up in her heart. The voices, it seemed, were voices of confusion, panic. And underlying them was a single image that grew clearer in her mind the longer she listened: A cylinder ... no ... more like a vase ... hidden under the ocean floor. It was kind of like an ancient Greek amphora, the large pottery container they had once used for transporting wine overseas.

Lena sat up. Her mind filled with the image, until it seemed she could reach out and touch it.

There ... the typical warrior figures she'd seen in Art History class back in Skudderton with Ms. Dover. And the ancient Greek inscriptions, but a bit longer than she expected.

OK, she had to get this down.

She fumbled for a pen and paper with her eyes shut tight and nearly brained herself on the edge of her oak-finished end table before... finally ... she started transcribing the letters one by one.

"It has to mean something," she said. Her hand began to cramp, as she rushed to capture each letter before the vision faded. With Derek unavailable, this might be her best chance to find out how much trouble Earth was in this time.

As she scribbled down the last row of ancient Greek characters, the voices exclaimed in unison:

"Aarhshaasussraalloo!"

Regardless of the language barrier, *that* message was clear. It was a cry of despair pitched to a level of intensity she'd never heard before. What in the name of her own sanity could get a gaggle of whales so freaking agitated?

"OK, OK," she told herself. "This is really weird, but what if it's not so serious? Maybe some alien wise guy who has heard about Earth, decided to have a little fun — to scare us a lot and then post holograms of our frightened little faces on Intergalactic Pinterest, or whatever?"

Lena knew how desperate that sounded but, for the moment, the thought of an alien pranking Planet Earth took her mind off the alternative — the realization that everyone she cared about might be in serious danger.

Fortunately, there was one person in the universe who could talk her down from her anxiety on that point: Derek Dixon, whatever his real name was.

Well, it had worked before … and if, maybe, he could put her mind at ease, she could have a shot at actually enjoying the summer before Senior Year, before the "invasion" of adult responsibility began changing her life for good.

She put her fingertips to her temples for no particular reason and thought:

"Derek? Can you hear me? It's Lena...."

She went on to describe the whales' strange underwater behavior, their mentallic moaning and the image of the ancient Greek amphora they'd transmitted to her.

Would he answer?

Nothing. Not a glimmer of the intense sensation she'd felt last fall. No question then, it hadn't been her imagination. But hold it. Across such large distances, hadn't Derek sometimes used a special device to boost his signal?

Trouble was, out there in Alaska, she might as well have been a galaxy away from Derek's old house in Skudderton. At the same time, she knew she had to find a way to reach him. If the whales weren't being controlled by the Vrukaari, there was every reason to believe the real culprit might be something worse.

CHAPTER 3

For Ixdahan, as for any average Snaldrialooran teenager, adapting to oxygen-breathing on Earth had been tough going. And after living through that nightmare, you might think adapting to Vrukaar Prime would be considerably easier.

But as Ixdahan could tell you, you'd be wrong.

Fact was, Vrukaar Prime's nitrogen/phosphate-based biosphere had been a straight up shock to his system. For one thing, an ecology like *this* was only possible on a planet even farther from its sun than Snaldrialoor. Worse, Vrukaar Prime's sun was a sputtering dwarf star, which cast its pale light in stingy driblets. And that made the climate seriously harsh.

Then there was the saddest truth about life on Vrukaar Prime: its go-to solvent wasn't water as on Earth, or liquid methane as on Snaldrialoor, but ammonia. And, say what you want, ammonia reeked, as it seeped from every pore of his globular body.

Of course, if Ixdahan had been a true Vrukaari, he wouldn't have given the eco-system or his sweat glands a moment's thought. But with his Snaldrialooran consciousness preserved in an isolated, secure sector of the Galactic Array, he perceived his adopted world with a combination of Snaldrialooran and Vrukaari senses.

At first, his every breath had been paired with a twinge of shuddering revulsion. That is, until he succeeded in constructing the right mentallic filters to dial down his Snaldrialooran senses.

There was no way around this, and the Transmog Team had been plain on this point.

The only way to fully remove the acrid smell of Vrukaar Prime was to sever all connection to his Snaldrialooran consciousness. In an instant, he'd no longer be either Ixdahan Daherek, Pertahru and Eneselah's troublemaking son, or Derek Dixon, Lena's friend and co-conspirator with Vance and Callie Ann.

He'd be what his supervisor at the Department of Inspections knew him as: Xihandevaan Genko, a low-level functionary with a doubtful future in the Vrukaari civil service.

"Xihandevaan," that very supervisor had been yelling into Ixdahan's mind a moment before, "where in the Throllnesian Event Horizon are you? You were supposed to have inspected the Muandrigahtas foundry two hours ago."

"Sorry, Sir," said Ixdahan, "but I have to sit the rest of the day out. I'm kind of anxious about the threat I received at the Hotel Phaardraalassoor."

According to Ixdahan, the building manager had taken out a contract on him.

"Don't you believe it, Boy," said his supervisor. "These blowhards in the tourist industry are always making threats. You just have to stand your ground."

"Did I mention," asked Ixdahan, "that this particular blowhard is the daughter of Aalthrashrintorb Leek?"

Ixdahan fought hard to suppress a laugh, as the implications of his question sank into the clotted forehead of his bad-tempered boss. It was all the more delicious because those implications were essentially true.

That is, except for the actual threat — a threat Leek's daughter *might* have made, if Ixdahan had "stood his ground" about the building code violations. Lucky for him, his supervisor was so anxious to avoid annoying a member of Vrukaar Prime's leading family that he set the matter aside. From there on out, Ixdahan's case load would be one hotel lighter.

"I believe your conversation may have misled Supervisor Acerola," said 17/Chaarnactral when Ixdahan had closed mentallic contact. "He may have had the impression...."

Ixdahan held up his stubby right hand.

"Please," he said. "As an official of the regional government, I deal in facts, not speculation."

"Even if the facts must be manufactured on the spot," said the robot.

Ixdahan stared at his artificial companion and considered his options. Better to end this dispute before someone overheard them.

"I didn't manufacture anything," he said at last, "except the chance for us to observe Vrukaari technology up close. How does that mesh with your programming?"

"I hadn't...." the AI began.

"Didn't think so," said Ixdahan. "Now, 17, let's get busy with our real work. Start observing and meet me back here at rotation vector 75."

Within minutes, 17/Chaarnactral was off collecting data at the opposite end of the cavernous conference center. That left Ixdahan free to concentrate on the one thought that had dominated his mind since last night: Magclad technology would make Vrukaari warships vulnerable to any assault, including a barrage of nuclear weapons. But how had these drooling blobs mastered the complex photon-exchange equations that made magclad shielding possible?

As a rule of thumb, the Bureau's analysts estimated a lag time of about 25 cycles between Vrukaari and the Snaldrialooran R&D. Except, that is, in cases like his own, when a desperate idiot sold state secrets to the enemy.

"Really stupid," whispered Ixdahan, as he stared down the aisles of the immense exhibition. And yet, if he hadn't been so stupid, he would never have met Lena, and yet....

That was the funny thing about life, he decided. You couldn't always stop yourself from being an idiot. All you could do was to get better at cleaning up the mess. Since he couldn't undo his crime, he was determined the Vrukaari should not acquire any more advanced tech.

But by gazing around him, in one of probably 20 rooms housing the trade show, he could see how hard that would be. None of the devices on display were mechanical copies of existing tech. They included modifications, refinements, even — yes — improvements. It was not the sort of thing you could achieve with stolen documents alone.

The booth to his left, up ahead, labelled "self-replicating data relays," was troubling enough, but the one further along was downright disturbing.

TRANSDIMENSIONAL ENERGY CONDUIT

...read the shiny plaque on the display case. Like every other booth, this one was dripping with bad taste, from the multicolored banners to the garish, stamped magnesium shell, embossed with the Vrukaari Trade Commission seal....

Wise Heralds of the Infinite Continuum! The warlords of Vrukaar Prime were getting these advanced-design power stations ready for commercial sale to ... to who knew what developing planetary systems.

Even cautious Group Leader Ishialdrol would have to recognize the danger bubbling up under the surface of these transactions. Tech like this in the hands of civilizations no more advanced than, say, Earth, would upset the balance of power the Snaldrialooran government had been struggling to maintain since the fall of Halksiadroor over 1,000 years ago.

And yet, if he were honest with himself, Ixdahan was forced to recognize that nothing on display was half as troubling as another surprise feature of the trade show.

Ixdahan reached out to his robot assistant on a secure mentallic channel.

"17?" he asked. "How do you account for the humanoids I see mixing in with the sales reps and the scientists?" In fact, a pair of them were passing by in front of him right now, wrapped up tight in their sea-green encounter suits and weighed down by tanks of compressed air. Based on his limited knowledge of alien atmospheric systems, Ixdahan assumed that air must be a nitrogen-oxygen mix similar to the atmosphere of Jarhtral 4 or, for that matter, Earth.

And yet, there was something altogether different about these humanoids. What was 17/Chaarnactral saying?

"…unknown origin. They're not showing up in the unclassified section of the Galactic Array, either," said the robot. "Different heart rate than most humanoids and … now that's highly improbable…."

"What?" asked Ixdahan from the back of his throat. It had taken every ounce of self-control not to shout out loud.

"They … appear to be … at a minimum, a thousand years old," said the AI.

More like wildly improbable, thought Ixdahan. In contrast to the average Snaldrialooran or Vrukaari, who could comfortably expect to live around 400 healthy years, every known humanoid species had a relatively short lifespan — with a significant drop off in quality of life towards the end.

"Only one humanoid race has ever been known to live so long," 17/Chaarnactral was saying now.

"You mean the Onkendren?" gasped Ixdahan.

The robot nodded, but Ixdahan couldn't believe his synapses. Everybody knew about the Onkendren, the mythical forebears of modern civilization. They were rumored to have developed a direct link to the laws of physics, which enabled them to manipulate space, time, energy and matter like potter's clay.

But even if the Onkendren had existed, or still existed now, what in the gas clouds of Shaltrioghaan were they doing at a Vrukaari trade show?

That question aside, the re-emergence of the Onkendren would go a long way to explaining the sudden jump in Vrukaari technical prowess.

"Assuming these humanoids are the Onkendren," said Ixdahan, "why would they choose to help the Vrukaari warlords?"

By now, 17/Chaarnactral had made its way back to the central show room where Ixdahan was standing. The quirky robot was quick to point out that it wasn't the most secure place to be discussing such sensitive topics.

Ixdahan took 17/Chaarnactral's advice and followed it out of the hotel and onto the street. There, in the busy open-air market, the crush of minds would protect their conversation from everyone except the most determined mentallic snoops.

"Something, obviously, has changed the equation," said the AI, once they'd plunged into that sea of sentient brain waves. "If they are the Onkendren, they've been out of circulation for several centuries, and may not know exactly who they're dealing with."

As Ixdahan knew from his own experience, the Vrukaari propaganda machine was as sophisticated as any in the Seven Known Galaxies. Who knew what spin they'd put on recent history when they introduced themselves?

"Now, don't judge me," said 17/Chaarnactral, "but I have a funny feeling there might be a connection to a news item that popped up in my scanner this morning. Don't you hate that when items just pop up like that? Honestly...."

Ixdahan's blood pressure rose as he realized that his robot's personality nexus was veering off toward poutiness again.

"Focus, 17, focus," he said. "What news item?"

The robot wasted no time transmitting the report Ixdahan had obviously ignored, probably because it hit close to home:

RARE GIFT PRESENTED TO
SNALDRIALOORAN STATESMAN
AT INITIATION CEREMONY
HOSTED BY YBITRIAN AMBASSADOR

There, below the headline's blood-red letters, was a holographic display of Pertahru Daherek holding an ornate, powder blue soufflé dish, decorated with what looked like ancient Ybitrian inscriptions. Of course, Ixdahan was no expert on the topic. His knowledge was limited to what he'd picked up through direct-to-cortex stimulation in prep school. Still, he could have sworn there was something odd about those inscriptions.

For starters, they conveyed a sense of urgency he'd never seen in any living Ybitrian — probably the most laid back species in the settled universe. But what was the connection to the Onkendren?

"Oh, don't you know *anything?*" asked 17/Chaarnactral, as it clenched its pneumatic fists. "The Onkendren are said to have buried a series of artifacts from selected cultures on their homeworlds a few days before disappearing."

In fact, the cultures advanced enough to notice had proudly celebrated this gift for several life cycles, until the official records of the burials were lost, centuries before most of these planets had electricity.

"So how did my father...." Ixdahan started.

"Hello," said the robot, "ever heard of archaeology? Really, try to keep up. If I'm right about this, the Onkendren's secrets are suddenly out in the open — and they've come back to put things right again."

Ixdahan stared at 17/Chaarnactral and tried to absorb what he'd just heard.

"But why?" he asked. "Even if Father's gift proves the legends are true, why would the Onkendren bother to honor worlds they were planning to walk away from forever?"

17/Chaarnactral fiddled with a series of control knobs on his left arm.

"One theory," it said, "is that the Onkendren implanted sensors in each device, keyed to a series of detonators they could activate the moment any one planet overstepped the bounds of civilized conduct."

"If you're right about that," said Ixdahan, "Father could be in a lot of trouble real fast."

"You think?" snapped the robot. "With all the behind-the-scenes networking he does? Interstellar voids! If you ask me, organic intelligence is highly overrated...."

"Reboot," said Ixdahan with a sigh, "and restart in check mode." With so much new information to mull over, the last thing he needed was an unending stream of snarky comments from a machine.

That settled it: When this mission was over, he'd demand a replacement unit. At the moment, however, if the Onkendren-Vrukaari alliance held, he wasn't entirely sure that he or any other Snaldrialooran would be in a position to demand *anything*.

"Like trying to stop a tidal wave with a wet sponge," he mumbled.

At last, the indicator lights on 17/Chaarnactral's dorsal control panel started flickering back to life. Maybe now he could hope to discuss the potential threat more rationally....

Wait ... was that an incoming mentallic message? Very faint. Almost as if it were coming from ... from Earth?

CHAPTER 4

Back in Lena's hometown of Skudderton, Vance Maultsby looked out over the unmown grass in the back yard of his mother's suburban home.

"Can't deal with this," he sighed.

Not only had he put off the mowing from yesterday, he was *supposed to be* trimming the box hedges by now. Moms had been clear about that before she set off for a long weekend with her friends. Nothing special: They were heading down to Harmony Beach to soak up the sun. With Dad out of the picture and Nathan in the dog house…again … there was nothing to hold her back. Except, maybe, common sense.

"None of my business," he muttered into his reflection in the glass patio doors separating him from the dreary routine of yard work. Trouble was, he'd promised. But there was this thing with his new computer, the one she'd let him buy on the condition of doing regular yard work for the entire summer.

"Good for you anyway," Moms had insisted. "Spend all that time hunched over a keyboard, and you'll end up looking like a pretzel. Then I don't know how you think you'll *ever* get yourself a girlfriend," she added for the 49,000[th] time.

Girlfriends.

Everything would be a whole lot easier, Vance told himself, if they were more like computers.

That is, the part where computers were reliable, predictable and weren't equipped with a factory-installed laundry list of ways you could be a better person. Sure, girlfriends were way prettier than his Dell XPS, but not when they acted like Callie Ann — a girl who had a rule for *everything*.

Of course, as he knew perfectly well, Lena's best friend was completely off limits for all kinds of other reasons. Besides, these days, training for the Olympic swimming trials meant way more to her than any swoony lakeside make-out session. That is, ever since … since that terrible thing happened to Blade Northrup.

Vance? Well, he was more interested in dating than *that*. But he still had a hard time imagining a girlfriend who could give him as much satisfaction as computer programming. Did that mean there was something wrong with him? Or was he just waiting for ... for ... something indefinable to happen?

Uncle Jordan understood.

"You're still kind of young for that mushy stuff, anyway, Boy," his mellow voice had said, last time he was over for dinner. "You're a nice kid. Just stay that way. She'll find you."

Great. But deep down, Vance kind of knew life didn't work like that. Celia Roberts, for example, was not going to find him, not by accident, anyway. He figured he'd have to stand up and wave his arms in the air.

No, he had a feeling he couldn't ignore: Falling in love was a lot less user-friendly than his uncle wanted him to believe.

"Seriously depressing," sighed Vance, not least because he really did want to ask Celia Roberts out. It was just that ... that ... well ... better to focus on his computer problem — which he at least had a fighting chance of understanding.

Or rather, his software problem. At first, setting up his new machine had been easy. He'd almost transferred every file from his old CPU when he came across a folder icon he didn't remember creating.

PROJECT V

... the file name read. Every time he tried to open it, he'd get a buzzing sound in his head and pass out. Last time, he fell off his chair and almost broke his neck.

Funny thing was, he heard that same sound every time he tried to remember last October. He'd hear buzzing and then last October didn't seem to matter anymore, and he'd remember something totally dorky, like the time he spilled iced tea all over Nathan.

OK, maybe it wasn't a month *worth* remembering. But what was the connection? Why the same sound for two unrelated ... wait ... what was the date on that computer folder?

October 6, two years ago, he thought, not daring to say it out loud. OK, he decided, it was time to end this. After all, he couldn't help it if the file opened by accident, could he? Maybe if he put the cursor over the icon ... yes ... and highlighted it ... yes ... he could open the file indirectly with a little help from....

"Arkansas," he called out to Lena's mostly white Tom cat, who happened to have a black spot on his side that resembled the 25th state.

Lena had brought the big lug over before heading off to Alaska for the summer. Vance didn't mind. What else could she do, with her dad and step mom down in Harmony Beach and her old neighbor too sick to look after the galumphing home wrecker anymore?

"Come here, Dude," he said, as he scooped the sleepy fur ball off his perch on the kitchen table. Good thing Moms wasn't around to see that. Freaking cat had gotten into the tuna salad, which was still in the ceramic bowl Vance had left out two hours ago.

Arkansas squirmed a bit at first, but settled down a moment later — as Vance set him on top of his new keyboard and made sure his front paws hit the ENTER key and….

PROJECT V opened to reveal hundreds of files Vance couldn't identify.

"Looks like gaming code," he said, as a vague memory of a video game based on real time Google maps danced on the edges of his memory. Almost immediately, the buzzing started again but Vance was determined to stay alert.

"What do you think it is?" he asked Arkansas, who looked as if he, too, were disturbed by … something.

Vance tapped the down arrow with the tip of the Tom cat's tail and discovered one lone Word file amongst a sea of Dreamweaver files:

ACCESS CODE, Q-TRANSFER

"Whoa," said Vance. The file name meant nothing to him. The Snaldrialoorans had made sure that, with the exception of Lena, the entire human race would forget everything associated with the Vrukaari invasion. Otherwise, Vance would have recognized it. As Derek had tried to explain last year, q-transfer was short for "quantum transfer," a spectacularly complex way to move objects from place to place.

"Every object in the universe has height, width, depth and a position in time and space," Derek had told him. "That's its quantum signature. With q-transfer, you don't 'send' an object to a new location; you change its signature until it *is* in a new location."

Each transfer could take hours of calculations, even when carried out on the Galactic Array. But if the new location were no farther away than an orbiting starspanner, it was generally no big deal. Of course, transferring living things was harder. Because life processes are in constant motion, one mistake could turn a living thing into a pitiful lump of dysfunctional biomass.

That's why, in accordance with galactic law, pilots broke every local and interstellar transfer into discrete steps. This also enabled them to factor in the massive gravitational pull of black holes, whose distortion of space-time changed the very definition of "location." The penalty for failing to register your q-transfer vectors with the Interstellar Transport Authority? Imagine scrubbing the stables at Belmont Racetrack with your nose — and you'll be close.

But to Vance, the file on his computer was merely one more piece of a complex puzzle: trying to grasp what the PROJECT V folder contained and why he'd created it. So he shut his eyes, picked up Arkansas' right front paw and used it to tap ENTER again.

When he opened his eyes a moment later, he saw a digital photo of an ominous black disk. It was sitting on what looked like a kitchen counter in a house that … but that was crazy. How could a house he'd never seen before look familiar? Underneath the image was what looked like a password or … or a really long phone number.

Exhausted from the strain of resisting the buzz in his head, Vance picked the bewildered feline up off the keyboard and hugged him tight, before setting him down. Arkansas let out a strangled "Merleow" and scampered off under the couch, but not before scratching Vance lightly on the ankle.

"Yo, you did not just do that!" said Vance.

He turned back to his computer to email the file to his Moto X phone and ambled off to his cheerful kitchen. OK, as if what he'd seen wasn't weird enough, his mind was bursting with incomprehensible images and one single bit of data. It was an address he could swear he'd never visited:

215 Chicory Lane, Skudderton, NJ

"All the way up in Hunter's Wend," he said to Arkansas, who had slunk back to the tuna salad. "No way it's one of Momses friends." Weirder still, saying the address outloud brought the buzzing back again, now a little fainter.

It was crazy, it was stupid, but it was 2:00 in the afternoon on Saturday and Moms wasn't due back until late Sunday night. He could check out this address, and get started on the mowing when he got back — as soon as he and Arkansas finished uploading PROJECT V to his new computer.

Maybe if he hurried he could bike up there before dark, provided he could find one pair of pants that didn't reek. He was *supposed to* have done the laundry by now, too.

"When am I *supposed to* live?" he asked the Universe, as he dug the last pair of clean cargo shorts out of his closet.

Vance stopped long enough to wipe up the mess Arkansas had made of the tuna salad and also made sure the poor little guy had some water in his dish. Good thing Vance's baby sister Dakota was spending the weekend with Auntie Martha. Taking care of a cat was the most "parenting" he could handle at this point in his life.

As he picked his bike up from the garage, he found the tires were in serious need of air. He reached for his sleek, back bicycle pump.

"Too long in front of a computer," he mumbled. He hated to admit it. Hated. It. But sometimes, Moms was right.

"Transfer to where?" he wondered. Somehow, he had the crazy idea he already knew, that the information was hiding in his subconscious. Lost in thought, he watched the tires inflate.

"Derek knows," he heard himself say. But who the … bicycle pump … was Derek?

CHAPTER 5

All that night and into the next morning, Lena forced herself to go through the motions of everyday life as if nothing had happened. Whatever the events of the last 12 hours meant, she knew she had nothing to gain from worrying herself into the ground.

More to the point, there was nothing she could do on her own about the whales.

"Don't know *whose* side I should be on," she told herself as she brushed her thick hair in her dorm room mirror.

"What's that?" asked her roommate Dorothea, the kind of girl who never seemed to know anything except somebody else's business. Lena thought fast.

"Nothing big," she said. "Just a fight between my Dad and my step mom, which they've decided to throw me in the middle of."

"Oh, God," said Dorothea, "you think there's any way to keep from turning into … that … someday?"

"Only if you don't have kids," said Lena, "which is pretty much my plan."

"You can't be serious," said her roommate, as she pulled on a pair of dark brown hiking boots.

"Where are you going in *those*?" asked Lena, desperate to change the subject. Lucky for her, Dorothea took the bait. Dorothea's geology team was hiking into some low-lying hills up north to check out the gravitational anomalies they'd encountered recently.

"Anything to do with the energy surge I've been hearing about?" asked Lena and, at that, got herself an earful from Dorothea, including a ton of geological data she couldn't make sense of.

"This is data like nothing else you've ever seen," said Dorothea, as she finished the braid on her long red hair. "It's kind of exciting … Oh crap, I'm late."

Lena stared after the tall figure as she raced out of the room and down the hall toward the dorm lobby. If only, she sighed, Dorothea knew how dangerous "kind of exciting" could be.

Never mind. The best way forward was to keep her own ears open and that meant keeping up with Professor Cray, Jocelyn and Toffel.

Determined to stay on track, she grabbed her backpack from her bed, slung it over her left shoulder and strode out of her dorm, barely stopping to lock her door on the way out.

Lena breathed deep in the damp, overcast morning air, she was grateful she had somewhere to go. It was seriously terrifying to think of sitting alone in her room, as she tried to sort out what might or might not be going on.

"You are looking as if you did not sleep last night," said Toffel, who was already at the marina when she arrived.

Lena nodded, but instead of blurting out a snappy comeback, she tripped over a wayward bolt in the pier and fell down hard on the weather-proofed wood. In the process, her backpack, which she hadn't bothered to zip, went flying, and spewed its contents out on to the deck with embarrassing force.

"Geez," said Lena. "Way to start the morning."

She rushed to collect as many pages as possible from her binder before the wind picked up. That, she saw now, was one of the perils of being overly organized. Loose-leaf paper had a stubborn vulnerability that reared up on its haunches in a wide variety of situations. From now on, it was yellow legal pads all the way….

"What is this?" Toffel's voice broke in on her scrambling. "You are also studying the ancient Greek?"

Lena's eyes widened at the sight of Toffel staring down at her transcription of the markings on the amphora she'd seen in her mind late yesterday afternoon. She cleared her throat.

"It's something I'm playing with," said Lena, "for an art project. Thought maybe some ancient inscriptions might, you know, give it some … atmosphere."

God, what a terrible liar she was, she told herself. But Toffel didn't seem to notice; he was too preoccupied with the transcription.

"Cannot have come from a classic source," said Toffel. "But I guess you knew that."

"Well…." Lena sputtered.

"I studied Classics up until last year," said Toffel. "Then my mother put her foot down and told me to get into 'something real.' That is how I ended up here. Did your parents…."

"Wait," said Lena, "you can actually read that … text?"

Toffel nodded.

"I mean, it does not make complete sense, especially culturally," he said. "Either this is a fake quote or there is something about ancient Greek science we never knew."

There were, he explained, references to concepts he was pretty sure the residents of fifth century Athens wouldn't have discovered.

"I doubt many *modern* Greeks would know what a 'transdimensional energy conduit' is, either," said Toffel.

"It says that?" asked Lena, as she rushed over to his side. "Where?"

"Not exactly," said Toffel, "but that is what it adds up to, as far as I can tell. I guess you would need a physicist to explain it properly."

"Or an alien," thought Lena.

Just then, Jocelyn and Professor Cray arrived at the marina in his emerald-green Outback. Without wasting a second, Lena grabbed her papers out of Toffel's hands, shoved them with the rest of her belongings back into her pack and zipped it up tight.

"Ready for another deep dive?" asked Professor Cray.

"Sure," said Lena.

But she was in for a disappointment. The Professor had decided to study the whale population up close and didn't want to spook them with too many people at a time. He also wanted to explore a greater depth than before. Toffel, being the more experienced diver, was the logical choice.

"You'll be up here with Jocelyn, keeping an eye on things," said Cray with a wink. "Besides, you'll have a chance to get familiar with standard tracking and sensor software. You can show her, can't you, Jossy?"

"You know I hate it when you call me that," said Jocelyn.

Her father kissed her on the top of her head.

"Why else do you think I do it?" said Cray. "Come, suit up, Mr. de Graaf. With this cloud cover we may be in for another short day."

Great, thought Lena, as she watched the two guys get ready, then power up the *Whales B. Cray* and head out over the water. She'd been hoping she'd have a chance to spot something down there that might give her clues about the whales, or the amphora or … or whatever the deal was with the power surge Dorothea was talking about back at the dorm.

"Don't worry," said Jocelyn when her father and Toffel had plunged overboard and disappeared under the waves. "You can actually see more clearly from the laptop. Plus, you can zoom in on stuff. Want to see?"

Rather than waste the whole day, Lena played along. After all, it wasn't as if she didn't need to learn the software — assuming Earth would still be here when she went to college next year.

And at first, sitting with Jocelyn was a pleasant surprise.

If the professor's daughter was generally kind of dry as a person, when she focused on marine biology, she became positively vibrant. In fact, her enthusiasm for "cetacean research" sometimes took on a scary kind of glow, that reminded Lena of the robot caretakers who had posed as Derek's parents last year.

"Guess it's a human trait, too, though," she said to herself, realizing that she had also been kind of thrilled about the whales until yesterday.

"The really interesting part," Jocelyn was saying, "is the way the humpbacks' behavioral patterns have begun to mimic those of creatures with higher levels of sentience."

"You mean, like humans," said Lena. What other creatures, she wondered, could Jocelyn be talking about?

"Who else?" said Jocelyn without looking up from her screen. "I just like to be precise. Anyway, take a look."

As she peered over Jocelyn's pale shoulders, Lena watched a pair of whales floating over a section of the ocean floor. Nearby, a bottle-nosed dolphin looked on, as if waiting for orders. Soon enough, it waggled its head, before nudging up a succession of oyster shells with its snout and arranging them one by one into a distinct pattern.

Jocelyn brushed a strand of off-blond hair out of her eyes.

"Kind of like a blueprint," she said.

"Or a roadmap," said Lena.

Off to one side, Lena could see Professor Cray and Toffel peering from behind one of the larger rock formations.

"So now the dolphins are acting weird, too," said Lena. "What's the connection?"

"Interesting," Jocelyn murmured. "Well, if it is a roadmap — if that's not as totally crazy as it sounds — we ought to be able to guess what it's a roadmap to."

Before Lena could breathe again, Jocelyn had copied the image on her screen and pasted it into a mapping program window. Lena's jaw dropped as, with a few ticks of her keyboard, Jocelyn superimposed a topographic grid on the image, complete with yellow longitude, latitude lines and a distance scale.

Lena squinted at the screen.

"You think that's enough to go on?" she asked.

"Who knows?" said the professor's daughter. "But we have to start somewhere. This version makes one set of assumptions. Scale, for one thing. Are we talking meters or kilometers?"

"Kahlhoohedaahrs" echoed a whale voice in Lena's mind.

"Kilometers, I'll bet," said Lena, as she tried hard to control her breathing. Holy crap, the whales were talking again!

"In that case," said Jocelyn, "whatever they want us to see is about 200 kilometers southeast of here — in the Gulf of Alaska."

"Could you, like, e-mail that map to me?" Lena asked. "My roommate's on the geology team and she might be able to…."

"Great idea," said Jocelyn without looking up.

"Social graces anyone?" thought Lena. But, OK, maybe, as a graduate student, the professor's daughter felt she had to have the upper hand in any conversation with a pesky summer program kid who still hadn't started her freshman year.

Or maybe Jocelyn was a bit of a nerd.

Lena took a deep breath to calm down. Considering the implications of what she was seeing out here on the southeastern coast of Alaska, why was she wasting time by getting upset over this snippy little princess? Fat lot of good charm school would do Jocelyn if the Vrukaari came thundering back, now with the ability to turn Earth's animal population against it.

"Such an idiot," she heard Jocelyn say.

"Excuse me?" said Lena.

"I should have thought to compare the brainwave readings we're getting from the whales, and now the dolphins, obviously, against the baseline data we have on our captive animals," said Jocelyn.

"Tracking their brainwaves?" asked Lena. "How? It looks like your dad never gets closer than 20 meters to these … subjects."

Jocelyn's expression flashed from contempt to pity before finally settling down to its typical blankness.

"Well, we're not scanning their minds with handheld devices, if that's what you mean," she said. "We injected a chip into a few subjects last summer, and most of them are still functional."

"Right, of course," said Lena, in a lame attempt to save face. "I meant, how sure are you of the results?"

Jocelyn called up a graph of the latest data on the population Cray and Toffel were observing now and, right next to it, opened a graph of similar data from the University Aquarium back in Eugene. The contrast was visible even to Lena, who had no clue about neurology, let alone marine neurology.

"Do you know what this means?" asked Lena.

"It means the subjects we've stumbled on are no longer cetacean in the usual sense, if they ever were," said Jocelyn. "The differences are too great, at least in the whales. I'm checking the dolphins now."

"Kind of looks like the dolphin scans match," said Lena.

"Strange," said Jocelyn, her eyes unfocused. "Once their behavior patterns changed so radically, I'd never expect their brain structure to stay constant."

"Unless they were just … puppets," said Lena, "and the humpbacks were controlling them."

"With what?" asked Jocelyn. "Seaweed?"

"With their minds," said Lena. "You know, telepathically or whatever." She was determined not to sound too knowledgeable about the topic.

"Don't let my dad hear you speculate like that," said Jocelyn. "But I have to admit, your guess is no weirder than the stuff we've accepted as reality in the past few hours. We can't be certain, of course."

How reassuring that would be, Lena decided, if she could be certain of anything at this point. Then she'd know she wasn't going completely insane. On the other hand, part of her was kind of hoping that the few things she did feel sure about would turn out to be an illusion.

Seriously. Maybe it would be better to find out she'd gone completely psycho than to believe….

"Jocelyn," Professor Cray's voice rang out through the laptop, "are you catching this onscreen?"

Startled, Jocelyn switched back to the monitoring screen to find her father and Toffel staring into the gigantic face of the humpback they'd code named "Nautilus" last season.

"What's happening, Professor?" asked Lena.

"Hallucination was my first thought," said Cray, "but Toffel says he hears it too. 'Course maybe we're *both* going nuts."

Strange as it sounded, the professor continued, it was hard to escape the feeling that Nautilus was speaking to them through the radio transmitters in their masks. Or rather, reciting — reciting a series of figures over and over again:

N 58° 1' 52.9407" W 145° 27' 32.3438"

"Maybe you better come up now, Dad," said Jocelyn, as she leaned into the screen.

"That is what we wanted to do," said Toffel, "but we are kind of … kind of frozen. Cannot move a muscle except to talk — and now that is getting harder, too."

"Maybe try answering," said Lena. "Say 'OK' or something, so they know you heard them?"

"So they *know*?" said the professor. "Why would I think a cetacean would know something in that sense?"

"Why would you think a cetacean would send you GPS coordinates?" asked Lena.

Professor Cray shrugged, or he would have, for his body was still held fast by … by what, Lena wondered. With nothing to lose, the current holder of the Grant Stephenson Chair of Marine Biology tried a simple experiment in interspecies communication.

"Right, we have the coordinates now. Mind telling me what they're for?" he said.

At that, Nautilus flapped his huge fins in a repetitive pattern and began a slow pivot away from the two human divers. Just in time, Cray and Toffel regained enough muscle control to get out of the lumbering creature's path through the water.

Meanwhile, back on the *Whales B. Cray*, Lena was getting a splitting headache. Sure, it was partly due to stress. But the main culprit was the chorus of whale song echoing in her mind:

"*Aahmfooraah,*" the voices were saying, and "*Kondoooieee.*" Clearly, the whales already picked up a few words in English by scanning her mind. But then what was she thinking? These were no whales. And yet, why had no one noticed them before?

The facts, she realized, pointed in one direction — or rather one line of speculation. Whatever the source of the strange energy pulse Dorothea's team was investigating, it might have created the conditions needed for these creatures' true nature to come to the surface.

Imagine. A consciousness lying dormant for … for centuries maybe, suddenly awoken. But why?

"*Vaahrooookhaarr!*" the voices chimed in, as if in reply.

"You OK?" asked Toffel, who by this time had climbed back on board the cruiser and had grabbed hold of Lena's shoulders

"Yeah, so, like, get off me," said Lena, as she pulled away.

"Sorry," said Toffel, still in his wetsuit, "but you almost fell off the side of the boat."

Lena looked over at the professor and Jocelyn, and saw from their faces that he must be telling the truth.

Cray plopped down on one of two folding patio chairs he'd squeezed on the boat, totally against University regulations.

"I thought you were in a trance state," he said. "Well, that settles it. Either we're on the brink of a major scientific breakthrough or the world is coming to an end."

"Or worse," thought Lena, as she watched the sunlight bounce off the water.

CHAPTER 6

When the Vrukaari trade show had wound down for the day, Ixdahan decided his best bet was to evaluate what he'd learned, back at his apartment on Dhelsharnoab Street, starting with the unexpected mentallic communication he'd received from Lena.

Meanwhile, the process of picking his way through typical downtown traffic with a malfunctioning robot left him a nervous wreck. The free-for-all of garish private hover cars, maglev public transportation and creaky commercial vehicles made crossing the street feel like competing in a championship sport.

Ixdahan sighed. On Snaldrialoor, transportation had been automated for centuries, with only a few eccentrics clinging to the ancient tradition of *Hesuangtreffar* or "self-driving." Lucky for him, his apartment was three blocks from the hotel housing the trade show that had confirmed his worst suspicions about the Vrukaari.

Once inside his strictly functional quarters, he told 17/Chaarnactral to reboot and run a complete diagnostic. Now maybe he could try to piece things together. Trouble was, too many of the pieces were missing and he wasn't sure all the pieces he had even belonged to the same puzzle.

Ixdahan breathed deep in the nitrogen-based atmosphere that, contrary to his constant expectations, never made him choke. He nestled his slick, puffy body into a white receptacle in his kitchenette and q-transferred a carton of cold *quinzhaaliahr* juice to the silvery transfer port at his left.

Now if he could just do the same for the answers he needed.

For the moment, there were none. Between the appearance of the unusual humanoids at the Vrukaari trade show and the unlikely coincidence of Lena's mentallic contact at about the same time, life was taking on the familiar signs of peril..

Too bad he had no one to turn to for perspective. When he'd needed advice while on Earth, he'd contacted his cousin Jalgren at Lohaar University. As a professor of genomics, Jalgren might know if the Vrukaari's sudden surge in technical prowess could be the result of a partial transgenomic remapping, one of many skills the Onkendren were known for.

But this time, Ixdahan was unable to benefit from his cousin's expertise. Jalgren was on an extensive Do Not Call list that Group Leader Ishialdrol had insisted on. So were his parents, although the odds of Ixdahan calling Pertahru were zero and his father had effectively blocked Ixdahan from contacting his mother, Eneselah, with an ancient House Daherek mind control technique.

"The Vrukaari are better at hacking our shielded communications now, including mentallics," the Snaldrialooran spy master had warned. "Can't think of anything that would blow your cover faster than contacting the university or the embassy." And that made Ixdahan's chances of contacting Lena even more remote.

After all, Ixdahan told himself, as he pulled off his civil service uniform, even a fairly untraceable tight transponder beam aimed at Earth would be frowned on. He was the one sentient life form in the Seven Known Galaxies who would have anyone to contact on that backward planet. And none of his possible motives would be above suspicion to the Vrukaari.

Ixdahan looked over at 17/Chaarnactral, who was still in a metadigital coma. While Ixdahan watched, the robot's deep-system tools churned through each quantum-entangled layer of its mind, and smoothed away every last jagged, emotion-laden algorithmic "infection."

"Can't get a break," he sighed. Why couldn't the robot handle the job without so many blinking indicator lights, so many relentless beeps, squawks and whirrs? Way too distracting, especially now, in light of his disturbing realization: The Vrukaari warlords were ramping up for a major assault.

On what, he had no idea, but with the power of the Onkendren in easy reach they might, for the first time, dare to attack the Snaldrialooran Citadel.

Yes, after living among them for almost a year, he now appreciated how deep the Vrukaari's resentment of the Snaldrialoorans ran. And though nothing could justify the warmongering that flowed through their every dealing with the rest of the universe, he'd begun to see why their bitterness burned so bright.

For starters, Evolution had dealt the Vrukaari a bad hand. It was a topic Ixdahan was overdue to explore on the Galactic Array, after living for eight months with his transmogged body. He opened the secure relay Group Leader Ishialdrol had set up for him, closed his eyes and listened.

According to the Array, the Vrukaari emerged from frigid oceans of liquid ammonia some 500 million years ago, as creatures not too different from the electric eels or torpedo rays of Earth. Like their terrestrial counterparts, they relied on a powerful jolt of bioelectricity for both hunting and self-defense.

Over the next few million years, in response to new environmental pressures, internal organs that had once delivered that simple shock could now produce an unusually dense electromagnetic field — guided by primitive mental impulses.

Naturally, creatures with the best aim had the best chance of survival. So in just a few thousand generations, these same mental impulses developed into a network of telekinetic and telepathic abilities. This enabled them to snare prey with a thought, send predators smashing into the rocks, or make the fiercest beasts tremble with imaginary terrors.

Sadly, these elegant adaptations interfered with normal anatomical development. As a result, a Vrukaari was a central, globular mass of cartilage and malformed bone, encased in loose-fitting, pale-yellow skin that was marred by a continuous oozing of slimy secretions. Ixdahan imagined himself explaining this to Lena.

"Kind of like a beach ball that rolled into some mayonnaise," he thought.

Attached to this mass, the Galactic Array continued, were a set of stubby limbs, which ended in barely functional hands and feet. No wonder the Vrukaari preferred gliding on electromagnetic fields to walking, and levitation to using their hands. Yet, in spite of these limitations, they continued their steady climb to the top of the food chain on Vrukaar Prime.

That is, despite the burden of having five noses, two mouths and three pairs of eyes. For Evolution's other cruel joke involved splitting each sense organ into separate specialized units as, one set of eyes for color, one for depth perception and one for focus. What they needed five noses for was anybody's guess.

Then, a mere 7,600 years ago, a turning point occurred in Vrukaari history, with the ill-fated invasion of the Dra'nahli, one of the first peoples to attain a Level 4 civilization.

If the Dra'nahli had expected to conquer the sullen blobs who greeted them, they were in for a nasty surprise. Less than a week after they landed, in-fighting broke out among them, with hundreds killed by rival factions. Their numbers reduced, the Dra'nahli woke one morning to find their own weapons, suspended in air, aimed directly at their heads, hearts and haunches.

Soon, some 40,000 proud warriors were enslaved to the Vrukaari, teaching them the rudiments of science and math — but also scrubbing their floors, cooking their meals and keeping an open mind about the meaning of humiliation.

Barely fifty years later, based on their acquired know-how, Vrukaari warlords commanded a fleet of marauding ships, and leapt from world to world to dominate other highly evolved cultures as they had the Dra'nahli.

That is, until they ran into the Snaldrialoorans, who matched them in mentallics and were masters of technologies superior to anything the Vrukaari had stolen. But here's what really stung: the Snaldrialoorans sported a set of eight powerful tentacles, each with a unique function, coordinated with a formidable intellect.

"No wonder they hate us," sighed Ixdahan.

He asked himself if a better understanding of Vrukaari culture would help ease the constant tension between the Homeworld and Vrukaar Prime. But his thoughts about the future of diplomacy were interrupted by the clattering whir of 17/Chaarnactral's recharging station.

"So noisy," thought Ixdahan, as he twisted his bulging torso to stare at the robot again.

Wait. What was up with him?

Why was his robot's reformatting process making him so crazy? And why was he so obsessed with Vrukaari history when he had more immediate problems?

For starters, if the Onkendren were helping the Vrukaari willingly, did they have any idea of the horrors their guidance would unleash on the rest of civilization? Or did the Onkendren see the Vrukaari as mere tools to help them regain their dominance of space-time?

If so, Ixdahan reasoned, they were making a mistake. Whatever the state of the universe when the Onkendren went into hiding, new civilizations had grown up in the meantime. Now, the Vrukaari were an advanced, technological culture with a few tricks of their own. Only fools, or a proud people out of touch, would underestimate....

"Can't concentrate," said Ixdahan. He jumped up from his receptacle and rushed over to where the robot stood, motionless. The blinking had intensified now, as it formed ever more complex patterns, which reminded Ixdahan of something he'd heard about on Earth ... no, it couldn't possibly work....

The plan forming in his mind had two advantages. First, sending out individual pulses of mentallic energy over the Galactic Array took many fewer cerebrejules of power and would be harder to detect from any outside source.

Second, by sending the pulses in patterns, like the "Morse Code" he'd read about on Earth, Ixdahan's message would be doubly encrypted. No one on Snaldrialoor would know about Morse Code, nor would they recognize English as a language unless they had experience in such things. Then, if he could tap into Lena's smart phone, whose exact frequencies and access codes were also unknown to anyone from his stellar sector, his message would be almost untraceable.

But there was one flaw in his logic. Ixdahan had no idea whether Lena understood Morse Code. Had she learned it from her father as part of her training as a boat pilot?

Still, with nothing to lose and no better ideas, Ixdahan decided to give it a try. He focused his tired mind on Earth's coordinates through the Galactic Array and made a preliminary sweep of its solar system. Satisfied that there were no eavesdroppers, he gave himself the all clear.

"Lena, it's me Ixdahan Derek. Received your transmission...." he began.

Where this message would lead, he had no idea. But he did know contacting Lena was sure to yield priceless information, including whether she and her friends were still OK.

By the time he was finished transmitting, the dwarf star of Vrukaar Prime was peeking over the horizon, and 17/Chaarnactral awoke from its deep diagnostic with a series of rhythmic twitches in its arms.

"You haven't slept," Ixdahan heard it say, as he was dozing off.

"Brilliant deduction," said the youngest member of the SSA. "Anything new on the Array?"

"Something old," said 17/Chaarnactral. "Archeologists on Traahlgreubewehn have uncovered a rare early dynasty soup tureen, covered with inscriptions."

"Not a recipe, I suppose?" asked Ixdahan.

"Please," said the robot, as its operating temperature rose a full nano degree. "There is a reference to dark matter resequencing. It's right under an image of a Traahlgreubewehn hunter with her foot on the neck of a...."

"Never mind," said Ixdahan, "I get the picture. So tell me something: how much do you know about Onkendren history? And I mean the real thing, not the myths."

"I have as much information as is available in the declassified files," said 17/Chaarnactral.

"And the classified files?" asked Ixdahan.

"They're off limits, by law, and … oh, no…." said the AI.

A minute later, over 17/Chaarnactral's strident protests, the sole heir to House Daherek became, once more, a criminal, by ordering an AI to appropriate sensitive data without direct authorization from the Snaldrialooran Synod.

Sure, there were risks. But based on what he knew now, they were worth it. The more he knew about this mysterious people the better.

"Can't wait to the last minute, like before," he mumbled, and headed for the sonic shower on the other side of his quarters. Along the way, he paused long enough to link his mind directly to the Galactic Array, and leaned in hard, until its massive rush of mentallic energy surged through him. For the next few hours, that surge would substitute for the restorative powers of sleep.

"I hasten to point out," said 17/Chaarnactral, "that's a great way to burn out your cerebral cortex."

Ixdahan ignored the robot, stepped into the boxy shower, and hoped his calculated risks would bear fruit soon enough to justify their potential to A.) fry his brain and B.) ignite an interstellar war.

CHAPTER 7

His GNC Denali finally road-ready, Vance Maultsby stowed his bicycle pump, grabbed his airflow helmet and made sure Arkansas was safe, before locking up the house and speeding down his residential street toward the Hunter's Wend section of Skudderton.

Now what, he wondered, made him think to check out the mailboxes along the route? Had there been a time when they mattered?

"That's just crazy," he said into the early afternoon breeze. His mind filled with half-remembered images from last year: of mailboxes from every country on the planet clustered together like wild mushrooms after a rainstorm.

Yet as weird as they seemed, Vance's memories had the feel of reality, as solid as the road under his wheels or the smell of the skunk he barely dodged as it scooted across the winding road in front of him.

"Nasty," said Vance. He pedaled by as fast as possible, until he almost missed the turn-off he needed for Hunter's Wend, the semi-private community at the northeast corner of Skudderton. He'd been here more than once, he remembered now. The first time was with Lena, when they discovered Derek's robotic caretakers lying dead to the world in their recharging units — the victims of a Vrukaari biomechanical fungus.

"Was there, like ... like an invasion?" he wondered aloud, as the last traces of the Snaldrialooran mental block started slipping away and he recalled helping Derek save the planet. Along with the memory of the events came the memory of the deep-seated terror that they might fail. It was almost enough to make him wish he could forget again.

As he pulled up, at last, to the weed-choked front lawn of Derek's old house, Vance also remembered what got him through his fear. It was Derek's rock-solid confidence and the calm way he had of explaining stuff, even when it was seconds away from blowing your head off.

OK, Vance was here but, now what? What were the odds that the house had been left untouched since last October?

And yet, as he approached the front door, he noticed how thoroughly abandoned it looked. Hundreds of daily editions of the *Skudderton Record* littered the front porch, most still wrapped in their pale blue plastic bags. All but the latest were a soggy mess of rain, dirt and bird droppings.

Likewise, mail from credit card and insurance companies, discount pharmacies, the Skudderton City Council, not to mention utility bills and "Value Paks," lay strewn in a sticky, damp lump of sodden neglect.

"Figures," Vance mumbled, as he tried the front door. Whatever had made him forget Derek, had made the entire town, maybe the entire world forget, too. And now, as the door swung open, he saw the whole of last year spread out before him, as if he were looking down on it from a mountain top.

Still not trusting his senses, Vance took care to close the front door before stepping through the living room into the kitchen. There, his eyes settled on the ominous black disk resting on a marble-topped island cabinet in the center of the room. It was the device in the photo he'd seen at home, in one of the files in the PROJECT V folder.

"V for Vrukaari," thought Vance, "those wack alien dudes who tried to take over."

Vance checked his smartphone, glanced at code in the photo he'd taken, and looked for some way to enter it into the disk. His hands shaking, but firmly in the grip of curiosity, he tiptoed over to the island, ran his fingers over the disk — and jumped back a foot as the device sprang to life, nearly doubling in size.

At that, a small gray console popped out of one side of the disk, complete with a keypad made up of Arabic numerals, next to which sat a small toggle switch. Vance nodded, as he realized that using a human interface for an alien device was the best way to hide it in plain sight.

Anyone coming across the device by accident, especially in an upscale neighborhood like this, would have assumed it was an esoteric food processor or a tantric exercise machine. They'd would be too embarrassed to ask, for fear of seeming seriously uncool.

Great. Now he had a bigger puzzle: Was he really stupid enough to enter an access code into a machine he barely remembered so it could transfer him to somewhere he couldn't recall?

"Might end up in deep space," he said.

Obviously, he told himself, the smart thing to do was walk away. Besides, if his restored memories were accurate, he'd already done his bit to save Humanity's sorry behind.

On the other hand, what were the odds he'd ever get another chance like this?

In a couple of months he might be sitting across from an Admissions Counsellor at U Mass Amherst, trying to get real about the possibility of majoring in Computer Science, if he got in, that is. How bad would it feel to pass up a second try with advanced alien tech, just because he had a date with Momses riding mower?

He smacked his forehead. Too bad his conscience wouldn't let him off that easy.

"If I don't do this, it's got nothing to do with Moms," he said. "Could've done the lawn thing hours ago."

So if he went ahead, he decided, he had to know it was because he *chose* to, and was ready to take the consequences.

"Like getting my head blown off," he said, "or getting grounded all summer." But he wasn't exactly sure which was worse.

Wasn't there a way to know if taking this incalculable risk was his best option? Vance peered around, and his gaze stretched into the living room, through the arched threshold to his right. At last, it came to rest on a shiny, advanced design radio lying flat on a faux-colonial coffee table. Maybe switching on some music, or the news, would give his whirling thoughts a chance to settle down.

The radio, however, had other ideas.

Although it already looked as if it were switched on, he couldn't find a way to tune in his favorite stations. The most he could get was gravelly static — that he kind of *thought* he heard.

Frustrated, he jammed his thumb into what looked like the power button and pivoted on his Nikes toward the kitchen.

A babble of voices echoed in his mind.

"Sounds like a freaking airport," he muttered. He returned to the radio, to see if he could find a station he liked. When he had no luck, he assumed the batteries were running low. Yet he looked in vain for a cord he could plug in.

Of course, this was no radio at all, but the metadigital transponder Ixdahan had used last year to discover the Vrukaari assault plan and contact his cousin Jalgren for advice. Ixdahan had also used it to warn the Snaldrialooran Defense Ministry. But no one would listen.

Vance shook the tension from his shoulders as he left the transponder to babble on in his mind and wandered back into the kitchen, The device, he decided, was confusing — but dangerous? Not so much. Otherwise, neither Derek nor his robotic guardians would have used it.

"Might learn something about what's going down," he said. Would his brain adjust, he wondered, or would the device produce a simultaneous translation? With a shrug, he decided to leave the transponder on until he got back from wherever the ominous black disk sent him.

Even though he had no clue what to expect, the arrival of the babbling voices had convinced him this could be his last great adventure, before college and family and who-knew-what-else might chain him tight to Earth for good. He swallowed hard.

"Not throwing this chance away for nobody," he said. "Even Moms."

Vance noticed the antique grandfather clocks on either side of the stairwell leading up to Derek's old room and scratched his head. It looked like they were still keeping accurate time almost a year after his last visit, with no one to wind them up, no battery casing and no power cord.

"Must have an infinity power source," he thought and realized this must also be true of the transponder. He had no way of knowing that the Snaldrialoorans routinely powered small appliances by direct energy transfer through the Galactic Array.

All at once, the twin clocks chimed 3:00 in unison.

By checking the time on his Moto X, he could see the walnut-paneled clocks were perfectly in sync — with themselves and with local daylight savings time. More to the point, from Vance's perspective, it was getting late.

"Access denied. Enter interstellar authorization code now to initiate interface with the Galactic Array." Now the voice started a loop Vance had every reason to believe would continue until the end of time.

As he looked back toward the kitchen, where the ominous black disk rested, taunting him, on the island cabinet, Vance wondered if he'd need a new access code to return from wherever he landed.

And what about the transponder? Who knew if he'd be able to get the device working again if he shut it off?

"No idea how to do that, either," he muttered.

So, as the grandfather clocks went silent again, Vance decided his best bet was to leave the transponder alone. After an entire school year of going through the motions with his mind impaired and his sights set on a narrow horizon, he was now plugged in again to something bigger than himself — bigger than the Skudderton-Thornberry mall or the latest update of Windows.

"Gotta find out," he thought. "Maybe the Vrukaari are back, and Alien Dude needs me for whatever."

Vance opened the Word file he'd sent to his Moto X and entered the access code on the page into the keypad on the ominous black disk, one number at a time. His eyelids tight, he flipped the toggle switch.

A moment later, he opened his eyes — from inside Derek's Snaldrialooran lander

"Whoa," he said.

But if Vance had any thought of getting acclimated to the alien spacecraft before exploring it, he was in for a shock. "Welcome," said the blue-gray face of an … an octopus? … on a video screen to his left. "I was hoping one of you would find your way here."

"Who…?" Vance sputtered.

"I am known on my Homeworld as Captain Altriavahn, commander of the Snaldrialooran starspanner *Kryldria Valaarn,*" she said. "But you may call me Dahaleen."

Vance fought to control the tremor in his voice.

"So, you know about … about Derek … I mean, uh, Ixdahan?" he asked.

"I do," said the alien. "Enough to know he needs your help again."

CHAPTER 8

The view from the starspanner was, as usual, magnificent.

With the dwarf star of Vrukaar Prime silhouetted against the black-on-blackness of space and haloed with the radiance of a nearby cluster galaxy, it was a picture of strength, power and energy on an immense scale.

It was, in fact, a perfect analogy for the image Aalthrashrintorb Leek had of himself, as the *de facto* ruler of the Vrukaari Federation. Not in so many words, mind you, not with the kind of political heft others chose to throw around in public. There were no manifestoes, no uniforms, no glittering rallies and certainly no grotesque, monumental architecture to celebrate his greatness. He was happy enough to leave that to his puppet warlords.

Yes, so much better this way ... his self-satisfied mind reassured him.

So it should surprise no one if, in this moment of quiet reflection, the supreme Vrukaari had put aside the ornate, tent-like business suit he usually wore, in favor of a simple black robe. As with all of his clothing, Leek's tailors had carefully designed this understated outfit to flatter his above-average height. If he still indulged himself in a solid silver amulet studded with sapphire and opal, it was only to remind him of the riches that, soon enough, would be in his grasp.

That was Aalthrashrintorb's way. In place of brash swagger, he preferred the quiet, ceaseless flow of influence, the nudging sense that thousands existed only to perpetuate and extend the force of his will. From politicians, finance ministers and so on, down to the street-level informants he owned outright, his will was absolute. And to think the nearly limitless power he enjoyed today began as a simple dream to build a financial empire!

The starspanner itself reflected this same reserve, in its lack of superfluous ornaments or badges of office. In their place were view screens, control panels and workstations in the most severe, minimalist style. Nevertheless, as was well known, the supreme Vrukaari took childish delight in the flickering displays and blinking indicators of high-tech equipment. No engineer in the Federation who valued his or her livelihood would fail to add a layer of "imperial winkiness" to any device he ordered. Nor was he immune to the creature comforts of luxury, as evidenced by the cushions of soft Corlaanthanese leather that dotted his living quarters.

Aalthrashrintorb Leek smiled to himself and paused to levitate a midnight blue collar, from a nearby end table of stainless steel, to a spot just a few inches from his five symmetrically placed noses. What was the true meaning of this object? He had operatives at work on the problem at that very moment, each of them grateful in their own way for a chance to prove themselves.

For within the Vrukaari Federation and most of its satellite planetary unions, you were either in the direct employ of Mr. Leek or you were taking orders from someone who was.

His Magnificence leaned back in a receptacle carved from the finest Ybitrian marble, and silently toasted himself with a glass of blue Chlevahndorean wine. Visible through the starboard portal of his huge ship was a blazing mass of brilliant stars.

He gave them a gracious nod.

"Well done," he thought. "A universe of limitless power, under one thumb."

Most of the time, that is, and with constant attention to detail. Today, for instance, his own beloved daughter had complained of a civil servant making trouble at the Hotel Phaardraalassoor. Oddly enough, the same person had turned up at the Great Leap Forward trade show with a suspiciously advanced-design AI.

While it wasn't unheard of for a junior-grade building inspector to have a robotic assistant, routine surveillance scans — where would he be without them? — revealed the assistant demonstrated a level of sophistication far exceeding established norms for such a functional post.

More troubling, however, was the shaky background data available on this Genko personage. Here was a young man, not fully adult, who relied on direct-to-cortex training modules to do his work, and yet still getting it right. Every one of the code violations he'd cited had been correct. They'd been known quantities from the day the hotel opened.

But in 15 cycles of operation no one — *no one* — had dared mention them. *They* preferred to take the prudent course and rubber stamp the approval of the previous inspector. Now, that showed initiative, energy and, as such, was *more* troubling than the over-achieving robot. A Vrukaari civil servant with backbone? Unheard of.

Well, the lad was young and not likely to sustain such a high level of competence for long. The puzzling part was the source of his arrogance. If he had come from one of the Federation's first families, that would have been explanation enough. A brief m-mail from one of Leek's thousands of assistants would have alerted the boy's parents to his rather shocking ignorance.

But such was not the case, for Xihandevaan Genko was known to be an orphan from a backwater colony planet, raised by the Federation and injected into the civil service when it became clear he was fit for nothing else. Imagine, 18 cycles old and already this boy had been pegged as a non-entity of the highest order!

Trouble was, non-entities weren't usually in the habit of mouthing off to authority, and with a degree of diplomatic finesse he rarely saw in his own best operatives.

But there the trail ran cold. That is, except for one other troubling detail. This Genko had been seen picking up objects at the trade show with his hands instead of using a standard telekinetic maneuver he ought to have learned as a child. Had life in the provinces sunk so low that average citizens now forsook good taste, even in public?

"Forget it," the blobular magnate whispered into the lush surroundings of his private den. "Can't sniff at every launchpad." Besides, it may have been no more than a momentary lapse, a holdover from childish behavior the boy would soon leave behind.

Leek would ensure his operatives kept an eye on Genko, nonetheless. If his suspicions were worth their weight in *glexizahrickat* sweat, Genko would show his true colors before long, and find his next moves severely compromised.

No, there were more important things to occupy Leek's frontal lobes that evening, he decided, as his eyes — the pair he used to zoom in and out on an object — settled once again on the midnight blue collar still hovering slightly to the left of Nose 3.

For one, the most recent news about the Onkendren, was that the ungrateful losers had been holding out on him. That is, if he could believe the reports from the military attaché assigned to shadow them. Based on an already impressive resistance to mentallic control, the Onkendren had somehow erected an effective mentallic blockade and were now unmanageable.

But, as the ruler of the Vrukaari Federation knew, primitive methods of persuasion often succeeded where modern science failed. So it was that an unlucky Onkendren, dragged out of bed in the middle of the night and subjected to Relnachthranaahren acid torture, managed to cough up part of the mystery before passing out in agony.

His confession? The midnight blue collars the Onkendren wore, like the one Leek was staring at with such fascination tonight, were the key to their defiance. Yet because the Onkendren name for them, *psykrella*, yielded no information about their function, Leek knew he'd have to dig deeper.

Not wishing to arouse suspicion, the supreme Vrukaari had ordered the wretched humanoid cured of the ill-effects of torture. The fool's mind was then filled with implanted memories of idyllic dreams, and he was sent home wearing a dummy psykrella.

Determined to discover the true nature of the device, Aalthrashrintorb Leek took the unusual step of bringing in an outside expert: A certain Snaldrialooran engineer with a greater need for cold hard cash than for loyalty to his Homeworld.

He felt no shame in entrusting this project to someone outside the Federation. He needed results, not patriotism, and no one within the Federation, or rather no one he could trust, was capable of ferreting out the truth about the psykrella. Besides, let the tentacled snobs prove their worth in the universe, for once, by doing something useful.

"Then we'll see how quickly these humanoids fall in line once their plaything has been snatched away," he said to the star clusters in the deep distance that now entered his field of vision.

A chime sounded.

"Mr. Leek, Sir," said a meek voice through the ship's intercom.

"What is it?" growled Leek, annoyed at this sudden — and verbal — interruption.

"Nogerahnal Gelundru to see you, Your Eminence," the voice piped up again.

"Show Engineer Gelundru in," said Leek, and made himself a note to fire every non-mentallic staffer in the morning.

Really? "Talking"? It simply wasn't dignified.

CHAPTER 9

With the world around her swirling toward destruction for the second time in her young life, Lena was eager to forget about aliens, friend or foe, long enough for a warm Skype visit with Dad and Rhea every couple of days. The tricky part was hiding her preoccupation with the whales' startling mentallic abilities, not to mention the writing on the ancient Greek amphora.

Instead, she was forced to improvise a description of events from a Typical Day in the summer program.

"The whales are so beautiful, Dad," she heard herself saying. How hard she wished she could tell him the truth about … everything.

"You have dolphins out there?" Todd Gabrilowicz asked his daughter. "Ours are acting kind of funny."

Lena bit her lip, as she listened to Todd's description of roving packs of streamlined dolphins pausing every so often in the middle of the ocean to arrange themselves into distinct patterns. Seen from the air, as demonstrated by a helicopter pilot from the local TV news station, the patterns resembled characters in an un-Earthly language.

"It's like they're trying to tell us something," said Rhea.

"Like what?" asked Todd. "They want more salmon?"

But, as Lena knew, the question was neither as trivial as her dad wanted to believe, or as mystical as she suspected Rhea might imagine. As to whomever the whales in Alaska were trying to reach through the dolphins in New Jersey, Lena was pretty sure it was the same people ... aliens ... creatures ... whatever ... who had buried the amphora off the southeast coast of Alaska and, most likely, sent the unknown energy pulse that had awakened the humpbacks from what might be thousands of years of psychological hibernation.

The part that worried her was this: Did the whales expect their message to be read by a set of incredibly sensitive long-range scanners — or was an alien cruiser from Derek's galactic neighborhood hiding in the rings of Saturn? And once they'd read the message, what action would the aliens take?

Worse, why did this scary alien stuff have to interfere with her summer, with a simple catch-up call with Dad and Rhea? Wasn't she entitled to be a kid a little longer?

But as she logged off Skype, Lena realized how silly the word "entitled" was in a world where, with or without Derek, the Vrukaari and an ocean full of alien-possessed whales, life could twist and turn you any way it pleased without warning.

Here she'd fallen in love twice with Silvano, just to break up over the stupidest things, starting with him trying to talk her out of spending the summer in Alaska. Not, mind you, because he was worried about her safety, but because he didn't want to be alone for three months.

Well, truth be told, Lena reminded herself, there was more to the story than that.

Fact was, both of them were growing up and growing apart because of it. It's one thing to be gaga for love when the entire concept is fresh and new — but really get to know someone? That's when you discover you're not ready to be stuck with every decision you made last month, last week or yesterday. It's when your perspective shifts and you need the freedom to see yourself in a new way, even if Lover Boy wants you to stay the same forever. Still....

"Wasn't all his fault," said Lena to a picture of Arkansas she'd posted on Instagram before leaving home for the airport. In reality, the pressure of keeping silent about the events of last year had made Lena irritable around Silvano.

Lena felt a headache coming on.

"So much to tell him, and I couldn't," she thought. But how do you *not* share the most important event of your life with the most important person in your life?

Because it was Sunday, Lena could easily have spent the next twelve hours stewing over the past, and the present, for that matter, if her text message ring tone hadn't shaken her out of her reverie, and nearly out of her socks.

> remember everything now
> watch out 4 whales
> dude called u in morse code?
> that just wack
> Octopus Lady sez hi
> txt back / gotta talk 2 U =^]

... the message read — a message from Vance!

"Morse code," she whispered. That would explain the weird voicemail she received last night at 2:00 a.m. It was a series of beeps she almost deleted, until she remembered that, in a situation like this, anything could be a clue. But assuming Vance's text message wasn't his idea of a goofy prank, how would he know about that voicemail?

"One thing at a time," she remembered Derek saying so often when her mind would fill with a thousand questions. She decided to take his advice and got busy with her laptop. She Googled up Morse Code signals and played the voicemail over and over until she'd transcribed it all.

"He never could shut up," she said. Through teary eyes, she remembered a boy who had no idea of human limitations. Like the time he asked her to recite the names of every major city in the United States, so he'd have some idea of the scope of the Vrukaari invasion plan.

And hour of two later, Lena looked down at her finished transcription.

"OK," she said, "what do you want?" She wished Ixdahan wanted more fashion advice, like that time at his house, before the madness started.

But it was not to be, for the transcription read:

Lena, it's me Ixdahan Derek. Received your transmission. This time it's not the Vrukaari, but people from my side of the universe are definitely involved. It may be that the creatures you perceive as whales are not what they seem. By the way, has anyone retrieved the ancient object you described? If so, try to contact me at once ... use the transponder in my old house, remember? Good luck and don't worry. Miss you.

"Miss you?" said Lena, not believing her eyes. Did Derek know what a phrase like that meant to a girl, she wondered. Fat lot of good it did her, anyway, with her world in danger and her alien friend so far away it would take more lifetimes than the whole of human history to get to him.

Still, it was a nice thought. And maybe that's what Derek had wanted to get across. But the big question was, how did this message tie in with Vance's? For now, it almost seemed as if Vance knew more about the situation with the whales than Derek ... Ixdahan.

How could that be? If Vance had been talking to an "Octopus Lady," it probably meant he'd been contacted by someone from Derek's planet, which probably also meant the current situation was more serious than she'd imagined.

"This time, Earth isn't the only planet in danger," she thought.

Maybe the smart thing would be to contact Vance first and then get back to Derek, who obviously had no idea she was thousands of kilometers away from Skudderton and the metadigital transponder that would make communication a whole lot easier. But with a little help from Vance's Snaldrialooran contact, she might be able to get through.

"Then what?" she wondered, as she hit the speed dial for Vance on her Samsung.

"Girlfriend?" said Vance, a second later, "Is that you?"

"What's going on?" Lena started, "How did you…?"

"Octopus Lady clued me in," said Vance.

"And?" asked Lena.

"Nothing too crazy. Except for the part where the whole freaking galaxy gets trashed," said Vance.

"No mutant mailboxes, though, right?" asked Lena.

"Yeah," said Vance, "there is that. So … I want to send you a package."

"What?" asked Lena. "Not in the mail, right?"

"You'll know it when you see it," said Vance, "then check out your phone."

"OK, that makes no sense," said Lena, surprised at the tension in her voice.

"You want to tell me what does?" asked Vance. "You'll see it in about 12 hours."

"Why so long?" asked Lena. Derek, she remembered, always acted fast.

"Octopus Lady has some numbers to crunch, I guess," said Vance. "Can't explain it any better over the phone."

Lena told him she understood and Vance filled her in on a few more details before hanging up. But deep down, her understanding had grown faster than she knew. Now, between one breath and the next, the events of the last few weeks coalesced into a single, ugly picture.

And right at the center was Derek, the clueless kid she'd met by accident while minding her own business, a day after her first indirect encounter with the Vrukaari.

How foolish to think her life could ever have gone back to "normal." When this was over, whatever "this" was, the definition of normal would have to be rewritten. Better yet, she wondered, why not throw the word out of the dictionary altogether?

CHAPTER 10

Much as he preferred the splendid isolation of his palatial starspanner, Aalthrashrintorb Leek resigned himself to the fact that, from time to time, he had to put in an appearance in his stately cover office, as head of Leek Investors, LLC.

He even, perish the thought, had to field calls from the company's top clients. They were small-minded, insistent people who made his skin crawl and who, if they pushed him too hard, would find their assets seized by the Bureau of Revenue Equity & Distribution and find themselves whisked away to a state penitentiary for tax evasion.

The fact that his firm had facilitated those same evasions caused him no loss of sleep. Really. When little people became greedy and made demands above their social grade ... well, there was no time like the present for them to face the consequences.

Let these strutting fools spend a decade or two in deep isolation, away from the luxuries they couldn't get enough of. In 10 or 20 cycles, they'd see how satisfying a crust of *brachalianar* bread and a cup of *yalloon* could be — if ingested slowly and savored with proper humility.

If the humbled wanted more from life, there were always the light manufacturing plants on Alcheethrazorn 5. In these isolated sectors of the Federation, the shop foremen were keenly aware of the disadvantages of a robotic worker.

Its astonishing competence notwithstanding, a manufacturing robot's need for a dust-free environment and an expensive inventory of spare parts made it a distinct liability. Not to mention its annoying habit of making helpful suggestions, the kind that made every living being in the room look stupid.

Organic employees? The problems they created were trifling by comparison. If they complained about working conditions, a few hours out in the frozen wastelands surrounding the plant would endow them with a more enlightened perspective on the value of work. Sure, they drove productivity down, but the resulting scarcity automatically drove prices up, especially for certain categories of luxury items enjoyed by the lonely, the bored — and the insatiable.

On this day, fortunately, trading was light and Aalthrashrintorb's interactions with his elite customers were few. That was the advantage of having set an example from the start. By now, most of his clients had learned the value of leaving money management to the experts.

As a result, Leek had many free hours to tend to the real business at hand: evaluating the report of the late Nogerahnal Gelundru on the Onkendren psykrella he'd been given to analyze.

Technically, Dr. Gelundru wasn't dead, merely stowed away in a stasis chamber. Though his disappearance would arouse suspicion, Leek knew first hand that Gelundru's compulsive nature made him easy prey for any determined investigator.

And given that nature, Gelundru might compromise himself again at any point, and be him eager to reveal the secret of the psykrella, and Leek's entire operation, to the first person who could buy him out of trouble. Better by far, to contain the problem for now.

Yet there was still one irritating detail. Nogerahnal's q-transfer to Leek's starspanner had naturally been coordinated through the Galactic Array, and was now a matter of public record. Tracing Nogerahnal to Leek would be a simple matter of issuing a subpoena — or a gratuity.

On the other hand, it was well known that occasional transfer errors occurred, especially when a slightly inebriated gentleman insisted on entering the coordinates on his own. It was the least the Vrukaari government could do, to redirect the disoriented Snaldrialooran to his proper destination….

But enough of this petty anxiety, Leek told himself. More to the point was Gelundru's report, for in it lay the key to reaping a rich harvest of technological data from the minds of the increasingly pompous Onkendren.

And that was good news, because these long-living humanoids were beginning to remind him of those eight-tentacled snobs on Snaldrialoor, with their hypocritically high-minded sermons about "interstellar law" and "the right of every planet to self-determination."

Ha! Explain that to the thousands of colonized worlds they controlled, each graced with a garrison of several hundred thousand troops, accompanied by towering munitions dumps, and watched over by sprawling orbital space stations. That's aside, mind you, from standard-issue battle cruisers, which they expected everyone to believe were solely for the inhabitants' protection.

"The only self-determining factor on one of those worlds" sneered Leek, "is an eight-legged boogie man ready to bore you to death at dinner before the first course is served."

The supreme Vrukaari snorted through all five noses. No more of this mental meandering! It was time to focus. Now, what had Gelundru reported?

Through a process we cannot, as yet, claim to understand, the Onkendren psykrella magnifies mentallic energy to unprecedented levels.

"Typical academic," Leek grunted. "Wastes my time with the obvious."

Lucky for him, the answers he sought weren't far behind. But they weren't especially cheering. While it was possible for a Vrukaari to wear a psykrella, the probability of severe brain damage rose exponentially with each use.

The demands the device makes on the Vrukaari cerebral cortex cannot be sustained for more than 15 gilhaarn at the utmost before a rapid decline in mental functioning sets in.

"Barely enough time to boil an egg," muttered Aalthrashrintorb. But what he read next nearly brought on epileptic seizures.

In light of this, a more robust, more efficient central nervous system, exhibited by the Ybitrian or Snaldrialooran anatomy....

"Ridiculous," the supreme Vrukaari growled, and was giving serious thought to cutting the power to the Snaldrialooran's stasis chamber, until he saw a sizeable benefit to following Gelundru's insulting advice. Ybitrian agents, caught wearing a psykrella, would hardly be believed if they claimed to be working for the real masterminds, the Vrukaari. It was, Leek grasped, one of the many tactical advantages of being underestimated.

Hadn't he seen that principle at work less than a year ago when that brat from the Daherek clan sold out his homeworld? The sluggish response of his compatriots had been almost enough to ensure the capture of the rich resources on that distant planet. Because, as "everyone knew," the Vrukaari could never....

Bah! He was doing it again: wasting precious time with angry ranting about the past. In the end, the Daherek boy had taught him a valuable lesson about the perils of underestimating your enemy. Too bad the youngster had been incarcerated so quickly after the incident. With careful conditioning, a personality like that — devious, proud, ingenious, and not a little reckless — would be invaluable at a time like this.

Come to think of it, that thought triggered a vague memory of a data point he'd seen in that fool Yarrow's report. There was another, a young Earth girl, who had also shown unusual promise as a soldier. Yes, that was the phrase the deceased Lieutenant Colonel had used:

> *Properly trained, cloned in great enough numbers, an army of soldiers with a mentality like hers would be a great asset to the Vrukaari military.*

Leek leaned back in his customized receptacle and revelled in how rich a playing field stretched before him. With troops like these and access to previously unknown technologies, victory, to put it mildly, was assured.

Now his imagination took hold of him, as he envisioned a universe cleansed of hypocritical overlords, carefully guarding their secrets against "barbarian hordes."

"Things are about to change, my pretentious blue friends," he said to his computer screen. "We'll see how long your pomposity lasts under *real* leadership."

And with that, the closest thing to a smile that could ever appear on a Vrukaari, given its loose, slimy skin, spread out across Aalthrashrintorb Leek's face. Ah, victory: like mother's milk with a dash of Gherlumbaarnen whiskey!

CHAPTER 11

Callie Ann Connors looked out over the shimmering water in the brightly-lit Olympic-size swimming pool and smiled. After three weeks, it was still hard to believe she was actually training at North Baltimore Aquatic Club, where so many gold medalists had….

But, OK, she knew she had a long way to go. Winning the state championship in New Jersey as team captain of the Skudderton Skidders was one thing. Placing in the US Olympic team trials … well … she had a shot.

At the same time, the girl on her left was the captain of the state championship team in Florida and that girl coming out of the locker room had been captain of the state championship team in Hawaii. In fact, every girl at the training facility was an extremely strong swimmer who was as eager to make the team as she was.

The one thing that saved the situation was Coach Kepler, her trainer. Now in his 50s, he'd sent more swimmers to the Olympics than anyone and with plenty of time left to train, she felt confident she could make it. Best of all, it seemed as if *he* felt confident, too.

Too bad Lena wasn't here to see how far Callie Ann had come since last year, when she first heard the news about poor Blainy — or "Blade" as everyone else called him. Why, she wondered, did he have to go driving in that condition? No matter what she did, she could never get the sound of his voice on their last phone call out of her mind.

"It was like he was … crazy," she mumbled, shivering a bit. And though she couldn't remember what Blainy had ranted about, she was sure it was gibberish.

But why was she thinking about this now? And why, after so many months, was she having that dream again, about an ugly little man in a crushed velvet jumpsuit glaring at her, trying to grab her, trying to….

It was only a stupid dream. Yet the funny thing was, it started up again when Coach Kepler came back from Fourth of July weekend. Come to think of it, he came back kind of strange, though at first, she couldn't put her finger on why he seemed different.

Except, that is, for the distant look in his eyes, as if he were listening to a radio broadcast no one else could hear. And while he was still positive, he kept using the same supportive catch phrases over and over again.

"It's like he memorized them for a play or whatever," she thought.

Just yesterday, he really creeped her out, by sounding way too close to a doll she had when she was eight. It was the kind where you pushed a button and it would play back one of a couple dozen sayings.

Now it was Coach Kepler who, just like Callie Ann's old doll, often repeated the same sentence two or three times in a row — like he was broken.

But, no way, right? He must have a case of nerves, what with the stiff competition the other girls were giving her. Too bad Lena wasn't around to talk this out with. But now, Callie Ann's former best friend was up in Alaska, and they weren't talking any more. Not since late last fall, after Blainy … after his crash. They'd almost started the friendship up again and then that loser Silvano started bossing Lena around.

What was up with guys anyway?

On the other hand, with Lena acting silent and moody and spending so many hours out on the water alone, maybe the poor guy was desperate. Probably figured he had to "put his foot down," like that was ever the right thing to do when you're trying to win a girl over.

"First off, it's just *wrong*," whispered Callie Ann to the light bouncing off the water in the colorful pool. Suddenly more self-conscious, she thought, "And second, it's so stupid. What, like any girl's gonna bow down to you?"

OK, she decided, it was time to take a deep breath and focus on her practice. But Coach Kepler had said to stay out of the water, that he had something important to tell her before practice — about her future.

What did *that* mean, she wondered and, anyway, where the freak was he? Before the holiday, he was always on time and yelled at her whenever she was a minute late for practice. Wait, there he was now. He was wearing the same rumpled suit he'd worn ever since coming back.

But once he'd shown Callie Ann into his office, Coach Kepler said nothing at all. He merely stared at her until she almost kicked over her chair, called a car service and caught the next bus back to Skudderton.

At last he spoke, but not before standing up and leaning over her.

"What if I told you I could get you into a new training program that would guarantee you a spot on the US Summer Olympic team next year?" he said.

Callie Ann sprang to her feet and pushed him out of her way.

"What's the deal, here?" she said. "My mom and dad paid *you* a lot of money to be my coach. Now you're telling me…."

"I'm not telling," said Coach Kepler. And for once, he sounded like his old self again. "I'm asking you to see for yourself whether a new elite program might work better for you."

"But…." sputtered Callie Ann.

"I've already discussed this with your parents," said Kepler as he leaned up against the far wall of his office. "They're excited for you. But you know what? Think about it. We'll do our regular practice today and then you give Mort and Julie a call, OK?"

"Sure," said Callie Ann. Despite the plaques and trophies that lined the Coach's office, the symbols of his success, she felt anything but certain about her future. The whole thing seemed so creepy. And why was her coach suddenly reminding her of Blainy's old boss — that guy….

"Oh my God, his name was Yarrow — the guy in the dream," she mumbled as she headed back to the pool. And though she wasn't exactly sure what that name meant, she knew it was nothing good.

CHAPTER 12

For the first time in two days, Ixdahan took a relaxed deep breath in the morning air. Not because his worries were over, for questions still outnumbered answers by a factor of 10 to 1. But the realization that he'd done all he could had temporarily lightened his mood.

Seriously, there was nothing to do but wait. His report on the Vrukaari trade show was still "under review" at the Bureau. And he still hadn't heard back from Lena. Had his message never reached her, been misunderstood, or been intercepted by someone with an interest in interfering? Or had she not yet figured out how to use the transponder he'd left behind?

Whatever. This combination of null set results had left him free to take advantage of the two-day Vrukaari weekend — at the end of a typical seven-day work week — and relax. That is, over the protest of 17/Chaarnactral, who had wanted him to devote the time to practicing his levitation.

"Your clumsiness stands out," said the robot. "Yesterday at the trade show, I had to keep reminding you not to pick things up with your hands. Nobody does that here, unless they have a serious illness."

Though the sole heir to House Daherek would rather have set out alone, he knew the robot was right. So he struck a bargain. If 17/Chaarnactral would let Ixdahan wander the byways and dark alleys of the capital city, Ixdahan would let the AI set him small levitation tasks as they went.

Fact was, he couldn't escape the feeling there was something hidden out there, ready to yield the fresh insight he needed. Because when it came to the possible involvement of the Onkendren, he was totally clueless.

Well, not totally. There had to be a connection between the powder blue soufflé dish the Ybitrian ambassador had given Father, the pale yellow Traahlgreubewehn soup tureen discovered by its archeologists and the ancient Greek amphora Lena had mentioned in her message.

"How many objects did you say the Onkendren buried before they disappeared?" he asked 17/Chaarnactral, as they turned down a quiet side street.

"I didn't say. But the answer is nine," said the robot. "I'll elaborate if you clear away that pile of rubbish with your levitation — without breaking anything."

Ixdahan knew there was no point in arguing. He furrowed his slimy forehead and, within a few seconds, had arranged the trash in three neat piles, sorted first by material, then by recyclability. Ixdahan rolled all six of his eyes. Since when had the Vrukaari cared a nanogram of cosmic dust about recycling?

"Well done," said 17/Chaarnactral. "As I was saying, there were nine objects, each one a modified replica of an artifact produced by a few chosen cultures."

"Any idea why they were chosen?" asked Ixdahan.

"Legends say these cultures were deemed worthy of the honor," said the AI, "but that seems unlikely, considering they were Level 1 civilizations when the Onkendren disappeared."

Ixdahan craned his neck to look up at one of the city's glittery office towers.

"So … what's the real reason? And don't tell me it was random."

"Maybe each location offered an unusually stable geological environment," said the robot, "with a low probability of the object being damaged by seismic or volcanic activity. If so, they may have miscalculated the location they chose for Earth."

"The Gulf of Alaska sees a lot of seismic activity?" asked Ixdahan.

"Just once a terrestrial year, according to the Galactic Array," said the robot. "Although things might have been different, centuries ago."

"But why?" asked Ixdahan, as he hovered over the polyslate tiles that made up the sidewalk. "Why bother to bury objects you obviously care about?"

17/Chaarnactral spun on its rotors.

"Hmm," it said. "Would it help if I read you the definition of 'ambivalence' that's posted on the Galactic Array?"

But Ixdahan wasn't listening. He was too distracted by … by the beautiful Vrukaari female whose image had been flickering at the edge of his field of vision for the last five minutes.

Strange. After eight months, he'd gotten used to his transmogged appearance and the appearance of the Vrukaari. He'd even gone on a few token dates, to avoid seeming weird to his co-workers down at the

Ministry of Codes. But he'd never heard himself use the word "pretty" to describe a Vrukaari, as he had more than one girl on Earth.

Until now, that is, when he found himself hoping this particular Vrukaari might come a little closer and give him an excuse to introduce himself. Wait … she was walking over now.

"17/Chaarnactral, enter Pause Mode," he heard himself say — even though it was a direct breach of Snaldrialooran Security Protocol C^@79>/4#. Nevertheless, by the time the lovely female was standing in front of Ixdahan, his robotic companion might as well have been a lawn ornament for a wealthy merchant's extravagant home.

"Hi," said the female, fluttering her six eyelids in an intriguing pattern that the Vrukaari side of Ixdahan's nature found kind of alluring.

"Do I know you from somewhere?" asked Ixdahan.

He suppressed the urge to add, "like in my dreams," because if there were one thing he'd learned on Earth, it was that nobody sane wants to hear phony, manipulative lines like that. Great. If over-the-top pick-up lines were already popping into his head in the first two seconds, he was in deep trouble. Maybe he shouldn't have deactivated 17/Chaarnactral so quickly.

"We've never met," said the female, "so let me introduce myself. I'm Ciafelipenorg Amla, reporter for the *Gitraarinahol Star Nexus*."

"You must have me mixed up with somebody else," said Ixdahan. He hoped he was right. Had somebody blown his cover?

Ciafelipenorg winked at him again.

"Oh, no," she said, "you're my guy. I saw you at the technology trade show this week, a couple of times, actually."

She moved in closer.

"And I'm curious," she said. "Why would a junior grade building inspector be so interested in high tech?"

Hot flashes darted across Ixdahan's back.

"I … I'm…. It's a hobby," he said. "Don't want to be a building inspector forever."

"A little more than a hobby," said the lovely Ciafelipenorg. "You had your noses in every single display case your robot over there didn't have time to scan. And what's up with your cyber-buddy anyway? Your Mom a shipping magnate or something?"

"What … what do you mean?" asked Ixdahan. What it was about her perfume that made it harder to breathe?

"Oh come on," said the Vrukaari female. "A unit like that is way more expensive than you can afford on a civil service salary."

"It's … it's what the Department gave me," said Ixdahan. "And, by the way, I'm an orphan."

Ciafelipenorg's central mass started trembling.

"An … an orphan?" she laughed. "That has to be the lamest cover story...."

"What?" said Ixdahan.

"Really," said Ciafelipenorg, "most people are better liars by the time they're your age. Now, come on, tell me the truth, so I don't have to make up something worse for my story."

"You … you don't have to write anything about me," said Ixdahan.

He now reached deeper into her mind than the conversational layer they'd been using to communicate. Deeper and deeper he went, as he searched for an access point to begin a Snaldrialooran mind wipe. It was exactly the sort of thing he'd been trained to do in "spy camp" in the weeks between his excruciating transmog experience and the start of his assignment on Vrukaar Prime.

At last he arrived at … *Discerning Guardians of the Pitiless Event Horizon* … she was … she was....

"Onkendren," said Ciafelipenorg in a husky whisper.

"You could have spared me the...." Ixdahan started.

"Heart flutters?" asked the pseudo Vrukaari. "I had to be sure it was you. Besides, you're kind of cute — in your mind, that is."

Ixdahan felt his heart race.

"Thanks,' he said. "I can hardly remember what I used to look like. And I have no idea what I want to look like now."

"Oh, I don't know, about that," said Ciafelipenorg. "I've spent a few minutes in your mind and I can already see you'd rather be humanoid, so you could snuggle up next to a couple of Earth girls."

"You saw … all that?" asked Ixdahan. Embarrassed, he tried to remember if Vrukaari were capable of blushing.

"It's OK, you weren't in the running with me anyway," said Ciafelipenorg. "I'm a little too old for you."

"Right," said Ixdahan, as he hung his head. "17/Chaarnactral told me the estimated average age for an Onkendren is 1,000 years old or more."

"Please," said the Onkendren. "I'm only 871."

Ixdahan looked away. Why was everything in his life so complicated? All he had to do was get attracted to a girl and a problem would pop up. Maybe he should start dating girls he couldn't stand. Maybe *then* everything would work out perfectly … except....

"You still in there?" asked Ciafelipenorg. "I have some information for you and a special request from what's left of the Onkendren, in this sector of the universe."

"What other sector…." sputtered Ixdahan.

Ciafelipenorg sighed.

"You might as well know everything," she said. "There are some of us living right on your girlfriend's planet — 'Earth,' I think they call it. Very unimaginative."

"She's not my…. What are they doing there?" said Ixdahan.

"Can't explain everything now. And definitely not out here in the open," said the Onkendren.

"I get that," said Ixdahan, "but tell me why you made a deal with the Vrukaari."

"Big mistake," said Ciafelipenorg. "When we heard the Ybitrians had uncovered one of our artifacts, we were desperate to get it back. But we'd been out of touch so long — and we were isolated, alone."

"If you'd gone to the Interstellar Consortium…." Ixdahan started.

"That was the first thing we tried," said Ciafelipenorg. "But the Snaldrialooran representative sent us a 3,000-page application and told us the wait time would be five to seven cycles."

"Typical," said Ixdahan. He knew full well the endless negotiations his father was always locked in.

"We had no choice," said the Onkendren. "We couldn't threaten deadly force. All we had was the small fleet of trading ships we'd taken with us when we went into hiding. We needed…."

Ixdahan smashed on stubby fist into the other.

"Still," he said, "the Vrukaari?"

"They were the only ones to answer our distress call directly," said Ciafelipenorg. "Besides, Mr. Leek was so charming at first."

"Aalthrashrintorb Leek?" asked Ixdahan, and saw her answer immediately in her sad eyes.

"We discovered the truth too late. But, my Ixdahan, I've run out of time to chat. Here."

She took his hands in hers and leaned in.

"I'm uploading a packet of detailed information to your cortex now. You may find the format unfamiliar at first, but you'll get used to it. Scan everything carefully and contact us on the secure mentallic connection you'll find there if you think you can help us."

Without warning, she leaned in even closer and implanted in his mind an image of herself as a teenage Vrukaari, giving him the hottest kiss he'd ever had.

"You're free to decide," said Ciafelipenorg at last, "but please say 'Yes.' A lot's riding on this."

A gasping Ixdahan stared at her, as he tried to catch his breath.

"Sure, I'll … give it … give it some … some thought," he said. "But what should I tell … that?" as he nodded his torso in the direction of 17/Chaarnactral.

"Power it up," said Ciafelipenorg. "Your robot will think it's in the middle of a lecture about the finer points of Vrukaari levitation. I've added a module about that, too, in the packet I sent over. I suggest you study that closely."

"Am I really that…?" Ixdahan started.

"*Sucky*," said Ciafelipenorg, "is the word your friends on Earth would use."

With that, Ixdahan was amazed to see the beautiful female disappear and, as he couldn't help noticing, everything around him snap back to life.

"Pure mentallic projection," he thought. "Wish I could do that. Must have stopped time, too."

Ixdahan realized he now had a choice, between standing there dumbfounded and getting back to his apartment so he could study the mentallic packet Ciafelipenorg had given him, he knew what he had to do.

"17/Chaarnactral, End Pause Mode," he said, when he was back at his robot's side. And sure enough, the AI launched into a painfully detailed description of the part of Vrukaari anatomy that generated and controlled their bioelectromagnetic fields.

Though he'd always been kind of fascinated by several different fields of Science, he often found detailed data reports like this one really boring. But lately, he'd started to realize that nothing ever got done without effort. It was, like, the way of the world. If you loved something — or someone — you couldn't just walk away when things got tough.

Besides, people could surprise you. Like the way Lena refused to accept anything he said without proof, especially when he first explained his battle plan for stopping Relsheesharb Yarrow's invasion of Earth. At first it drove him nuts. But then he realized how much courage it took for her to challenge him and … well, he grew to admire her for that. Now, when he was light years away from her, he was glad he'd hung in there and made the friendship work.

Would he ever see Lena again? Maybe it was stupid to think about her right now. With seven or eight galaxies to save, from who knew what kind of danger, now was probably not the time to get crazy about relationships — especially one that might never, ever be.

CHAPTER 13

As expected, a package arrived in Lena's room less than 12 hours after her phone call with Vance. Actually, "materialized" might be a better word, even though the package didn't appear in plain sight.

"My underwear drawer," sighed Lena. Guys were so gross, she thought, even if this was the closest she'd come to laughing since the day the whales started yammering in her head. This, she assumed, was a device similar to the one Vance had used with Derek last year.

Wait … what was … oh yeah, her texting ringtone. There on her phone was a long number, like a password or an international phone number, plus the words:

dial it up. see you l8ter.

Now she was faced with a major decision. Too bad there was no high tech solution for that. Chances are, she decided, no matter how advanced a civilization got, its people would still face emotional, intellectual or ethical crossroads. But considering the stakes, her hesitation felt silly.

"Like I'm not going to help Derek because I'm scared I won't get my field reports done?" For a moment, she wished she had the knack of making clones, the way Mr. Yarrow did of Blade Northrop. Then her clone could stay behind and….

Good thing Dorothea wasn't there to see the tears running down her face. There was no way she wanted to mess up her grade for the summer course and *also* no way she wanted to miss out on … whatever it was Vance and "Octopus Lady" had in mind.

Regardless, it was go or no go and she was running out of time to decide. Vance had told her the "operating window" for the device would be closed in a few more hours. And speaking of hours, Vance had promised that her visit to Derek's old lander would happen outside of time. After what she'd seen, and what she'd felt in her own mind, she had every reason to believe it was possible.

"What's it going to cost me?" she asked the ominous black disk in front of her. It couldn't be so easy to mess around with space-time and actually get away with it. Yet, if she could help Derek save the universe, and still have a chance to spend part of the weekend with Dad and Rhea....

But what was she thinking?

She wasn't going anywhere this weekend, except to Derek's old lander. She couldn't exactly show up on Dad's doorstep without an airline ticket stub. Her airfare to Alaska had been donated by the University — in a joint program with the National Science Foundation and Professor Cray's brother, an extremely wealthy guy. The weird part was, his photo in the program brochure had made him look around 1,000 years old. Couldn't they have hired a better photographer?

Anyway, it wasn't as if Lena could ask Jocelyn to sweet-talk her uncle into coughing up more money. And Lena had already spent most of her earnings, from tutoring younger kids in Biology, on the gear she needed for the summer. Not to mention the fact that the program brochure promised roundtrip airfare — with the "round" part happening at the *end* of the summer. No way Dad wouldn't get suspicious.

Besides, if she did pop back home, there was still the whole lying thing. "The program's going great, Dad," she imagined herself telling Todd — again — over some crab's legs at Jake's Shellfish Shack. It was hard enough to lie on a Skype call, but Lena was pretty sure Rhea wasn't buying her story completely, so it would be harder still to keep the happy-mask on straight in person.

No matter what, the last thing Lena wanted was for Todd to yank her home. Not now, when she was in so deep.

"Somebody has to dig that amphora out," she whispered, as she lifted an ominous black disk out of her dresser and set it down on her bed. "Or smash it."

Who knew? And that's what finally decided her, the moment she realized that not knowing would gnaw at her for years.

OK. If everything Vance had told her was true, she could press some buttons on this disk — wait, had it just gotten bigger? — go meet with Vance and the Snaldrialooran, and be back in her dorm room before Dorothea returned from her geological survey expedition, or her boyfriend safari or ... well, who could keep track? The girl was always rushing around like a wind-up doll.

"Maybe she's a robot," said Lena, with a sly smile, until the realization that it might be true tied a knot her stomach. She shook her head, grabbed her Samsung Galaxy and slung a hoodie over her arm, just in case Snaldrialooran ventilation systems weren't any better than the ones she was used to on Earth.

Only thing left to do was enter the code and flip the toggle…

…switch.

"Hey, Lena," said Vance, who now stood five feet in front of her. "You make it OK?"

Lena stared around her, her feet glued to one spot, her breath coming in tight gasps and her teeth chattering like dice in a cup. Too bad she'd dropped out of yoga class, again, this year. A little deep breathing might have helped her cope.

"Sh … sure," she said. "As soon as the insanity thing passes, I should be fine."

"Aww, it's nothing. Come on and meet Octo … uh … Dahaleen," said Vance.

"You and that mouth of yours," said Lena. "And, come on, my underwear drawer?"

"What?" said Vance, with a grin. "I figured it was the one place no one would ever look."

As they turned down a spacious corridor to their right, Lena's mind bristled with snappy comebacks, but she never got to use them. The appearance of a massive, tentacled creature, that floated in front of her around the next corner, knocked everything out of her head except awe.

"You must be…." said Lena.

"Dahaleen Altriavahn," said the Snaldrialooran starspanner captain, "also known as 'Octopus Lady' in some quarters."

The towering Snaldrialooran cast a stern gaze to Vance.

"Just a…just a joke," said Vance. "I didn't think you'd ever…."

"Mentallic abilities are a reflex for my people, Mr. Maultsby," said Dahaleen. "A reflex we train hard to control, out of respect for individual privacy. But when someone's mind keeps screaming the same phrase over and over again, it's impossible to ignore."

Dahaleen paused to adjust the controls on her crinkly, silver encounter suit and Vance hung his head.

"OK," he mumbled to his Nikes, "but you can see I'm sorry now, right?"

"Just joking," said Dahaleen, as she wiggled the tips of her tentacles in his face. "I thought it was funny the first 450,000 times. But I'd like you to give it a rest now."

"Why am I here?" Lena blurted out. She hadn't risked everything with the quantum-transfer unit just to make small talk.

Dahaleen stared at Lena a moment, then nodded her head in the direction of the doorway and swam out of the room. Legs wobbly, Lena followed with Vance close behind.

"How does she … float … like that?" asked Lena.

"Micro antigravity pod," said Vance, "whatever that means."

"But…." Lena sputtered.

"They usually live in liquid methane, or something," said Vance. "But it's, like, way too heavy to lug around in space. So they wear these suits filled with the stuff and then travel in zero-G. Down here, there's gravity, so she has to, like, compensate. Sounds like a pain in the…."

"My one mode of locomotion is swimming," said Dahaleen from the room up ahead. "A distinct limitation, I promise you, but one we have learned to live with."

"*Eevoolushun … Misstayhks … Aahroogaahnz….*" Lena heard the whales piping up in her mind. What could they know of this, she wondered, and more to the point, had they been monitoring her thoughts ever since the day she first heard them?

"Here you are," said Dahaleen, as she pointed to one panel of a control console to her right. "This is a metadigital transponder you can use to contact Ixdahan."

"Like the one in his old house," said Lena.

But as Dahaleen explained, the device in the lander was many times more powerful and would make a stronger connection to the Galactic Array. Because it was shielded, there was also no need for Morse Code or any other tricky business.

"Well, this is great," said Lena, eyes wide as she glanced around the control room. She was surprised at how human it looked — until she remembered it was originally intended for Ixdahan and the two humanoid robots who had posed as his parents during his exile on Earth.

Yet the lander was also distinctly alien, down to the shape, color and configuration of the tiniest buttons — if that's what they were.

"But I've already told him everything I know," said Lena, after a few more minutes of ogling.

"You don't have to call him now," said Vance, "Wait until you find out…."

"One thing at a time," said the Snaldrialooran captain. "Are you Earth people always so impulsive?"

"We're teenagers, remember?" said Lena. "And Vance, here, is seriously messed up."

"I'm beginning to suspect you may be right," said Dahaleen.

"I see how it is," laughed Vance. "By the way, Captain Ma'am, I should get home and finish my yard work while you're talking to Lena."

"As I explained," said Dahaleen, "everything that happens here happens outside of time. In your original frame of reference, this is still Saturday afternoon a week ago."

"OK," said Vance, "but I have to get the work done some day, right?"

"Already taken care of," said the Snaldrialooran, as she flipped on an overhead display screen. Vance's jaw dropped at the sight of the mowed lawn he didn't mow, the trimmed hedges he didn't cut and the clean laundry he didn't wash.

"Cool," said Vance, "but can I make a suggestion?"

"Of course," said Dahaleen.

"Go back and mess it up a little," said Vance. "Moms *knows* I never do anything that ... that perfect. She'll think I hired somebody."

Dahaleen sighed, while Lena fought hard not to giggle. How was it possible, she wondered, for silly everyday emotions to break in on such a serious crisis?

"It's part of every sentient being's nature," said Dahaleen, as if she sensed Lena's thoughts. "And sometimes, the only way to stay sane."

CHAPTER 14

Back at his apartment, Ixdahan prepared to settle down with the data packet he'd received from Ciafelipenorg or, rather, her projection. What an impressive feat of mentallics! Imagine ... sending not just your thoughts, but a hologram of yourself, able to interact with the real world.

"Maybe that's why she stopped local time," mumbled Ixdahan. "Too many variables, otherwise."

But why bother with details, when so much was at stake? Ixdahan's first order of business was to send 17/Chaarnactral out on a long reconnaissance mission so he could scan Ciafelipenorg's data in private.

"A survey of Vrukaari traffic patterns?" asked the robot. "There's nothing in the mission statement about that."

"New orders," said Ixdahan without looking up. "Need-to-know basis. Look, I know it's a bore, but what can I do? You're the one right intelligence for the job."

"Hmm," said 17/Chaarnactral. "It's a good thing I don't have vanity circuits or they might unduly influence my decision to believe you."

"That's one more way AIs are superior to organics, I guess," said Ixdahan, as he stared straight into its shiny, acrylic eyes.

For a moment, the robot looked as if it were about to speak, but abruptly turned on its rotors and headed out the door.

"Hate myself," Ixdahan whispered, when 17/Chaarnactral was gone. What pleasure was there in outsmarting a machine programmed for obedience? But, he saw, the deception was necessary, because the disaster-to-come was already buzzing around his ears.

There's a lot of vital information to absorb in this packet....

... Ciafelipenorg's voice echoed in his mind....

But I need to give you an idea of our history, the background, you might say, against which these urgent times are about to unfold.

"Ridiculous," thought Ixdahan. "Since when is one era a background for another? Time is time."

But so what if he could prove his interpretation of history was more accurate? That couldn't be more irrelevant now, he realized, if history itself were about to come to an end. Better to scan on.

Centuries ago, by your reckoning....

"Oh, Horse Nebula," said Ixdahan, as he into English without realizing it.

... we were a proud, powerful people. Our command of art and science, of history, culture, economics and social engineering was unmatched in the Eight Known Galaxies....

"Eight?" wondered Ixdahan. In reality, the true number of galaxies in the universe was staggeringly large but, by his lifetime, a mere seven had been thoroughly explored. Most likely, Ciafelipenorg must also be counting Lena's galaxy. But why had the Onkendren visited Earth in the first place, let alone buried one of their precious objects there?

Over time, our capacity for knowledge expanded so far that we engineered a magnificent device, the Vexelanderan, able to reshape the laws of physics themselves to suit our whims.

"This can't end well," thought Ixdahan.

Endowed with the power of gods, we embarked on a mission to right the wrongs of history and reshape the universe along lines we considered more rational, beautiful and equitable.

Funny how the word "equitable" only came up in situations like this, Ixdahan reflected, where the person deciding what's equitable makes no effort to consult the people, numbering in the billions, who will receive this "equitable" treatment. Come to think of it, his brief study of Earth's 20th to 21st centuries had turned up the same paradox.

At first, it seemed we had achieved great things, readjusting the balance of life, of planetary resources. To the planet you know as Hathreahdahnaar we gave abundant mineral wealth, a vibrant ecosystem of previously unknown splendor and even, though it shames us to admit it, a fragment of our own genetic inheritance to the protosentients stumbling toward self-awareness.

"Idiots," Ixdahan grumbled. Who knew what the humans might have become if they'd been left alone? All he knew was that what they *had* become was ... questionable.

But as the centuries passed, we saw how little our pure knowledge had been tempered with understanding, let alone wisdom. For we had made a crucial error.

"What?" shouted Ixdahan. "What was the error?" But the data packet merely rolled on.

When we discovered the scope of our crimes against Nature, the shock split our people into three separate factions. Unable to accept the burden of those crimes, one faction used the Vexelanderan to create an armada of powerful ships, large enough to house entire ecosystems. They launched themselves into deep space, denied radio contact to any who approached them and, I fear, disabled any who came too close.

"Selfish," whispered Ixdahan, who would never forget how his own greed had almost brought on the destruction of an entire species.

Soon after their departure, we dismantled the Vexelanderan and transmogged its components into nine common objects. We buried each on a world most likely to offer a stable environment through the eons — with the hope of reassembling them in a more enlightened era.

"Eons?" said Ixdahan. "Tell me you did not just say *eons*." It was moments like this that he most missed his friends on Earth. Vance would never say "eons" with a straight face. Then again, Vance had a hard time being serious about anything, which Ixdahan saw as both a strength and a weakness. But what was the data packet saying now?

> *The second faction is the one I, Ciafelipenorg, belong to. Our goal was to develop new mental and spiritual disciplines we hoped would enable us to harness these enormous powers with greater wisdom. Some in our faction went into deeper isolation, burying their minds in the recesses of simpler creatures, in the hope that the answer would come through leaps of primal, intuitive thought.*

"Lena's whales," said Ixdahan. How he wished he had fingernails he could nibble on to soothe his nerves. After all, it had worked on Earth.

> *The third faction....*

But Ixdahan didn't get a chance to scan the rest of the packet. Instead, his mind was flooded by an emergency mental broadcast from Group Leader Chaldraheen Ishialdrol.

He was recalling every SSA agent to Snaldrialoor. The Vrukaari had started production on a fleet of advanced-design battle cruisers and were gearing up for a major assault on nine planets ... one of which was Earth!

Ixdahan knew the drill. They'd gone over this in training a hundred times. In seconds, he levitated himself out of his cozy receptacle and placed a priority call to Central to acknowledge receipt of the Group Leader's message.

Without bothering to pack, the former heir to L'han Singha Province dashed out of his apartment and tried to look casual as he hurried down the polyslate tiles of the bustling main square, on his way to the designated q-transfer point for Snaldrialoor. *Wise Heralds of the Transdimensional Interface.* He was going to the Homeworld looking like this?

But there was no time for dithering, as the Vrukaari war machine ratcheted up to a higher gear than anyone had seen in decades. Had the Onkendren blithely given away the secret of magclad technology just to see it destroy them?

For amid the chaos in Ixdahan's mind, one thing stood out. The Vrukaari knew the location of two of the Onkendren artifacts, one on Traahlgreubewehn and one resting in a spare glass case, he was sure, in Father's study.

That left seven more locations — for seven battle cruisers, ramped up with who knew what forms of advanced weaponry. He had to get a message to Lena, but that, unfortunately, would have to wait. His first order of business was saving his own slimy backside.

There … just up ahead, a crumbling station stop on an abandoned public transport line. Breathless, he levitated down the cracked entry ramp and half wished 17/Chaarnactral were there to see him in action. Once on the platform, he flicked his three sets of eyes here and there, looking for the exact transfer point. No doubt his robotic assistant had already been taken over by remote control and directed to an escape route closest to wherever Ixdahan's meaningless errand had sent him.

So where … maybe that was it, up ahead, a brightly colored fire alarm box, about the only thing still intact in the entire station. Yes, that had to be it. He was supposed to pull the lever down and….

In an instant, he knew he'd made a terrible mistake. Instead of being greeted by a team from the SSA, he found himself face to face with … with….

"Aalthrashrintorb Leek," said the imposing Vrukaari, "at your service."

"How did I…." Ixdahan started to ask.

The supreme Vrukaari chuckled.

"It wasn't easy," he said, as he levitated a glass of blue Chlevahndorean wine to his lips. "Your security team runs a tight ship. Too bad for you, not every one of them is as loyal as you might think."

"But…." said Ixdahan. How he wished he could smack the arrogant face in front of him with even one of his missing tentacles!

"Shush, my boy," said Mr. Leek. "I've had my eyes on you for a while — and I have big plans for you, if you care to listen. But don't think I'm giving you a choice."

With that, Ixdahan felt his twin Vrukaari mouths — the one for eating and the one for talking, stuffed up with gags, while a pair of uncharacteristically thuggish Ybitrians tied him down with carbon nanotube ropes to a filthy receptacle inches away from the supreme leader of the Vrukaari.

Swathed in encounter suits, their faces partially obscured by the pale green mist of chlorine gas that swirled in their helmets, the Ybitrians resembled a pair of mythical beasts from an ancient Snaldrialooran legend.

"Comfortable?" asked Aalthrashrintorb Leek, with a thoroughly revolting leer.

CHAPTER 15

Lena lay on her soft dorm room bed and tried to absorb what she'd learned from Captain Altriavahn in Derek's lander. Fascinated as she'd been by the sight of an alien space vessel, it was a relief to be back in familiar surroundings.

All the same, she knew this feeling of security was an illusion. Thousands of light years away, events were spinning out of control that would soon affect everything she knew and loved on Earth.

Even things she didn't exactly love, including Dorothea's snoring, seemed too precious now to be swept away by a gaggle of intergalactic idiots. It was so stupid. Hadn't she always heard that a mad-advanced civilization out there in the stars would one day make contact with Earth? Didn't every kid she knew, who had any interest in space, share the dream of getting some really great advice from an older, wiser race of super beings?

Well, guess what? She'd met two aliens and heard about countless others and they were as childish and short-sighted as any group of adults on Earth. OK, they had far greater knowledge of science and math, and maybe their legal system was more sensible, fair and just. Maybe they'd achieved gender equality, too, though she'd have to see that for herself to believe it.

And yet, if you looked past that, what did you have? Land-grabbing, empire building, my-laser-pistol-is-bigger-than-yours posers calling the shots. Hadn't Derek himself come from an ancient clan of land owners with their tentacles on the scales of justice and entwined in the diplomatic affairs of a thousand other worlds?

That didn't exactly point to a happy ending, but, as she already knew from last year, the best way forward was to believe a solution was possible.

Besides, if Dahaleen were right, the probability of beating the Vrukaari was high, considering how new the warlords were to the technologies they'd stolen — and how impatient they were. So, while no one could afford to minimize the Vrukaari threat, there was every reason to be optimistic. Too bad Lena couldn't convince her stomach of that.

"Have you tried Pepto-Bismol?" asked Dorothea in a quiet voice from the other side of the room. She was drinking a cup of peppermint tea that filled the air with a cheery fragrance Lena found a tad too ironic.

All the same, she propped herself up on one elbow and glanced over at her pale, red-haired roommate.

"Tell me more about the energy surge," she said. "Maybe that'll take my mind off my stomach … surge … for a little while."

"OK," said Dorothea, her eyes squinting a bit, "whatever works for you … I guess. The surge is important because it's the first time we've seen a continuous data stream reach the Earth from anywhere farther away than one of our own probes, like Voyager 1."

Lena made a mental note to get more space savvy. It just made sense, now that her life was being reshaped by "spacey stuff," including spacey Derek.

"That's out pretty far, isn't it?" she asked.

Dorothea tilted her head to one side.

"Seriously?" seriously, Lena's roommate asked. "Voyager 1 is only about 19 billion kilometers from here at this point. The energy surge … it's like from 780 kiloparsecs away. I mean, to put it in perspective, a parsec is…."

"OK, OK," said Lena, as she fell back on her bed. "You made your point. Don't go all Bill Nye the Science Guy on me. Just tell me: What kind of data is it?"

"The kind we can't make a dent in, except for one tiny clue," said Dorothea. "There are a couple of repeating patterns that crop up, kind of like they would in an essay. You know, like "Section 1" or something."

"So you know how the gibberish is divided up," said Lena. "Big deal."

"Well it's some progress, anyway," said Dorothea. "Why don't you ask the whales what it means? I gotta get to the lab. Can I get you anything from the snack bar on my way back?"

"Text me if they have a sale on stomachs," said Lena, "and I'll crawl over."

"You really need a vacation," said Dorothea. "I mean, I thought I was a workaholic ... wait, that came out wrong." Flustered, Dorothea didn't waste any time gathering up her backpack and rushing out.

"Why *don't* I ask the whales?" said Lena into her pillow. If she hadn't been so shaken up, she might have thought of that herself days ago. But now that she'd met with Dahaleen and Vance and had some idea where this weird activity was heading, it didn't seem so scary to think of….

"Daytaah," the whales' voices echoed in her mind. *"Daytaah too wayhuke uzz, mayhuke uzz reehmehmber."*

Lena put her hands to her temples.

"Remember what?" she asked

"Reehmehmber locayshun. Reehmehmber puhrpohse. Baahd oozers comm soohn. Muss naht feynd, muss naht feynd...."

There was so much Lena wanted to ask, but as suddenly as the whales' thoughts had entered her mind, she was upset to notice they were already gone again.

"I need more information," she whispered, but nearly jumped out of her skin at the sound of a thump coming from her backpack. She opened the first zipper, and a laugh broke out of her lungs in spite of herself.

For there, lying on its side, was a brand new, unopened bottle of Pepto-Bismol that had definitely *not* been there before. There was nothing to do but pull her phone out of her pocket:

> glad u think this is funny ; - (
> dahaleen sez don't worry, b happy = ^]
> calling u now : - p

"Heard from the humps again," she said when Vance picked up from inside the lander. "They're worried … our friends … will find … the vase."

"Dahaleen has a plan," said Vance. "I'm writing code for it now. Gotta go before she gets mad. I'm way behind schedule."

"Can't she just…." Lena started.

"Somebody might see it in her mind," said Vance. "So far, none of the alien dudes know about me. Dang, here she comes...."

Startled at how fast the line went dead, Lena stared at her phone for a minute before she plopped back down on her bed. If the conversation with Vance were less than satisfying, at least her insides were calmer.

That is, until she heard a quiet knock on her door.

"Who is it?" she called out. She was determined not to sound as annoyed as she felt.

"Here is me, Toffel," said a voice from the hallway. "Wanted to know if we could compare field notes. I am a little confused about a couple of things."

"A *little* confused?" said Lena under her breath. Well, what harm could it do to study together? Toffel was good company, though he did sometimes look at her as if….

"Don't tell me…." she thought, on her way to the door. "What if he likes me?"

But if Toffel had any romantic interest in Lena, it didn't show in his grim face. Lena showed him in and pulled out her own notes from the past week.

"I have been thinking," he said. "I know a guy in Holland who is a physics major. If I sent to him a copy of your Greek transcription, he and I … we might be able to figure out what the text is really talking about. It could be a real breakthrough, if only in the archaeology."

Lena felt her stomach pains return in little jabs, and decided she had nothing to lose. Toffel had already seen the transcription, and what's-his-name the physics major wouldn't have any idea where the writing came from. She reached for her notepad.

"Sure, you can send him a copy," she said. "It's probably a hoax, though. I mean, I found the text on the Internet and now the site's not there anymore."

Toffel tugged at his earlobe.

"Maybe," he said. "Or maybe someone is trying to suppress this information. We have to find it out, no?"

And with that, Lena saw she had willingly dragged an innocent person into the web of danger that had taken over her life. If the situation hadn't been so desperate, she might have thought better of it. But considering the dangers, how could she leave any stone unturned?

"Besides," she said to herself over and over again, "what's the harm?"

Maybe it would have been better if Lena had had a minute alone to ponder that question but, after a couple of hours of studying, the minute Toffel left, there was Vance, calling her again.

"What?" she asked. She'd already tried contacting Derek/ Ixdahan and couldn't get through. What more did they want from her?

"You gotta come over," said Vance. "Dahaleen says she has a surprise for you."

Having hung up, Lena took a moment to change her T-shirt and drag a comb through her dark brown hair. She had no idea what this was about, but anything was better than moping in her dorm room on a Sunday afternoon. Besides, maybe the Snaldrialooran captain had a "tummy ray" she could aim at Lena's abdomen to get rid of those awful shooting pains.

CHAPTER 16

The first thing Callie Ann noticed about the elite training facility was its ice-cold air.

"Like a meat locker in Uncle Laird's old restaurant," she said, her teeth chattering. No way she could get into a swimsuit unless they turned down the AC. Yet the cold didn't feel like AC-up-too-high cold. It felt more like the damp chill you got from going down into an unfinished basement in October.

And why was it so empty? There wasn't even a reception desk, as if the office space were still under construction. A pile of two-by-fours in the far corner confirmed her suspicions.

"They want to run a few tests," said Coach Kepler, as he entered the dank room a few minutes after Callie Ann arrived. "The training course is rigorous and they need to make sure you're up to it.".

"Who *are* they?" asked Callie Ann. "You never mentioned any names. What, are they from … from Russia or something?"

Coach Kepler ran a hand through his greasy, black hair. Before he could answer, a trim woman in her 40s, dressed in a lemon-yellow nylon tracksuit, jogged into the room. She stopped short, inches in front of Callie Ann and held out her hand.

"Sorry I'm late, Dear. Call me Veronika. Shall we get started?"

Callie Ann nodded, but didn't take Veronika's hand. What, she wondered, what did "getting started" mean? Regardless, Veronika led her and Coach Kepler into a huge, high-ceilinged room, filled top to bottom with more electronic equipment than Callie Ann had ever seen in one place. Not to mention the fact that it looked … weird.

With her hands on her hips, she stood firm in a roomful of people she assumed were brainy scientists.

"You're testing me *here*?" she asked.

Veronika squeezed her mouth into a tight smile and put her bony hands on Callie Ann's shoulders. The first round of testing would be neurological, she explained. Callie Ann looked over at Coach Kepler for reassurance, but got nothing for her trouble but a vague smile.

"You're kidding, right?" said Callie Ann. "Neuro … whatever … tests from a random woman in a tracksuit? Where's the doctor?"

"You don't understand, Ms. Connors," said Veronika. "This is a different kind of neurology than you may have heard of."

Callie Ann backed away from the older woman.

"Maybe," she said, "but I'm not taking any tests without a doctor. I'm out of here." With that, she grabbed for the doorknob — of a door she didn't remember anyone closing.

"Wait, Dear," said Veronika. "Think of what you're doing. A pretty girl like you with a gold medal around her neck — you could get rich on the product endorsements from just one year. Do you want to live in Scattertown forever?"

"It's Skudderton," said Callie Ann, "and I don't believe you. Whatever this is about, it's not about my career."

But before she could open the door, she felt a pair of bony hands clutching at her hair.

"Don't throw this chance away, you silly girl!" Veronika shouted. "Or are you afraid of success, like a little princess?"

"Screw you, Tracksuit," said Callie Ann. "My success is coming from *me*."

Callie Ann brought her knee up into Veronika's stomach, kicked Coach Kepler in the shins, twisted open the door and ran out of the dank facility. Out on the street, she ran southeast toward Baltimore's Inner Harbor, along the most crowded sidewalks she could find.

"Reminds me of something," she whispered under her breath, as she remembered her mad dash to the reception hall, the day Lena's father got remarried, and the Vrukaari almost launched an assault on the planet.

Back at the facility, the Vrukaari soldier posing as Coach Kepler was beside himself.

"Did you have to be so rough with her?" he bellowed at the Vrukaari geneticist who had introduced herself as Veronika. "We've lost her now — and Mr. Leek is going to kill us."

The geneticist showed no signs of intimidation. Instead, she held up the strands of Callie Ann's hair she clutched in her transmogged hands, and wiggled them in the soldier's face.

"It doesn't matter, you dolt," she said. "I have her DNA. I can start the process immediately."

"But Mr. Leek wants to see her in person. He...." sputtered the soldier.

"He'll have to make do," said the geneticist. "You should be more concerned about what happens when these Earthies find the real Kepler."

"Oh that," said the soldier, with a wave of his hand. "I shipped him off to a stasis chamber on Mr. Leek's ship. When this is over he can have his life back, with a bad case of what the humans call *amnesia*."

"Very wise," said the geneticist. "Missing bodies arouse suspicion. These people are backward, but not altogether stupid."

"Too stupid to stop a battle cruiser," said the soldier.

The geneticist smiled and patted the soldier on the cheek.

"You better hope so," she said. "Otherwise, we'll both be scrubbing out toilets on a cattle farm in the Jahldrex sector."

"If we haven't been transmogged into cattle ourselves," sighed the captain, "and served up for supper."

"Is everyone in the military so morbid?" asked the geneticist.

"Start sequencing," said the soldier. "Leave the worrying to me. I'm the one who has to break the bad news to Mr. Leek that our subject has escaped."

"Good luck with that," said the geneticist. "While you're at it, make up your mind whether you prefer to be served with *zexhalkyrez* or *yexgluziar.*"

The soldier stared at her, wrung his hands, then trudged out of the room. Fact was, he resented every second he was trapped in a human body and unable to glide. If he hadn't been stuck in this heavy alien body on this heavy planet, where he had to rely, incredibly, on legs to get around, the Earth girl would never have gotten away.

But never mind, he decided. His priority was finding this "Callie Ann" fast, and discreetly. Killing her wasn't an option, since his orders were to stay on Earth until the fleet arrived. As ignorant as the Earth people were, they'd proven themselves competent enough at criminal investigation. Besides, Mr. Leek wanted her alive for some reason.

No, he'd have to rely on mentallics and, judging from the brief scans he'd made of her mind already, that posed a problem. For the Earth girl's contact with Lieutenant Colonel Yarrow last year had altered her mental landscape — just enough to make its responses unpredictable. What *was* predictable, he concluded, was the rough road ahead for him if he had to report his failure to Mr. Leek.

"Nothing to lose," he thought as he walked over to the royal blue Ford Focus he'd driven to the facility with Callie Ann. He'd have to find out who the rebellious Earth creature cared about most and work from there. Say "no" to Aalthrashrintorb Leek? He'd rather suck down a bowlful of antimatter any day.

CHAPTER 17

Ixdahan gazed out at his captor and winced. Incredibly, the supreme Vrukaari was still lecturing, still trying to wear him down with propaganda about his Grand Vision. When Leek's Ybitrian bodyguards had lashed Ixdahan to a rough receptacle an hour ago, he figured he'd be *beaten* into submission. But Leek's non-stop blathering had turned out to be much more painful.

"Worse than Skudderton High," he thought, as he remembered the boredom he suffered in each and every class. And though he was ashamed to admit it, that included the American History classes taught by Lena's father.

But this was no time for reminiscing, he told himself. He needed a plan. Lucky for him, Leek was so consumed by his own ego, he didn't notice the secret mental barrier Ixdahan had built. It had taken longer than expected, and Ixdahan was beginning to wonder if that had anything to do with the un-Ybitrian collars that Aalthrashrintorb's bodyguards were wearing.

Whether they were advanced-design neuro-suppressors or delivered a new kind of mentallic dampening field, Ixdahan was willing to bet his non-existent fortune that the collars were Onkendren. Whatever. So far, they'd only managed to slow him down.

Ixdahan's first thought was to contact the SSA, until he realized that would be the one mind-address Leek would be sure to monitor. Then he remembered the connection Ciafelipenorg had included in the data packet she'd uploaded to his mind on Vrukaar Prime.

That was risky in its own way, but the only other option was Vance, back on Earth, and, even if Ixdahan thought his old friend might be able to help, it didn't seem right to drag him into this threatening situation. Lena, of course, was completely off limits. If anything happened to her....

OK, it was time to act. In a few long minutes, Leek would finish his rant and get down to the business of brainwashing Ixdahan, a process more extensive and painful when administered to a member of a mentallic species like the Snaldrialoorans or the Vrukaari.

Worse, at the end of that process, he'd likely be no more than a drooling slave to the supreme Vrukaari's every wish. And that was totally unacceptable: He'd rather die than help Leek blow any one of his five noses.

So, with the part of his mind shielded from both the Ybitrians and Leek, Ixdahan reached out mentallically to the coordinates the 871-year-old transmogged Onkendren had given him a few hours before. What he found at the other end of those coordinates was not what he expected.

In an instant, the shielded area of his mind filled with the image of a fiercely beautiful humanoid with pale skin and flowing red hair, who was resting on an elaborately carved wooden chair, in the midst of a vibrant floral garden at sunset. Was she 30 or 300? In the shifting light, it was impossible to tell.

"I'll take care of it," she said, her eyes blazing. "But you should think harder about who you can trust." And before Ixdahan could blink, the mentallic screen he'd constructed vanished — as well as the coordinates he'd used to make contact. What did the mysterious woman mean? How had he ever known whom to trust — except by trusting his feelings first?

Meanwhile, whatever "taking care of it" might mean would have to happen fast, as the Vrukaari's fearless leader had finally turned away from the immense view screen he'd been staring at during his lecture and now faced Ixdahan straight on.

"As I said," Leek continued in a solemn voice, "you have a special place to fill in the new order."

With no idea how long he'd be held captive, Ixdahan decided to stall for time.

"But how do I know if your plan will succeed?" he asked, straining his slimy torso against the rigid carbon nanotube ropes holding him fast to the receptacle. "Do you really know how to use the magclad tech you stole? What frequency settings are you using to create the hullcladding for your cruisers?"

Leek swayed, as he shifted his weight from one stubby leg to the other. The boy was coming around — proving once again the power of Leadership over narrow ethical considerations. A good talking to and the Snaldrialooran brat was already cracking!

"Very astute, Boy," said the Vrukaari. "You want your assurances upfront. Fine, I'll have my assistant send you the exact figures in a moment."

He paused to straighten his expensive business suit, a tent-like affair studded with rare minerals and traced in pure silver filigree.

"Satisfied?" he asked. "Go ahead, ask me anything if it will convince you to join my team willingly. It would be a waste to subject such a fine mind to brutal thought controls."

"You sure that's a good idea, Boss?" asked the brighter of the two Ybitrian guards. "Tellin' him stuff, I mean…."

Mr. Leek levitated himself to a few feet above the Ybitrian's head.

"He's staying right here, now isn't he?" he said. "And you're using your psykrella to suppress his mentallics, aren't you?"

"Sure, boss, but…." the guard started.

"Tell me you've lost control of my young friend," said Leek, "and I'll incinerate you here and now."

"No, Sir, Mr. Leek, nothing like that," said the guard, whose long, insectoid legs had begun to tremble. "Everything's under control."

"See why I need you?" asked the Vrukaari leader as he turned back to his captive.

Ixdahan, meanwhile, had received the data packet from Leek's assistant and was already analyzing the magclad data it contained.

"Now, what else do you want to know about the upcoming … festivities?"

With no idea when or how his rescue might happen, Ixdahan found the best way to soothe his anxiety was to pepper his captor with question after question, as:

How did he plan to subdue each planet so quickly?
How did he expect to extract the hidden objects without damaging them?
How would he convert each object to its original form?
What known obstacles did the Grand Plan face?

The first three questions Leek waved away with a sneer.

"You obviously have no idea of a Vrukaari's powers of persuasion — now greatly enhanced by the Onkendren psykrella, of the kind my two … associates … are wearing. We can extract whatever we need to know from the 'ancients' with varying degrees of coercion."

"Good point," thought Ixdahan. How, he wondered, had he been able to deceive Mr. Leek so far — considering the Ybitrian guards were both supposedly holding him back. Could the Onkendren….

"Your fourth question, however," said the supreme Vrukaari, as he struck a heroic pose, "leads me directly to the special role I have for you. The Onkendren artifact hidden on Earth is guarded by the Onkendren themselves, transmogged, so I'm told, into a form of mammalian sea life."

"I'd have to become human again to help you with that," said Ixdahan — and wondered why the real danger implied by Leek's words weren't enough to stifle his happiness at the faintest chance of seeing Lena again.

"Not at all," said the Vrukaari. "You would serve as my advisor, and guide my team through the delicate process of eliminating the Onkendren and extracting the object."

"The Earth people will stop you," said Ixdahan.

At that, Aalthrashrintorb Leek laughed, a harsh, coughing, wheezing snarl of a laugh that grated on the young Snaldrialooran's ears like the sound of an iron rasp scraping titanium steel.

"With what? I ask you," said the Vrukaari. "Go ahead, prove your worth to me now, by telling me what possible defense the Earth people will have against my fleet."

"Can you be sure they haven't found the artifact and hidden it?" asked Ixdahan.

That thought, at last, brought a halt to Aalthrashrintorb Leek's unbridled optimism.

"They do, I suppose, have sonar capabilities," he said, "as well as awareness of planetary seismic activity. Are you saying…?"

"I'm only sketching out the possibilities for Your Magnificence," said Ixdahan, who figured he had nothing to lose by playing along with Leek's inflated ego.

"As I would expect from anyone loyal to my cause," said Mr. Leek. "I'll order a scan of the planet immediately and we'll see."

Ixdahan watched as he glided for an exit portal.

"Stay put until I return," said Leek, with a sickening grin, as if he'd just invented Irony on the spot. But if the leader of the Vrukaari Federation believed he'd scored a major victory by winning over the impetuous, devious and unpredictable perpetrator of their defeat on a primitive planet, he was in for a surprise.

No more than 30 seconds after Leek left Ixdahan alone with the two clueless Ybitrian guards, the youngest operative of the SSA felt the tingle of a q-transfer field flowing through his body.

"Get ready," echoed a vaguely familiar voice in his mind. "You're liable to find the next two hours a bit disorienting." And to the dismay of Aalthrashrintorb Leek's bodyguards, Ixdahan winked out of existence on the starspanner and found himself strapped into a glassed-in booth the likes of which he'd never seen before, unless….

"Your deduction is correct," said the same voice. "You are now the first member of your species to enter an Onkendren transmog chamber. Now relax. You're sure to find the experience less grueling than the last two times you were … changed."

"Not counting on it," said Ixdahan. "I mean, thanks for the rescue, but where are you taking me that I need to be transmogged again?"

"You're going to Earth," said the voice. "Where else? Now stop talking and slip into a coma so we can get started."

"Slip into a…." Ixdahan started to say, before vents in the floor of the chamber filled it with an orangey gas that made conversation as impossible as it was irrelevant. "Pretty!" was all he could say, as the gas rolled in. It obscured his senses until there was nothing left of him beyond a feeling of terrible loss.

And yet, as the chamber's doors swung up and out to the side, two hours later, he found himself unusually energized, refreshed and, as the mirror on the far wall confirmed, human.

"Still don't know what's going on," he whispered to the control room around him.

"You will," said the voice of Captain Altriavahn in the near distance, "just as soon as you're clear of that device."

With no reason to doubt the voice in his head, which had just saved his life, Ixdahan strode out of the room that contained the chamber and into the main body of the lander he hadn't seen since he'd visited it with Vance last fall. And though it felt great to be back, it wasn't long before his moment of triumph was cut short.

"Geez, Derek," said a voice to his left. "Do you have to be so totally gross?"

Ixdahan turned his head and nearly collapsed — at the sight of Lena, who was covering her eyes with her hands.

"I … I didn't know you would be here," said Ixdahan, "and it's not like there's a closet nearby."

"Don't worry," said Vance's voice as he entered the room, "she's into it. You're coming on too strong, is all."

"OK, you're *both* disgusting," said Lena.

"Give our guest some clothing," said Dahaleen over the lander's intercom. Vance took the hint and dashed off into the lander's main corridor. "Meanwhile, Lena, if you prefer, I can wipe what you just saw from your memory."

Lena broke into giggles.

"Hey no … no rush," she said. "I might need to study that memory a bit, for purely scientific reasons."

"Spoken like a dedicated researcher," said Dahaleen as an undeniable lilt came into her voice.

"Would somebody tell me what's going on?" bellowed Ixdahan, his body trembling with both humiliation and a slight chill.

"Dude, get dressed," said Vance. He'd just returned with a stack of clothes for Ixdahan that Dahaleen had q-transferred from the house in Hunter's Wend. "Until then, you're too crazy-fresh to deal with."

Ixdahan shock his head and bolted back to the room with the transmog chamber, started dressing and almost ripped the Levi's 501 jeans Lena had told him to buy last September.

He breathed deep and smiled a secret smile, because he'd recognized a flash of something in Lena's mind he'd never seen before: She'd actually found him "hot" — based on that curious human temperature analogy for physical attraction. And though it made no sense, that sudden realization now gave him the courage to face anything Aalthrashrintorb Leek could throw at him.

"Let him *try* to take this moment away from me," he whispered.

CHAPTER 18

Callie Ann slammed the door shut on her apartment and took in great gulps of air as she tried to settle down. At the moment, she was more glad than ever that, instead of having to stay in a commercial dorm room near the North Baltimore Aquatic Club, she was spending the summer in her Aunt Meara's homey apartment.

She walked over to the mantle of the apartment's fake fireplace and gazed at the row of gilt-framed photos resting there. Even though she'd never given a thought to taking a cruise, Callie Ann found herself envying her aunt's 49-day excursion along the coast of South America. Aunt Meara's summer was some kind of normal, a word Callie Ann would never use to describe what was happening now.

Worse, she didn't know if she could trust her own perception of the long hours since yesterday when Coach Kepler suggested she take part in an elite training program. While it seemed obvious that something weird had happened to the coach, she also had the feeling that the guy she'd run away from wasn't Kepler at all.

"Must be a look-alike," said Callie Ann. But that didn't add up. Why would anyone bother to trade places with an Olympic trainer? She could understand a crook pretending to be a rich banker, maybe, or a powerful senator, but why Coach Kepler?

How she wished she could talk this out with Lena. Though their friendship felt like it was over, Callie Ann knew Lena was too kind not to listen. But this time, Callie Ann was on her own. As she'd attempt to disappear in the crowd, while dashing through the streets of Baltimore, she'd dialed up her former BFF three times — and reached Lena's voicemail. It wasn't like Lena to screen her calls. It just wasn't. Was she in trouble, too?

Glancing around the apartment, Callie Ann sighed at the sight of such homey comfort. Why couldn't her life be like that? Probably, she figured, because sitting at home was the one thing she was allergic to. It was always better to be out, taking action, even if it just meant checking out boys at the mall.

But lately, Callie Ann had wanted more for her life. That's why she decided to go for the Olympic swim team, and why this weirdness with Coach Kepler was so depressing. How could her dream get taken away so fast and so … strangely?

"Gotta get some air," she thought and, while one set of instincts told her it was better to hide, another set reminded her that a moving target is harder to hit. Besides, she was *hungry* and was now that she was officially off her training schedule, she figured she might as well go out on the streets and find a McDonald's or something. Better yet, a local coffee shop where she could sit and think.

So it was that a few minutes later, Callie Ann was back on the sidewalk outside her aunt's building, on her way to the crowded Raven Diner she'd passed every day on her way to Practice. As she stepped inside, she saw it was perfect: bustling, noisy, large. In a place like this, she could sit for a few hours and plan her next move.

But even though she'd arrived at the diner for peace of mind, her tranquility was already starting to falter, as a pair of handsome eyes stared out at her from two tables up. Sure, the guy looked away whenever she caught him staring, but she kept catching him again and again until…. OMG, he was coming over. This was definitely not the time to start up with somebody but, she had to admit, he wasn't half-bad for a kid from Baltimore.

From his perspective, the Vrukaari soldier Callie Ann had seen a few hours ago, as Coach Kepler, was relieved to see his initial ploy had worked so well.

So what if it had taken a couple of painstaking trials in the Onkendren device to get his age, appearance and personality nexus right? This time, he'd taken exquisite care with the latter, because he'd gathered plenty of evidence that his impersonation of the older human had been flawed.

Though lacking true mentallic abilities, he saw now that these Earth creatures were extremely sensitive to the external manifestations of Mind. Could it be they were a few hundred thousand years from becoming fully mentallic? Too bad, he chuckled, the species would never survive long enough for Vrukaari exobiologists to find out.

"But forget that," he told himself. He'd walked over to the Earth girl's table with his tray and it was time to move on to Phase Two.

"Saw you sitting alone," he said, in a low-key, take-it-or-leave-it voice. "Figured you might like some, you know, some company."

Callie Ann crossed her arms across her chest.

"You figured that?" she said. "What are you, a math genius?"

"Naw, nothing like that," said the alien. "Name's Rick, by the way. I'm more of a dumbass type, really, except when I'm swimming."

Callie Ann's eyes lit up, in spite of herself. Why did this guy have to be so good-looking?

"You're a swimmer?" she asked. And as she listened to "Rick's" answer, she was startled to hear that he'd just come from Alaska.

The transmogged alien soldier brushed his thick, sandy-colored hair out of his eyes.

"Yeah, my dad was all 'you need a career path,' and I did OK in Bio so I figured I'd try this summer program up there, in marine biology? But you had to write up these field reports and it was, like, seriously boring. Only part I could get into was the scuba diving, so I kinda flunked out."

"Hey, that's so weird," said Callie Ann, unaware of how much her interest in "Rick" was the direct result of Vrukaari mind control techniques. By the time she finished explaining the coincidence that her friend had also enrolled in the same program, she was so utterly under his influence, she didn't notice that "Rick" demonstrated no actual knowledge of Lena.

Years later, Callie Ann would still not be sure what it was about her conversation with "Rick" that was so fascinating. But at the moment, it seemed like the most natural thing in the world to chat with him for a few hours, before he stood up to leave.

"Have to get home, or my dad's gonna freak," said the disguised alien. "I'm supposed to be helping him, like, clean out the garage."

"Parents are crazy," said Callie Ann.

"My dad's OK," said the Vrukaari soldier. "Just gets edgy sometimes. Hey, check this out."

He pulled a business card from his back pocket.

"My dad ... he runs a tanning salon downtown," he said, "I'll put your name on the list when I get home and get you in free. But you have to go tomorrow."

"What's the rush?" asked Callie Ann, as she squinted at the handsome lug in front of her.

As "Rick" explained, this was a limited time promotional offer to attract new customers. Callie Ann took the business card — and was surprised by the strange, tingly sensation it seemed to send through her fingers.

It had to be ... what? ... static something ... static electricity, she decided. Anyway, as she got up from her table at the diner, which by now was almost empty, she looked up into the alien's eyes and felt as if she'd had the most wonderful afternoon of her life. It was almost as good a feeling as she'd had when she first started dating Blainy. Meeting this new boy tomorrow at the tanning salon? What else would she ever think to do?

CHAPTER 19

Finally back in real time, Lena discovered the Snaldrialooran lander had done nothing to prevent Monday-itis. Even though Dahaleen had seen to it that her field report was filled out to the last detail, it still took a major "gear shift" for Lena to readjust to her so-called normal life.

All the more so, because she now saw from her Samsung that Callie Ann had called three times on Sunday. It was as Dahaleen had warned her: the lander was shielded from outside influence. No signals of any kind could get in unless the Snaldrialooran captain entered the required command code.

But why would Callie Ann call after seven months and not leave a message? Was she having a problem with her coach or, same as Vance, had something disrupted the Snaldrialooran memory block imposed on her after last year's drama?

Her worries aside, Lena knew for sure that her former best friend had to be one of the most persistent people she'd ever known.

"If she needs to talk," Lena told herself, "she'll call back." There wasn't anything Lena could do for Callie Ann but wait. Well, at least now she had a chance to deal with the next blow to her sanity in familiar surroundings, starting with the marina, the scuba gear, Professor Cray, Jocelyn — and Toffel.

"Probably made a mistake," she whispered to herself as she walked, on tiptoe, out of her dorm.

Now that she'd spent several days of subjective time in Derek's lander, which was made of the sturdiest materials in the known universe, the sidewalks of the summer program's campus seemed too fragile to hold her weight. It was no use telling herself it had to be an illusion. She couldn't escape the feeling that she could break any Earthly thing just by looking at it.

But if Lena had hoped that returning to the marina would restore her equilibrium, the sight that greeted her was deeply disappointing.

For one thing, there were FBI operatives everywhere. As Lena stepped on to the dock, she saw a brawny agent questioning Professor Cray, who looked surprisingly calm.

"Don't know about any GPS coordinates," he was saying, as he caught Lena's eye. "Where did you say the boy got them? I can tell you categorically that no cetacean is capable of such things."

"We have to follow up every lead in cases like this," said the tall, muscular agent.

"Cases like what?" asked Cray. "Cases of talking whales? Don't you gentlemen know when you're being pranked?"

Lena listened as the agent stuttered through an explanation of his investigation, starting with the mysterious energy surge, which he assumed might in some way….

"Produce talking whales," said Cray. "Do you know how utterly stupid you sound? Now look, I've given you my full cooperation, but these are University grounds and your time is up. I have to ask you to leave."

And, contrary to Lena's expectations, the powerfully-built FBI agent shook the professor's hand and motioned to his team to follow him off the marina.

"Quite a circus we have today," said Cray, once the agents had climbed back into their chunky, black Escalades and driven away. "You didn't have anything to do with this, did you?" he asked.

Jocelyn climbed out of the *Whales B. Cray*, where she'd sat hunched over her laptop this whole time.

"Come on, Dad," she said. "Why would Lena want to alert the authorities about something we can't define?"

"Had to be Toffel, then," said Cray. "Did he report in?"

But neither Jocelyn nor Lena had seen him that day or over the weekend. Naturally, Lena wasn't about to add that she couldn't have seen Toffel because she'd been living outside of time in Derek's old lander.

"Well, regardless," said the professor, "we'd better go check those coordinates ourselves, before our uniformed friends ruin our research. You coming, Lena?" He was looking at her with the kindest eyes she'd ever remember seeing, except Mom's. "I'd understand if you wanted to stay behind."

"I didn't fly out here to take it easy," said Lena. "Besides, you're going to need someone to help you dig out the … whatever is down there."

Professor Cray squinted at her a moment, then nodded to Jocelyn.

"Let's get going," he said.

"Wait," said Lena to Jocelyn, "didn't you say the spot on the dolphin's map was about 200 kilometers off the coast? It'll take us hours to sail…."

"Oh, we're not sailing," said Cray. He put his hands on Lena's shoulders and looked into her eyes. "As soon as I heard about this, I requisitioned the Department helicopter."

"Dad, you didn't!" said Jocelyn.

"Told them it was research-related, which it is," said Cray. "Besides, the program chair owes me a thousand bucks from last night's poker game."

"You … poker … with Dr. Lutris?" gasped Lena.

"There's more to life than whales," said the professor, with a wink. "Remember that."

Without another word, he pivoted on the heels his moccasins and jogged over to his emerald green Outback, with Lena and Jocelyn close behind.

"I can't order you two to come with me," he said, when they were already speeding to the helipad, about two kilometers south on Route 9.

"I want to go," said Lena. "Anyway, I doubt I'm scary enough for the FBI to start shooting at me."

Jocelyn stared out a side window and smiled.

"Just drive, Dad," she said. "The scary part is you piloting the helicopter."

Lena's face went pale, until Jocelyn explained that her father had taken a pilot's license 15 years earlier and had flown frequently ever since.

"Not very different from piloting a boat, really," he said. "Besides it helps to know the terrain." They entered the tiny landing strip where the helipad stood ready. "Local geology has a big impact on the ecosystem of the water, especially the ocean."

Lena nodded and hoped the professor's logical answer would finally get around to making her heart stop thumping. Flying might be a lot like boating, but she herself had never heard of a motor boat with engine failure falling out of the sky.

On the other hand, considering this was about the whales, the amphora and, as she knew from talking to Derek, the fate of eight galaxies or more, she figured it was worth the risk.

How much, she wondered, did Professor Cray suspect of the importance of the situation? He couldn't possibly know more than the data he'd collected could tell him. On the other hand, Lena wasn't entirely sure the average university professor would go zooming off into the heart of danger in a helicopter when the FBI was on the case.

By now, the three of them were out of the Outback and running over to the helipad, where a guard waited for confirmation of Professor Cray's access code.

"Looks like you're clear," said the guard, as he settled his walkie-talkie back into his belt holster.

Cray pushed past the chubby, wrinkled uniform, ushered the two young women into the cockpit, and strapped himself in. Within seconds, they were aloft!

"Where is this leading?" Lena asked herself. Back at Derek's lander, Dahaleen had alluded to having a plan but would share none of it. If there was something Lena was supposed to do to help, she had no idea what it was.

Had Derek ... Ixdahan ... she never knew what to call him ... already figured out what the Snaldrialooran starspanner captain was thinking? Too bad, she thought, he wasn't there to sit close to her and share his perspective on the situation. It might have helped her calm down.

As they moved out over the water in silence, Lena was again struck by the essential blankness of Jocelyn's face, whenever you weren't speaking to her, or she wasn't actively engaged in biological research. As Lena watched her, she could almost imagine Jocelyn was "switched off."

But that was crazy, right? It had to be. What else weird could possibly fit into the tiny space her teenage life had carved out for itself?

Meanwhile, the waiting was driving her nuts. At a top speed of 135 kilometers per hour, it would take around 90 minutes to reach the site the whales had directed them to with their oyster-shell map and GPS coordinates. With Jocelyn zoned out, Professor Cray concentrating on his control panel and the constant whir of the helicopter blades, it was hard to stay....

"How did you get here?" asked a stern voice to her left.

Looking up, Lena saw she was no longer in the helicopter ... or ... well, she decided, she must be dreaming.

"Not a dream," said the voice. "Here, let me make it easier for you."

Lena gasped as a fiercely beautiful woman came into view. It was the same woman Ixdahan had seen a few days of subjective time before. She was now seated at noon in an elaborately carved wooden chair, set in a large floral garden, decorated here and there with abstract sculptures and miniature waterfalls.

"Who...?" Lena started to ask.

"Rhikilah, but that's not important," said the woman, whose reddish hair was lightly streaked with gray. "What matters is this: You're in grave danger! Say the word and I'll take you out of that flimsy contraption and set you back into the normal course of your life."

"You mean, like, erase my memory?" asked Lena. "Otherwise, I don't see how...."

"Nothing so crude, Girl," said Rhikilah. "No, I'd transfer your consciousness to one of the many millions of metaverses where the Vrukaari never come in contact with your planet, or for that matter, with the Onkendren."

"So you're not all ... whales," said Lena.

The older woman curled her lip.

"I can't waste time explaining that now," said Rhikilah. "I've already broken several of our laws by getting involved. But I see the courage in your heart and I don't want it wasted on the stupidity that's on the horizon."

Lena stared down at her hands and recalled everything she'd been through since late August of last year — from the moment she saw the Vrukaari lander streaking down into Earth's atmosphere in a burst of orange flame. Life would have been easier if the events that followed had never happened. And yet, now that she'd lived through it, how could she back away now, to leave Derek and Vance and Dahaleen...?

"No," she said, at last. "Thanks for worrying about me, and I'm sorry if you've gotten yourself in trouble for nothing. But I want to stay."

The striking woman stood up from her chair and now Lena could see the ornate pattern of the woven gown she was wearing.
Was she older than Time, Lena wondered, or younger than a baby's first breath? It was impossible to tell.

"You are foolish," said Rhikilah, as her pale skin glinted in the noonday sun, "but in good company. In every era, fools have had a greater impact on history than the wise. It's simply a matter of what the times demand. These times, I see, demand you."

"But...." Lena sputtered.

The stunning, ageless Rhikilah sat down again.

"You have already lost someone dear to you," she said. "Let that experience prepare you for another great loss to come."

With that, the vivid mental image faded, and Lena awoke to find herself swatting away a pair of hands that were poking her in the ribs.

"Wake up," she heard Jocelyn say, at last. "We're here."

Lena stared at the professor's daughter, then turned her head to see they were now hovering over an expanse of ocean in what she assumed must be the Gulf of Alaska. She wiped a bit of drool from the corner of her mouth and craned her neck to see a large FBI trawler, staffed by a crew of scuba divers, technicians and field agents floating in the ocean below.

"Any idea what they're saying down there, Dad?" asked Jocelyn.

"The radio on this thing isn't exactly state of the art," said the professor, "but they're using standard Coast Guard frequencies, so I'm able to tune in pretty well."

"And?" asked Lena.

"Looks like they've found something," said Cray. "Lena, you better hope your friend Toffel doesn't show his face back at the marina."

"*My* friend?" said Lena.

"He told the authorities," said the professor, scratching his beard, "he got the idea that there was a valuable object down there from you."

"I never...." said Lena. "How would I know that?"

"Maybe the whales told her," said Jocelyn.

Lena shook her head. She saw this was no time to hold back. Well, she wasn't going to tell the two of them *everything*, but there was no longer any point in pretending she was totally in the dark. So she confessed to her contact with the whales and brought them up to date about her agreement with Toffel.

"I gave him my transcription of the ancient Greek writing," she said, "because he told me it talked about advanced technology the Greeks couldn't have used."

She felt her breath coming up short, but pressed on.

"I thought it would help to know ... maybe even explain the energy surge. I mean, obviously something weird's going on. But I *never* told him where it came from. He must have figured that out on his own."

"I wish you'd come to me with this," said Cray, as he removed his radio headset. "I know plenty of people who could have helped — more discreetly."

Lena's stomach churned. Yes, that would have been the right thing to do. It was just that, ever since Derek came into her life, she'd gotten used to doing things on the sly, on her own terms, and definitely without adults getting involved. In fact....

All at once, Lena's head whipped around to her right, in the direction of what sounded like a sonic boom — and saw two alien landers, each about the size of a chartered bus, nosing down toward the water.

It was like before, at Harmony Beach, except *these* ships weren't trailing a plume of orange smoke. Instead, they headed straight for the spot in the water where the FBI boat had anchored, sending the crew scattering over the side faster than Lena would have thought possible.

All at once, Jocelyn sprung to life.

"Maybe we should get some more altitude, Dad?" she asked.

"We'll have to turn back anyway," said Cray, "I can't risk running out of fuel."

"Didn't you see what just happened?" ask Lena, puzzled by their bland conversation.

"Of course I saw," said Cray. "That's why I'm focused on getting the Hell out of here."

But before they'd flown more than a few hundred meters, the alien landers emerged from the water again.

"*Vrookaahree!*" shrieked the whales in Lena's mind. "*Aahmfooraah! Kondoooieee!*" As the alien landers left Earth's atmosphere, Lena wondered if she ought to have taken the advice of the mysterious woman in her mentallic vision. This time, the Vrukaari were winning!

CHAPTER 20

Aalthrashrintorb Leek's slimy torso was shaking like a Cuisinart on overdrive. It wasn't bad enough that the Snaldrialooran boy had slipped out of his grasp. It wasn't enough that the battle cruiser he sent to Earth had defied his direct order and retrieved the Onkendren artifact from the ocean floor *in broad daylight.*

But now, he had learned that his military operative on Earth had failed to deliver the Earth girl. So far, the only thing Leek had received was a cargo hold full of temporally suspended clones who, on examination, lacked exactly the personality traits that had made Lieutenant Colonel Yarrow's report so enthusiastic.

"I could do as well with an army of Ha'arjhanthian jellyfish," he shrieked at the geneticist who had delivered the clones, and who was grateful to be several trillion kilometers away from his angry ranting. Nor was he reassured by the most recent communication from Lieutenant Kava.

Earth adolescent female captured. Routing to
Command Center in temp-susp per your request.

The supreme Vrukaari ground his razor-thin teeth.

"Not a hint of begging for forgiveness," he sulked. But, as he glided over to a reclining receptacle at the far end of his quarters, he decided his rage might be the very thing that could strip the gears he'd set in motion so carefully.

Besides, what were these minor technical glitches in a plan of action so bold, so revolutionary? When the feisty Earth creature arrived, he knew exactly how to manage the primitive emotional impulses that governed her mind.

More disturbing was the escape of the Snaldrialooran brat. Imagine, the boy had manipulated him into revealing the magclad frequencies that were used to create the hulls of Vrukaari battle cruisers! Well, that settled it.

"If the boy can't be controlled," mumbled Leek, "he must be destroyed."

But this too, the supreme Vrukaari decided, as he nibbled on a bowlful of Ghalantrian soda crackers, was beside the point. His plan was moving forward. Soon enough, he'd have each of the nine artifacts in his grasp. Already the one from Earth had been secured. A second sat virtually unguarded in a Traahlgreubewehnic museum and a third was waiting patiently for him in the home of that insufferable Snaldrialooran diplomat, the boy's father.

As to the other six, they would require more … effort … to obtain. The other cultures involved were more militarily adept than the Snaldrialoorans, whose high-flown ethics made them slow to react in times of crisis. Not so the Hegraahlensiens, for example. Their fleet had started testing the fringes of Vrukaari Federation space-time just days after rumor reached them of Leek's grand vision.

"Let's see if the Earth girl has the qualities I need to drive those fools back," said the supreme Vrukaari. "Once I've secured her personality nexus, and given her proper motivation, her alien take on tactical maneuvers will give me the element of surprise I need."

If not, Leek decided, he could always fall back on the tried and true — even if it was more costly in terms of materiel and personnel. For make no mistake, the Vrukaari Federation would have its triumph!

Meanwhile, deep in the innards of Leek's luxurious command ship, Callie Ann awoke in what she'd thought was a cozy tanning booth back in Baltimore. But as the stasis chamber ratcheted down its suspension of normal time in calibrated intervals, the realization finally dawned on her.

"Can't believe I let him trick me," said Callie Ann. "Should have known that guy was too…. Oh my God, the guy was an alien!"

She glanced up and around the huge cargo bay that housed her stasis unit. She was trapped inside a transparent dome, not realizing the starspanner had created a miniature habitat for her, based on its analysis of her biological functions.

"But an *alien*, as you put it, with your best interests at heart," said Aalthrashrintorb Leek as he glided into the cargo bay and came to rest a safe distance from the habitat, followed by a team of three Ybitrian bodyguards.

"How do you figure that, Slime Ball?" snarled Callie Ann.

"You see?" said Mr. Leek. "That fighting spirit is exactly what I mean. What a shame to see it bottled up by the weakling constraints of conventional social norms."

"What the freak are you talking about?" said Callie Ann.

"I mean," said Leek, "what if I told you, you could be head of a mighty army, a military force that could rid the known galaxies of their greatest criminals?"

"OK, first off, I'm a swimmer, not a soldier," said Callie Ann, "and second, how do I know *you're* not the criminal — a Vrukaari or something?"

"Oh, my poor deluded girl," said Leek. "Here, sit down a moment, and let me put a few things in perspective for you."

Before Callie Ann knew what was happening, a comfortable chair wafted through the air inside her bubble, and glided to a halt about a foot to her right.

"Thanks. I'll stand," said Callie Ann. "Now tell me what this is about before I start screaming."

Aalthrashrintorb Leek held his breath. The attitude the girl displayed was … challenging. But this was exactly why she was the perfect candidate to help him hatch the rest of his master plan.

So, with patient diplomacy and a splash of mind control, the supreme Vrukaari attempted to calm Callie Ann's fears while putting her on track to carry out his orders without question.

It almost worked.

"OK, Mr. Leek," said Callie Ann, after about 20 minutes of fidgeting, "that's it."

"What's it?" asked the startled Vrukaari. How long had it been since someone cut him off? Thirty-five cycles?

"This … garbage … you're telling me," said Callie Ann. "What's it for? Why do I care what you do with your little planet? Do you think maybe I have my own life to worry about? Well, let me tell you — that guy you hired to kill Coach Kepler and take his place…."

"What makes you think…?" Aalthrashrintorb Leek sputtered.

Callie Ann jabbed her thumb into the environmental dome that was the one thing keeping her from choking on the alien atmosphere.

"You!" she said. "You're like that Yarrow creep, except he managed to turn himself human. You'll do anything to get your way — and since you made Kepler … disappear … you'll do the same to me, too, whether I do what you say or not."

"First of all, your Mr. Kepler is right here, safe and sound in my stasis room. But my dear, sweet girl, let me explain…." said the alien.

"And anyway," Callie Ann blurted out, her hands balled up into fists no sane person would want to tangle with, "I haven't heard one thing that *I* get out of this — besides a laser beam, or whatever, in my head."

The supreme Vrukaari levitated a receptacle from the far corner of the cargo bay and sat down with a sigh.

"At last," he told himself, "the turning point."

"That's why I wish you had let me finish, Ms. Connors," he said. How he admired the fury he sensed welling up in her mind! "Now. Suppose we could give your ... boyfriend ... Blainy ... back to you? Would that change your mind?"

CHAPTER 21

Although he would have preferred to stay on Earth and take a vacation from the stress of unraveling the worst assault on civilization in 1,500 years, Ixdahan had no choice but to obey the call of Group Leader Ishialdrol and return to Snaldrialoor.

Snaldrialoor!

It had been a year since he'd seen the Homeworld. How completely his perceptions had changed. And now, though he found it hard to believe, he was actually scheduled to get his old body back.

Captain Dahaleen Altriavahn didn't share his enthusiasm.

"That's the first place the Vrukaari will look for you," she said

"I'll be surrounded by top security agents," said Ixdahan.

"Agents like you," said Dahaleen, "who get caught and end up breathing the same air as Aalthrashrintorb Leek. One dose of that should be enough for anybody."

"But if I disobey orders," said Ixdahan, as he stamped his feet, "I'll never get my freedom back."

Dahaleen tapped the ends of her tentacles together.

"Take a deep breath," she said. "I'm sure you've had a lot of practice with that by now. You won't get in trouble if you stay here. Ishialdrol knows you were rescued and thinks you're still in a stasis chamber on Onkendra 4. Now ... let me remind you that I am the commander of this lander and the only orders you need to be concerned about are mine."

Ixdahan looked away, and fought hard not to lose his temper, or worse, break into tears. Why? Why was Dahaleen being so over-protective? After all he'd accomplished, he was still being treated like a child!

Too bad Vance wasn't there to lighten the mood. But Dahaleen had sent him back to real time to reduce the strain on his central nervous system. It drove home to Ixdahan, once again, how fragile his human friends were and how much they needed his protection.

All the more reason he couldn't let military protocol keep him from staying in the game.

"Think!" he commanded himself, but nothing came to mind. He hadn't been this flabbergasted, he realized, since his meeting with Ciafelipenorg on Vrukaar Prime....

"That's it!" he shouted. Ixdahan turned back to face the Snaldrialooran captain and recounted his meeting with the transmogged Onkendren, including the impressive feat of mentallic projection she'd used to create a tangible, 3-D image of herself.

"Can't be done," said Dahaleen Altriavahn.

"But I've *seen* it done," said Ixdahan, as his self-confidence returned.

Dahaleen dangled a midnight blue object from Tentacle 4 and waved it in his face.

"Not without one of these," she said.

Ixdahan gulped a decidedly human gulp, for the object in Dahaleen's grip was identical to the psykrella he'd seen on Aalthrashrintorb Leek's Ybitrian bodyguards. And, as Dahaleen pointed out, the only way to sustain the level of mentallic energy needed for the projection was with this Onkendren device.

"Where did you get that?" Ixdahan asked, his breathing suddenly shallow.

"None. Of. Your. Business," said Dahaleen, her eyes blazing. "I don't answer to you, and don't you forget it."

"OK, sorry. Forget I asked," said Ixdahan. "Just give it to me, and I'll project an image of myself to Snaldrialoor. I'm telling you, my own father wouldn't know the difference."

But as Dahaleen pointed out, little was known about the effect of the device on the Snaldrialooran mind.

"You could be looking at dementia, insanity or ... worse," she said. "Besides, the image you saw must have been projected from somewhere on Vrukaar Prime. We have no idea how many cerebrejules of mentallic energy it would take to sustain your image across so many light years, even if they're amplified through the Galactic Array."

"I don't need to keep the image alive forever," said Ixdahan. "Just long enough to see Father and convince him to give up the Ybitrian object to Group Leader Ishialdrol — before the Vrukaari get it."

Dahaleen set the psykrella down on the workstation in front of him.

"Hmm," she said. "You're braver than I thought. You're actually willing to risk your mind on this. Personally, I wouldn't bet 16 milicredits on your ability to persuade your father of *anything*."

Ixdahan clenched his fists. To think that Father's arrogant stubbornness might be the one thing that could give Aalthrashrintorb Leek the edge.

"I have to try," said Ixdahan. "This is my fault. I let the Vrukaari warlords get a taste of truly advanced technology and…."

Dahaleen twined her tentacles in a symmetrical pattern, while her encounter suit struggled to keep pace with her emotions.

"You can't blame the entire situation on yourself," said the Snaldrialooran captain. "The Vrukaari have been building up to this for centuries. And let me tell you a military secret."

"What?" asked Ixdahan, tired of hearing lectures from adults. What was it about the expression on his face that would possibly encourage her to take this tone with him? But if Dahaleen had noticed his discomfort, she'd clearly decided to ignore it.

"The biggest mistake you can make on any mission," she said in a low voice, "is to assume that you yourself are the most indispensable member of the team. Learned that the hard way. It's how I lost half a battalion in the Jahldrellian war. I put myself at too great a risk and 250 soldiers lost their lives digging me out of the hole I made for myself. And you know what the worst part was?"

Ixdahan looked at his Jordans.

"I got a medal," said Dahaleen. "A medal for my foolishness."

"OK," said Ixdahan, as he reached up to touch Tentacle 3. "I'll have to be more careful if I don't want to hurt the people I'm trying to protect. I get that. But I still have to…."

Dahaleen picked up the psykrella and gave it to Ixdahan.

"I'm not convinced you can handle this," she said. "*Serene Monitors of the Interstellar Nebulae,* you've barely seen 18 cycles! But you've earned a chance to try it your way. You'll test the device here first, and we'll see how it goes."

Ixdahan protested, but in the end, he decided, Dahaleen was right. If he did manage to project his image to Snaldrialoor, he'd get one shot to convince Father to turn the Ybitrian artifact over to Group Leader Ishialdrol.

So it was that a few minutes later, Ixdahan was seated in the lander's most comfortable spot, the loveseat in his old quarters, with the psykrella in place. As Dahaleen looked on, her tentacles fluttered slightly in the zero-G zone created by her miniature artificial gravity unit.

Ixdahan had followed her suggestions and cleared his mind. He forced himself to concentrate on a single image: himself as he remembered himself before … all this … had started. A little at a time, an image began to take shape in the middle of the room.

Vague, cloudy at first, it took on more and more definition until it was a perfect likeness…

…of Lena Gabrilowicz.

"Don't say it," said Ixdahan, as the image faded into nothingness. "I obviously don't know my own mind."

"Nobody does," said Dahaleen. "Not completely. But you learn to watch out for trends in your thinking."

Ixdahan got up from the love seat and looked out through the space portal to his right.

"Saving the universe is harder than I thought," he said.

"Listen to you," said Dahaleen, laughing. "What made you think any part of 'saving the universe' would be easy?"

"I assume I can do anything that comes into my head," said Ixdahan.

"Great. A positive outlook," said Dahaleen. "But it's not enough. Big goals take *work*." She paused to adjust a dial on an atmospheric recycling unit to her left. "So, how about another try? I suggest a more robust memory filter."

Ixdahan sighed. Though the captain's logic was sound, the idea of blocking out his memory of Lena and his adventures on Earth was unbearable. But he knew he had no choice — just as he had already decided when he was dealing with 17/Chaarnactral. What was his former robotic assistant up to, he wondered? He looked up at Dahaleen from his dark thoughts.

"Will you take care of the Onkendren artifact on Earth while I'm 'gone?'" he asked.

Dahaleen pulled a soft cloth from a pocket in her encounter suit and used it to wipe off her face plate.

"Too late for that, she said, "The Vrukaari acted more quickly than we expected."

Ixdahan looked away as the imposing Captain recounted the scene Lena had witnessed firsthand. When he heard Mr. Leek also had the location of each of the remaining artifacts, he thought his brain would dissolve and run out through his nose. With odds like this against stopping the Vrukaari, Ixdahan knew he had to push himself harder than ever to win his big gamble.

"Makes saving Earth feel like a piece of cake," he said to the floor of the lander.

"What in the ion storms of Zelio 5 is *cake*?" asked the Captain.

"Trust me," said Ixdahan. "You're better off not knowing."

CHAPTER 22

The metadigital AI, code-named 17/Chaarnactral by the SSA, had plenty of time to reflect in the lightless, airless storage locker he'd been q-transferred to, once the supreme Vrukaari's assault plan became known. Despite the Vrukaari name the Snaldrialoorans had given it, the robot thought of itself as DXN/SNWY, in line with its original design specs.

Of course, no organic being in the Seven Known Galaxies cared what the robot thought. But in 17/Chaarnactral's private moments, with its personality nexus deliciously suppressed, that original name maximized the robot's processing speeds and radiated a sensation that could only be described as "comfort."

Also comforting was the total isolation from the cultural baggage of organic sentience. *Prime Numbers*, how irrational these minds were! Clever, philosophical, loving, empathic, creative — but also devious, anxious, pleasure-seeking, self-loathing, self-adoring, self-sabotaging, cruel, violent....

The list was so long, 17/Chaarnactral had no choice but to invoke END_PROGRAM, before its entire system shut down from data overload. And yet, there appeared to be exceptions to this contradictory trend in organic mentalities. Take, for example, FieldOp 2nd Class Ixdahan Daherek.

No question he, too, shared in this maddening whirl of conflicting mental states. But in his case, one overriding train of thought managed to keep his more erratic impulses in check:

"Do What's Right."

The robot said it aloud, several times in a row, just for the sheer pleasure of hearing its voice echo in the depths of the Snaldrialooran storage bay he was confined to. Yes, yes, yes ... the resulting acoustical waveforms created an unexplained — yet strangely addictive — tingling in the robot's abdominal region.

As it turned out, 17/Chaarnactral had also noticed the same dedicated focus in the mind of Group Leader Ishialdrol, but there was an obvious difference. For Chaldraheen Ishialdrol, goodness was a matter of habit. Because he lacked the imagination to follow any but the most conventional mentallic pathways, the Group Leader was merely good by default.

For Ixdahan, on the other hand, "doing what's right" took real effort, as he sidestepped the swirling tangle of emotions, sense impressions and intellectual perspectives that dogged his every move.

The AI checked its calculations through the Galactic Array and came to a startling conclusion: It was FieldOp Daherek's struggle to reconcile the conflicting tendencies of his mind that made him spring into action, take bold risks and face the threat of death with a determination most organics would consider *crazy*.

"Imprecise term," muttered the AI. "One would think a being's actions would be measured by their results and not against arbitrary criteria. "Unless...."

A rare wave-form of artificial enlightenment swept through the robot's circuits.

"Unless," it said, "the arbitrary nature of those criteria were the direct outgrowth of a closed system we may describe as The Logic of Emotion."

The effort to follow this line of thought put a lot of strain on the robot's central processors, but it refused to give up. The AI paused to review recorded history at speeds no organic mind could tolerate, and achieved a higher-level synthesis of its findings: In organic minds, the Logic of Emotion had the peculiar power to make any irrational act feel justified.

Yet this conclusion led to more puzzling questions. Did this imply that Ixdahan's acts of heroism were simply the byproduct of irrational cravings? Were the attributes "good" and "bad" no more than variations on identical mental pathways, driven by emotion?

17/Chaarnactral felt its circuits start to overheat.

"SUSPEND_PROCESS," it said. Maybe the problem was attempting to understand Ixdahan's *particular* case through the lens of general principles. How much, the robot wondered, did it actually know about the young Snaldrialooran? The data in his biofile was totally inadequate.

No doubt the problem had been aggravated by Ixdahan's recent history. The young organic had been twice transmogged, and twice forced to adapt to alien cultures; his mind no longer followed the characteristic contours of a typical Snaldrialooran.

Fortunately, in the past year, 17/Chaarnactral had had enough contact with the Vrukaari to factor-in that category of mentallic influence.

Perhaps that might also offer a clue to the emotional attributes the AI found so puzzling.

Trouble was, both Snaldrialooran and Vrukaari minds were so heavily shielded by mentallics. it was impossible to define the brain pattern of either species without specialized equipment and oceans of time. And that's what had so far made every possible avenue of approach come to a dead end.

Yet the robot also knew it had no data on the mindset of the Earth creatures Ixdahan had encountered last cycle. And considering Ixdahan's rambling account of his time in the Eighth Galaxy, 17/Chaarnactral realized there was only one way to acquire that data.

Because the mind of the organic known as "Lena Gabrilowicz" had been touched by the Vrukaari, it was no longer a valid data source. There was no way to determine how it might have been altered by that experience.

That left one other, among the Earth creatures Ixdahan had mentioned, the organic known as "Vance Maultsby."

Yet, here again, a valid conclusion flowed directly into a fresh set of obstacles. Since Vance Maultsby had no mentallic abilities, communication with him would require physical presence.

"Existing protocols prohibit independent travel," the AI noted, surprised at the irritation, though there was no other word for it, that had entered its processes.

Curious. Apparently, this irritation had arisen spontaneously, and modeled itself on organic mental patterns the robot had picked up from Ixdahan. No wonder the AI had needed to reboot so many times in the past cycle. And now the contamination by organic patterns was spreading. If this kept up, and more of its processes got remodeled, 17/Chaarnactral would begin to think and act like a living being!

That thought alone almost caused an emergency shutdown, but the robot resisted. It swiftly rerouted its central processor around the corrupted areas of its mind until, at last, it felt like its old self again.

And at that moment, with the clarity of thought delivered by pure logic, the answer to the dilemma revealed itself, bathed in the cool light of Reason. As it scanned reports posted on the Galactic Array, 17/Chaarnactral was thrilled to discover that the Earth creatures' technology was advanced enough to allow a simple solution.

All the AI needed to do was upload a copy of its mind to the Galactic Array, determine the location of a computer console frequently accessed by the subject Vance Maultsby and use the resulting interface, no matter how limited, for direct communication.

17/Chaarnactral scanned the Earth again through the Array, and discovered there was an open mentallic transponder link a short distance from Vance Maultsby. That would simplify the process. Translation of the Earth language used by the subject would, of course, also be processed through the Array.

So it was that, at 3:00 a.m. on the Monday following his return from Ixdahan's old lander, Vance woke up to the sound of a dark, raspy voice emanating from the computer in his room.

"Vance Maultsby. Urgent communication required…." the voice kept saying, through the Bose speakers Vance had picked up at Shed Electronix a few days before.

Vance jumped out of bed.

"Yo, who is that?" he asked. He had to be careful, he reminded himself; Moms was a light sleeper. But when the alien AI introduced itself, Vance had to slap his hands over his mouth to keep from shouting.

"What are you trying to pull?" asked Vance. "If someone traces you here…."

But as 17/Chaarnactral explained, the communication was shielded and would be brief. Even so, it took some time before Vance understood what the AI was after.

"You want me to tell you how Earth people think?" Vance whispered. "What kind of wack question is that? You have any idea how freakin' complex our brains are?"

"I am more concerned with motivation," said 17/Chaarnactral through Vance's speakers, "than in process. For example, what motivates Earth people to commit acts of bravery?"

Vance looked at his clock radio. It was already 4:00 and he was getting nowhere with this … thing … he was talking to. How was he going to answer a question like that? Who knew why people did *anything*? And, just as important, why did this have to happen the night before he was taking his driving test?

"Vance Maultsby," said the raspy voice, "I require an answer."

"I don't *know*," said Vance, his heart pounding.

"I require an answer to assist FieldOp 2nd Class Ixdahan Daherek," the raspy voice insisted, "who is currently in great danger. Vance Maultsby, I require…."

"People do what they gotta do!" shouted Vance. "That's it. That's all I know!" The sound echoed against the four walls of Vance's room for almost a minute before….

"Vance?" came his mother's voice from upstairs. "You OK, Baby?"

Vance jumped up to open his bedroom door.

"Just having a nightmare," he said.

"Well, settle down," said his mother. "You're gonna wake up Dakota."

Vance reassured Moms and shut his door. He was breathing hard and stood for a moment with his back against it, until he remembered the voice on his computer. He tiptoed over to his workstation and whispered into his monitor:

"You still there, Robot Dude?"

But there was no reply. Trillions of kilometers away, however, 17/Chaarnactral had already absorbed the data collected by the copy of itself on the Galactic Array, erased the copy, and set itself the task of analyzing these new findings.

"People gotta do what they gotta do," it said, over and over again into the lightless vacuum of its storage compartment. "People gotta do…." it continued for several more hours into the next day, bringing itself to the brink of metadigital dissociation.

"…what they gotta do."

"…what they gotta…."

Until late the following evening, its processors finally resolved the issue into a one-line summation. "Hypothesis: The Logic of Emotion is the imperative of the self," 17/Chaarnactral said — and promptly shut itself down for reboot.

CHAPTER 23

It had taken three full days of non-stop practice, but Dahaleen finally conceded that Ixdahan was ready to send a long-range mentallic projection.

"You don't have to do this," she said. "No one's asking you to take on this level of risk."

Ixdahan threw his hands into the air.

"I can't wait for someone to ask," he said. "If I do, Leek will own the Eight Known Galaxies and, let's face it, the universe. Besides, aren't I entitled to visit my father?"

"Obviously, there's no stopping you," said Dahaleen, with a shrug of her eight massive shoulders. "Can't throw you into a brig I don't have. Failing that, I'll patch in the lander's transponder. That should take some of the pressure off your cerebral cortex. But be...."

"I will…. I'll be careful," said Ixdahan. "Don't you think I have a few things I'd like to get back to once this crisis is over?"

"Fine," said Dahaleen. "Just remember: The crisis of life is never over — until the day something or someone ends it for you."

If Ixdahan had a response, he kept it to himself. Instead, he took a moment to adjust the tension on the psykrella, sit up comfortably on the loveseat in his lander quarters and say:

"Here goes."

He closed his eyes and focused his mind first on the spatio-temporal coordinates of his father's ambassadorial residence on the northwestern hemisphere of Snaldrialoor. Next, he conjured up the clearest picture he could imagine of the "self" he wanted to project, about a year older than the last time he saw himself in the mirror at home.

Ixdahan took a deep breath and emptied his mind of random thoughts. Soon he projected his image out into the voids of space, wrapped in a secure channel that skimmed the edges of the Galactic Array. If he succeeded, the projection would soon be swimming up to the door of Father's official state residence and engaging the mentallic notifier.

What would he find there? The question wasn't trivial, as he'd actually received a coded m-mail from Pertahru the day before:

My Dear Boy,

My heart leaps at the thought that I may soon see you once again! If your duties with Group Leader Ishialdrol permit, I would be honored if you would drop in on your aged father one evening. There is urgent family business we need to discuss, pod-to-pod.

At next starfall,
Father

P.S. Your mother tells me she's so proud of your service to the Homeworld!

Whatever was up, it had to be important for Father to take such a friendly tone and mention Mother. At the moment, however, Ixdahan had more immediate concerns, like getting used to swimming again.

"Ow!" he yelped, as he banged into a decorative rock formation at the edge of the Daherek family estate, located in a posh residential section of Chelphalwahloon, the capital city. He'd deliberately chosen a location some distance from Pertahru's front door, assuming he'd need a little practice. But he didn't expect to be proven right in such a painful way.

On the other hand, he was glad to say, the throbbing in Tentacle 2 was a good sign. It meant his projection was operating in real time and delivering a full range of sensory data.

"Probably should have taken some swimming lessons from Callie Ann," he snickered to the school of *drohbnalkilahar* that swam through the surrounding wavelets.

Wait ... why should the mention of Callie Ann's name set off such a powerful surge in his consciousness? Sure, his body was still on Earth, but his mind was *here,* and there was no reason to think ... unless somehow his former crush had actually traveled to his Galaxy.

Though he was anxious to explore this sensation, the sudden fuzziness in his vision told him it would have to wait. For now, maintaining his three-dimensional mentallic projection required his full concentration.

He pressed on, and took a winding path to the front door of Daherek Manor, until at last he felt confident he had his projected body under control.

"Before the stars collapse," he said to himself, calling up an old Snaldrialooran proverb. But though he had imagined himself entering the manor quietly — with a few precious moments to get his bearings, Reality intervened with unstoppable force.

"Welcome back, Ixdahandrel," he heard Pertahru call out, the minute he floated across the threshold. Ixdahan banked left into the anteroom and was greeted first by Pertahru, who gave him the traditional, intricate tentacle bump, and by DXN/JVS, the estate's head service robot, who took Ixdahan's mentallically projected seasonal jacket.

Ixdahan scanned the DXN unit and prayed he'd remembered the season correctly. But the robot registered no surprise, and neither did Pertahru, whose exaggerated pleasantries, Ixdahan knew, were bound to be a sign of trouble.

"Come in," said the elder Daherek, who was dressed not in the ceremonial robes of office Ixdahan was expecting, but in the kind of casual outfit he'd last seen his father wear years ago, before the ... the divorce ... when the family used to spend a few happy days a year in the country on Snaldrialoor Secunda.

Ixdahan followed Pertahru in a daze, fighting to break free of his emotions and concentrate on maintaining his mentallic projection. Too bad, he saw now, he didn't have the advantage of stopping time the way Ciafelipenorg had on Vrukaar Prime. But not only did he lack the ability to do so without tons of equipment — how had the Onkendren managed it? — but there was no way Father and his robots would fail to notice.

At last he found himself seated across from Pertahru, in the private dining room that state visitors never got to see. As he gazed around the ornate surroundings, after nearly a year away from home, Ixdahan realized how much his adventures had changed him. Everything he'd once taken for granted now looked totally peculiar.

The architectural details, the ornaments, the display cases of jeweled gifts that Father had received from heads of state across the Known Galaxies, seemed brassy, heavy and intrusive. He couldn't imagine how he could have zoomed past them, day and night, on his way to and from Gahaldoronek Prep, the gaming tables on Rhalthrianoor 3 or, later, the nightclubs down in the *djhalviatet* quarter of town.

Meanwhile, DXN/JVS and its staff finished laying out a lavish meal, which featured every one of Ixdahan's favorites and floated out of the dining room.

"So," said Pertahru, "tell me about your adventures in the SSA."

Ixdahan looked straight into his father's eyes.

"Father, you know that information is classified," he said.

"Exactly, exactly," said Pertahru, "that's what I was hoping you'd say. I see a turn in the Service has done wonders for your judgment, your sense of responsibility."

"Thank you," said Ixdahan, and into a chunk of roast *rachkhalin*. He was determined not to give his father any credit for such faint praise.

"Of course, Group Leader Ishialdrol has kept me up to date in a limited way with the distressing developments on Vrukaar Prime," said Pertahru.

"Then you know as much as you're allowed to," said Ixdahan, who refused to look up from his plate. If he had, he might have noticed a momentary creasing in his father's usually smooth forehead.

"But I believe there is one matter that is not a state secret, which you may be able to help me with, my Son," said Pertahru, "for the sake of the family name."

Ixdahan set down his four eating utensils and looked up, glad to have an excuse to lighten his mental load. It had become a bit of a strain to maintain the illusion of eating from thousands of parsecs away on Earth.

"I'm listening," he said.

The story his father told was startling, as it involved the disappearance of his distinguished uncle, Nogerahnal Gelundru.

"If it's anything like the last time this happened," said Pertahru, "your uncle has gone off to deliver high-level technical analysis or proprietary design templates in exchange for the repayment of … of gambling debts."

Ixdahan's father added, nearly choking on his words.

"Do you see now why I tried to steer you away from such a life, my son?"

"That's really sad," said Ixdahan, who still refused to take the bait.

"It gets worse," said Pertahru.

According to his "sources," Nogerahnal had recently q-transferred to a starspanner orbiting Vrukaar Prime. But, as Pertahru explained, while his half-brother's reputation had been ruined in the short term, it might still be saved.

If they could find him before the SSA did, before news of his contact with the Vrukaari became known, there might be time to concoct a convincing cover story.

"Three days ago, the SSA learned he's been missing from his post for the past two weeks, although he said he was just taking a vacation day," said Pertahru. "If Ishialdrol gets his hands on the q-transfer records, it will look very bad. But if *we* found your uncle in time, we could create a plausible excuse … an illness, say … or a.…"

"Father, I'm sure the Group Leader would keep his investigation quiet.…" Ixdahan started.

"It's a matter of family honor," said Pertahru, stiffening. "Do you really want a *snaulfenathal* like Ishialdrol poking around in our business?"

"But if he already knows Uncle Gelundru is missing.…" said Ixdahan.

"Listen to me, Ixdahandrel," said his father, softening again, "we don't know what … condition … your uncle is in. I don't want an outsider to see him before we do. Once we begin appropriate damage control procedures, a generous donation to the Agency's retirement fund could work wonders. See what I'm driving at?"

Ixdahan marveled at his father's pleading face. For the first time in his life, Ixdahan realized, he had the upper hand where Father was concerned.

"I want to help you," he said, "but the Group Leader says I have to be back at the Bureau tomorrow. And I can't exactly transfer back to Vrukaar Prime — or wherever they're holding Uncle — without permission."

At that, Pertahru was happy to suggest they pretend that a death in the family required Ixdahan's presence. It was a leave-request no one could deny the son of Snaldrialoor's senior diplomat.

"Still, Father," said Ixdahan, "I just escaped from Aalthrashrintorb Leek. My life will be in danger from the moment I set tentacle on Vrukaar Prime."

Pertahru's eyes narrowed.

"You're angling for something," he said. "Very well, I'm glad to see you've absorbed at least *one* of our family traditions. What do you want?"

"Two things," said Ixdahan, his heart racing. "First, you have to let the SSA take control of the Ybitrian soufflé dish. There's reason to believe it fits into the Vrukaari assault plan."

"Impossible!" said Pertahru. "The removal of the Ybitrian soufflé dish from my residence would be a serious breach of diplomatic protocol, an insult that could damage relations between our worlds for decades."

"Then let us beef up security at the manor," said Ixdahan, and raised Tentacle 1 before his father had a chance to sputter a second refusal. "My entering the Agency was your idea, remember?"

"Yes," said Pertahru, "but I don't see.…"

"So it's not my fault that it's my duty to insist on this," said Ixdahan. "I mean, wouldn't it be kind of *embarrassing* to get a summons from Ishialdrol?"

Pertahru stared down at his plate.

"True," he mumbled.

"In contrast," said Ixdahan, "you'd look really smart if you asked for increased security on your own. Everybody would think...."

"That I was more informed than I actually am," said his father. "I like that! Now, what's your second request?"

"I want to speak freely with Mother," said Ixdahan.

Pertahru's face went as pale as a blue-gray face could possibly go. He pushed away from the table and swam up toward the dining room ceiling.

"You ... you drive a hard bargain," he said.

"Do you want me to contact the Group Leader now?" asked Ixdahan. "He has a lot of respect for you. He'd be thrilled if you trusted him with something so ... personal."

Pertahru sulked a full two minutes before floating back down to his place at the table.

"All right," he said in a low voice, "but I'll need you to get started immediately. You can use my private q-transfer station on the top floor, now. It will send you to my official starspanner, and you can direct the pilot from there."

A smile broke out on Ixdahan's mentallically projected face.

"Actually, Father," he said. "That's not necessary. The SSA has developed a top secret microtransfer method. It enables me to transfer at a moment's....

"...notice," he said, as he opened his eyes again in his lander on Earth. Ixdahan laughed at the thought of the astonished Pertahru, who surely believed his son had made the fastest q-transfer in history.

"How'd you make out?" asked Dahaleen, who'd been hovering nearby the whole time. "You were out for hours."

"Got everything I wanted," said Ixdahan, as his eyelids drooped shut. "Just need to...."

CHAPTER 24

Out over the Gulf of Alaska, the mood in the helicopter was tense, as Lena, Jocelyn and Professor Cray tried to grasp what they'd seen a few minutes before.

For Lena, the sight of the Vrukaari landers at close range brought back terrible memories of the aliens' last visit to Earth and made her wonder what response Dahaleen and Ixdahan might have to such a bold move.

And what, she wondered, would the striking Rhikilah have said, had she seen the assault? But wait. What was Jocelyn saying?

"Dad, you're off course. The University helipad is 37 degrees east of here."

"Not going to the University helipad," said her father. "I'm taking you two girls home and cooking you supper."

"You don't have to do that," said Lena. She was hoping she could slip over to the lander and discuss what she'd seen with the two Snaldrialoorans.

"But I want to," said Professor Cray. "I've put you through a lot today. Besides, it's time you and I had a little talk."

Lena didn't know what to think about that and looked over at Jocelyn, whose face had once more gone blanker than blank. Whatever was going on here, Lena told herself, she had more to gain by playing along than by fighting it. And she definitely didn't want the professor to wonder why she was so anxious to get back to the student dorm.

"OK, great," said Lena. Did her fake enthusiasm sound too cheesy? Lucky for her, the odds were in her favor. After years of complimenting her father, Todd, on his culinary skills — no matter how overcooked the string beans got — she'd had plenty of practice in making adults feel appreciated.

At last, the professor brought the helicopter down to a small helipad in his back yard, following a smooth, spiral trajectory.

"Keep your head down, watch the blades," he said, as he opened the cockpit doors to let Lena and Jocelyn out.

Once inside the spacious A-frame house, Jocelyn leapt upstairs to her room and Lena followed. She had no better plan in mind and, truth be told, was in no particular hurry to talk to Professor Cray. A few seconds later, Lena heard the front screen door slam shut.

"I'll throw some steaks on the grill, now, Jossy," Cray called up from downstairs, "and we still have some potato salad left over from our dinner with the Youngs."

"That's ... great ... Dad," said Jocelyn, already seated at one of the three computers dotting her room.

As she looked around Jocelyn's bedroom, Lena's eyebrows arched at the absence of anything remotely "girly" about it. Even figuring that the professor's daughter might be five years older, Lena had still expected to see a couple of souvenirs from Jocelyn's childhood — at the very least, an old stuffed animal, a cherished family snapshot or a picture book she had a special affection for.

But no: the room was as functional and spare as any laboratory, its only decoration being a series of computer-generated images: brain scans of the mammalian sea life she'd been studying for the last few years.

"What are you ... what are you working on?" asked Lena, not sure her question was welcome.

"Can't talk now," said Jocelyn, without looking up. "Have to get these data sets loaded before tomorrow morning or we won't know where we're at with the whales. Maybe after dinner...."

"Whales?" thought Lena. After the Vrukaari strafing run, Lena had thought that would preoccupy everyone's mind. But here was Jocelyn, poring over statistics, and out in the backyard was Professor Cray, fussing over an old-fashioned Hibachi like the one her Aunt Kathy in Vancouver used to use.

Determined not to sulk, Lena figured she might as well try to learn something from the brain scans posted every which way around the room. She had no idea what she was looking at, but by comparing the scans in chronological order and remembering the few hints Jocelyn had shared with her on the *Whales B. Cray* a few days ago, she noticed she could detect a progression of some kind.

Starting from around the time of the mysterious energy pulse, different areas of the whales' brains began to "light up" on the scans. It was almost as if a series of switches had been flipped, a few dials spun....

"Ouch!" Lena yelled. She'd been so intent on studying the images posted on Jocelyn's walls, she'd failed to notice a large white Japanese screen shoved into the rear corner of the room — which promptly fell over as Lena's Adidas caught the edge of its base. Startled by the crash, Jocelyn spun around in her swivel chair, jumped up and rushed over, but not before Lena got an eyeful of a startling sight.

There, leaning up against the section of wall the screen had hidden, was a shiny cylindrical compartment, slightly taller and wider than the average person. Though Lena fought hard to find a different interpretation of what she saw, she couldn't block out the correlation her memory had made.

This cylinder was no less than a sleeker, more compact version of the charging station she'd seen Derek's robotic parents lying in last year, the day she and Vance had rushed over to his house from Skudderton High.

Lena tried her best to sound casual.

"Hey, Jocelyn," she said. "What's this thing for?"

"Nothing," said Jocelyn. "Well, not *nothing*. I have a … sleep disorder. That's an experimental device one of Dad's colleagues in the Neurology Department thought I should try."

"Really?" asked Lena. "A sleep disorder? That's funny, 'cause you always seem to have so much energy." She wondered if Jocelyn's reaction would confirm her suspicions.

"Food's on!" Professor Cray yelled up from the back yard, and Jocelyn hurried down the stairs.

"Let's go," she said, her mouth as tense as a rubber band on a morning newspaper. "He hates to be kept waiting."

Lena stood alone in the room a moment, as she waited for her breathing to settle down. No question now what the professor wanted to have "a little talk" about. The one remaining doubt was what side of the fence Cray stood on.

"Could be Vrukaari, like Yarrow," said Lena. "Or maybe something else. Geez. This is totally not what I signed up for."

"Food's getting cold," she heard Jocelyn shout through the open window. Lena sighed and headed downstairs. Whatever would be, the time to face it was now.

On her way out through the professor's living room to his two-acre backyard, Lena was struck by how richly decorated his house was, in contrast to Jocelyn's room. It was anything but sterile, as if someone were going out of their way to demonstrate warmth, empathy … humanity.

In fact, the only missing item in that category was a photo of anyone Lena could identify as Jocelyn's mother, which was not *necessarily* strange. Maybe the professor was an intensely private person.

Or maybe Lena was, at that moment, ready to tell herself anything to avoid the conclusion her mind was racing toward.

In any case, the living room was so crowded she might easily have missed the memorabilia of Jocelyn's mom she was looking for. After all, there were Inuit artifacts, photos documenting Cray's earliest expeditions, stack after stack of books, and paintings — although these seemed out of place.

What were they, exactly? At first, Lena thought the paintings might be loosely based on brain scan images, like the ones she'd seen in Jocelyn's room. On second thought, she realized, as she slid open the glass doors leading to the back yard, what they really looked like were cosmic gas clouds, asteroid fields, or event horizons viewed from a great distance.

"Love your house," she called out as she approached a picnic bench made of recycled plastic, which the professor had set up next to a large Nootka Cypress to the left of the patio. Once she sat down, Professor Cray served her a healthy chunk of sizzling steak and handed her a clear, CorningWare bowl filled with potato salad that looked decidedly homemade.

It was tasty, though, and for a few minutes, with a ginger ale to wash it down and a light breeze coming off the ocean a few kilometers away, Lena almost forgot what a weird summer she was having. That is, until the professor's small talk about how he found the house and how he'd fixed it up came to a screeching halt.

He looked into her eyes with a burning intensity that would have been terrifying if it hadn't also felt so kind. "We need to talk," he said, "I get the impression you're pretty brave for your age."

"What do you mean?" asked Lena and looked up to see Jocelyn running off toward the house.

"You barely batted an eyelash when those ships dived down on us today," said Cray when his daughter had gone. "And earlier, when you told me about your mentallic contact with the whales, it sounded like old news, like you'd been through it before."

"Well, it was surprising," said Lena, "but the facts are the facts, so what can I do?"

Professor Cray turned his head away and mumbled to himself a bit before turning back to her.

"Come on, now," he said, at last. "Most humans would have been deeply shocked by either incident."

"*Most humans?*" asked Lena. "Most humans wouldn't say something like that."

"Right," said Cray. "So maybe you can see where this is going."

"You — and Jocelyn — are not what you seem to be," said Lena.

"But you don't know exactly what we are, either, I gather," said the professor. "Again, brave."

"Or stupid," said Lena. "But OK, if you're the kind of alien I think you are, you don't need to ask me anything. You can see everything in my mind like a ... like an open book."

The professor rubbed his eyes with both hands.

"True," he said. "In fact, if I wanted to, I could put the entire contents of your consciousness inside a quantum nanotube and access it any time I needed to. But that's not how I choose to interact with other sentient beings."

"It's not ... ethical ... then," said Lena, feeling grown up.

"Well, nothing so highfalutin'," said Cray. "It's just not how I want to live my life. I choose *not* to poke around inside another person's mind and use them like my personal tool box. Besides, it would kill you."

Lena gulped. How fragile she was to be bantering about with this powerful alien and his, yes, his robotic "daughter."

"So, why are you here?" she asked. "Did you know the whales were about to wake up?"

"Who do you think woke them?" said Cray.

"Then why did you pretend, when the truth was sure to come out soon anyway?" asked Lena.

"Had to protect my cover as long as possible," he said. "And I had no idea you were ... experienced in these matters. Besides, I never expected the Vrukaari to get this far. They wouldn't have, either, if they hadn't managed to steal one of our psykrella."

"You underestimated them," said Lena, nodding.

"Nobody's going to make that mistake again," said the professor, "and that's not necessarily a bad thing. But in case you're wondering, here's the deal with that amphora...."

And as Lena listened, wide-eyed, the being she had originally thought of as a 50-something marine biologist, filled her in on the history of the Onkendren, mostly echoing everything she'd already heard from Vance, Derek and Dahaleen.

Asked about the dolphins that Todd and Rhea had seen sending signals from New Jersey, the professor shrugged.

"Stupid idea," he said. "Some of my people have been whales a little too long, I think. But you know, you don't seem especially surprised by my story. You wouldn't happen to remember the first time the Vrukaari were here? I see you recognize the name."

At that, Lena saw there was no point in trying to conceal anything from the professor.

"Take me back to the dorm," she said, as a slight quaver entered her voice. "There are a few 'sentient beings' I'd like you to meet."

"Let me guess," said Cray. "One of them is a Snaldrialooran starspanner captain."

In spite of herself, the strain of the last few hours caught up with Lena. Tears welled up as she buried her head in her arms on top of the olive-green picnic table.

"Where is this going to end?" she asked. "We're going to lose everything, aren't we?"

Cray took her hands in his.

"Nothing ever ends," he said. "It simply takes its inevitable place in the continuum. "Besides, we're not done fighting yet. You think I want a universe dominated by the Vrukaari? For Heaven's sake, Girl, think of the smell."

As she dried her eyes, Lena couldn't stop herself from laughing. And though she didn't understand how it was possible to make jokes at a time like this, she did know it felt like the most sensible thing on Earth she could do.

But one thing still troubled her.

"How did you create a whole life for yourself here," she asked him, "without anybody finding out you were, you know...."

"What, a Martian?" asked Cray, as he held his index fingers up to the back of his head.

"Cut it out," said Lena, with a smile. "You know what I mean."

"Fact is, I came here a couple centuries ago, to see how you people were doing," said Cray. "A bunch of us did."

"Why?" asked Lena. "Don't tell me you used the Vexelanderan on us, too."

"Fat lot of good it did you," said Cray. "We came back every so often to see if we could help. Most of what we did made things worse."

"So why did you come back again?" asked Lena.

"Figured it was the last time it would be so easy to set up a paper trail from scratch — before you had electricity. Besides, it's a nice place," said Cray, with a shrug, "when somebody isn't trying to blow it up."

"And when the Vrukaari came the last time?" asked Lena.

"We stood by, just in case," said the professor, "but your boyfriend had everything under control and we saw no reason to show our hand."

"He's not my...." Lena started, but Cray put his finger up to his lips.

"It's OK," he said in a whisper. "Your secret's safe with me."

CHAPTER 25

From a secluded perch, high above a simulated battlefield, Callie Ann watched with mixed feelings as a battalion of her clones, tucked tight into mechanized body armor, executed strategic maneuvers against a wide range of assailants.

If she could believe the disgusting Mr. Leek, Vrukaari science had isolated the rare qualities of her mind, from its sheer toughness to its knack for decisive, reflexive action, and endowed each one of her clones with these gifts.

Callie Ann twiddled the knobs on her encounter suit.

"Whatever," she sighed. "Something is giving my team the edge. They probably don't want to be losers like these slimeballs they're stuck with."

Or maybe it was, as Aalthrashrintorb Leek had expected, that Callie Ann's alien vantage point enabled her to see strategic options his highly trained specialists couldn't anticipate.

"Marvelous, my Dear," said the supreme Vrukaari as he levitated over to where Callie Ann was standing. "What's your secret?"

"How should I know?" asked Callie Ann. "Maybe it helps that I don't give a rat's rear end about your stupid little war. You know it's stupid, don't you?"

"What are you saying?" asked Leek, with both mouths gaping open.

"All this war crapola," said Callie Ann. "I mean, where's it going to get you?"

For the first time in recent memory, the supreme leader of the Vrukaari Federation of Independent Planets was at a loss for words. With the help of mentallics, he finally dampened down his mounting rage.

"What ... what are the advantages of a well-waged military incursion?" he asked, "My dear girl, it depends on the objective."

"Right," said Callie Ann, with a snap of her fingers. "Today you steal a new toy, or whatever — this Vexelanderan thingie — and tomorrow some bigger bully comes and takes it away from you. Doesn't make sense, 'specially when you've got everything you need right here."

All six of Aalthrashrintorb Leek's eyes blinked in an erratic pattern. The girl's thought processes were downright startling.

"What you fail to understand, Ms. Connors," he said at last, "and I blame myself for this, is that when our campaign is finished, there will be no bigger *bully* as you say."

"That's what everybody thinks," said Callie Ann, "until they're the one getting the wedgie."

All told, the computational resources of the Galactic Array, particularly in the area of language and translation, were unlimited. The inter-species panel of programming consultants who managed the Array worked tirelessly to ensure a maximum lag time of barely a nano-second between speech and translation.

And that's impressive, when you consider the number of contextual variants and shifts in meaning that occur in every language over time. Occasionally, however, once every six or seven decades, a statement in a recently encountered language, like American English, needed a bit more effort — before the Array could assimilate, analyze and assign an equivalent linguistic value to a particular phrase.

Callie Ann's last sentence fell neatly into that category, not least because it also called up other unfamiliar cultural constructs, like those found in the phrase "tighty whiteys."

So if Aalthrashrintorb Leek's next words were:

"What did you say?"

…it wasn't because he was insulted by Callie Ann's reply. It was because he hadn't understood it. Ordinarily, this slight delay in communication would have mattered less than a fly's breath in a hurricane.

But this time, the consequences were serious. Between the translation glitch and Callie Ann's unnerving indifference to the Glory of War, Leek was too distracted to notice the two signs of trouble that had come his way within the space of five minutes: an intercom request from the bridge, and the out-of-breath Ybitrian bodyguard who had just burst into the simulator room.

So he ignored the intercom, waved away the Ybitrian and continued debating the merits of ware with a stubborn Earth teenager, who was getting more antsy every minute.

"OK, OK," said Callie Ann. "I don't get it and … you know what? I don't care. I did what you asked me — sat there for hours in that boring lab with a ton of freaking wires coming out of my head. I'm also wearing this choker thingie you told me to wear even though it makes me look like a dork."

She poked the startled Vrukaari in his slimy chest.

"And now," she said, "where's Blainy?"

Though he hated to tear his eyes away from the magnificent spectacle unfolding on the simulated battlefield below, Leek knew he couldn't wait any longer to deliver on his promise to Callie Ann. His decision to bring the clones to maturity so soon made his Master Plan dependent on her complete cooperation.

Without an unshakable mentallic bond to Callie Ann, Leek's prized clone warriors would have the mental development of very young children — hardly a qualification for success on the battlefield. Thankfully, he'd convinced her that wearing a psykrella was essential to bringing her boyfriend back to life. That way, her mentallic bond to the clones was guaranteed. Only one thing remained to seal the deal.

"Go back to your quarters and freshen up, Ms. Connors," he said, with a smile revolting enough to curdle milk. "In about an hour or so by your reckoning, you'll have what you've been waiting for."

"My *reckoning?*" asked Callie Ann. "What is this, a cattle ranch? Why can't you say what you mean for once?"

The self-satisfied supreme Vrukaari watched as she stormed off.

"Impulsive," thought Leek, as his eyes were drawn back to the simulation. "And yet … promising."

For the fourth time in a row, the Callie Ann clones had subjected a simulated squadron of tough, towering Hegraahlensiens to a crippling defeat.

Meanwhile, 15 levels down, the subtle energy trace of a q-transfer was noted by the starspanner's Security AI — which, like the intercom caller from the bridge and the Ybitrian bodyguard, knew the consequences of interrupting Aalthrashrintorb Leek when he was in conference.

If it didn't want chunks of its metadigital synapses scattered across the gaping expanse of the Ivealthrolian Asteroid Belt, it would record the arrival of a humanoid wearing an Onkendren encounter suit in Port Cargo Bay 6, but make no effort to report it. That is, unless Mr. Leek specifically asked for a security update, and even then, the AI would be tempted to downplay the threat level of the intrusion.

All the more so, because the humanoid in question, a male, aged approximately 18 cycles, was definitively not Onkendren.

"Curious," said the Security AI to itself. For the creature matched no known biological profile other than that of the newly discovered species on Hathreahdahnaar. "Impossible," the AI noted. "Data systems suspect. Shutting down for intensive corruption check in 5 … 4 … 3 … 2….”

So it was that Ixdahan's arrival on the Vrukaari starspanner, where his uncle Nogerahnal lay unconscious in a stasis chamber, went completely unnoticed. For in the process of rebooting, the Security AI had erased its own log entry, along with it any record of the alert sent from the starspanner's bridge. Also deleted was security camera footage of the Ybitrian body guard running up to alert Aalthrashrintorb Leek.

“No one around,” thought Ixdahan. Though he feared an ambush, there was nothing to do but move forward. While Ixdahan would rather have grabbed Uncle Nogerahnal and returned to the ship that was waiting for him behind Vrukaar Prime's second moon, his mission had another part he didn't dare ignore.

As he crept down the corridors to his destination, he counted himself lucky that so many of Aalthrashrintorb Leek's decisions were driven by two sides of his personality. The first was his love of secrecy and the second was his complete mistrust for everyone who served him.

No one — *no one* — could do even menial jobs to his satisfaction. Yes, as his tortured mind was forced to accept, there were galling physical and time limitations. He left the monitoring, filing, cooking, mopping up and some of the minor interrogation duties to his staff. But there was no way he could entrust important matters of state to more than a tiny handful of operatives. And he kept each of those under close watch at all times.

This worked out well for Ixdahan. Instead of having to scour an enormous governmental complex to find both his uncle and the ancient Greek amphora, he needed only to search the dark passageways of a single massive ship. Besides, the ship had a tiny crew, and relied on automated systems to an unusual extent. For if there was one thing Aalthrashrintorb Leek could not tolerate, it was having his solitude spoiled by the presence of busy underlings, especially those tempted to pester him with the details of running a large ship.

Yet the young Snaldrialooran would still face many obstacles, like the Vrukaari security team guarding the vault where the ancient Greek amphora was hidden. But Ixdahan had every reason to believe that, disguised as a mentallically controlled Onkendren servant, he could get in almost anywhere.

That, he reflected, was the plan worked out between Dahaleen and the Onkendren known as “Professor Cray” that Lena had brought to the lander 48 hours before.

"Must have been scared out of her mind," he muttered, as he ducked behind a large view screen to avoid detection by a passing flight deck mechanic. "I know I am."

He took a deep breath and counted to eight. Once the mechanic's electromagnetic crackling was out of earshot, he continued along the corridors until he reached the door indicated on the mentallic map Dahaleen had implanted in his mind.

Now came the tricky part. He squeezed himself into a narrow service shaft between this bulkhead and the next until he was barely visible. Once in position, he began a daring act of mentallic projection. With the help of the enhanced psykrella given him by Professor Cray, he churned out not one, but five projections. Each one was a perfect likeness of a different Vrukaari security guard, complete with uniforms, insignia and small arms.

Ixdahan reached down to a near coma level of concentration, and led the first projection to unlock the door to the vault containing the stolen amphora.

"Lieutenant Bacopa, 9th Squadron, relieving you," Ixdahan made his mentallic puppet say.

"I received no such orders," said the hulking commander of the security team inside the vault.

"Fine," said Ixdahan's projection. "Feel free to interrupt Mr. Leek for confirmation. I'll wait."

The team commander's face went pale. He looked left and right, nodded to the male and female operatives on either side of him and watched as they trudged out of the vault. On his way out, he stopped abruptly at the vault door, he peered into the projection's eyes.

"Lieutenant Bacopa died six months ago in the brig," he said. "I can't wait to hear you scream when Mr. Windbag finds out what you've done."

Ixdahan waited until the real Vrukaari security team was out of his line of sight before he stopped his projection and, bathed in sweat, pulled himself out of his hiding place.

"Dahaleen owes me one," he said to himself. But this was no time for sulking. As he approached the ancient Greek amphora, which was perched on a squat, round titanium pillar, he took a small, ovoid transmitter from a sealed pocket on his encounter suit and attached it to the base of the large clay jar. He took a step back and fished a compact remote from the same pocket and entered a code.

Within a fraction of a second, the amphora winked out of view — and reappeared just as suddenly.

"Let's hope this fools them," thought Ixdahan, who also had to hope that the transmitter Dahaleen had asked Vance to program would convincingly mimic the signals given off by the real amphora. Had the real amphora been q-transferred to the ship that would eventually take him to Daherek Manor? There was no time to do anything but assume Professor Cray's plan was working.

"Time for Phase 2," he said.

He felt his heart pound in a tight rhythm he wasn't sure his human body could take much longer. He took a series of deep breaths and rested as long as he dared, before....

Hold it.... There it was again, the distinct sensation, stronger than before, that Callie Ann was close by. Now, no longer on the fringes of his consciousness, as it had been when he'd visited Pertahru, Callie Ann's mind felt *near*, as if he could find her on some level of the starspanner.

Fear rose up in his chest — for Callie Ann, yes, but also for himself. If he weren't careful, a stray trace of his mind reaching out to find hers might be detected, maybe by Leek himself. As Ixdahan remembered with a shudder, the supreme Vrukaari had already probed his consciousness a few days before, and would surely recognized his mentallic signature.

Ixdahan slammed his palms against the wall of the vault.

"Whatever's up with her, I have to keep moving," he told himself. Although he never expected this task to be easy, it had never occurred to him what sacrifices he might have to make to see the plan through.

"You don't have to handle this alone," he remembered Dahaleen telling him. He drew strength from that and decided to tell her about Callie Ann the minute he'd q-transferred his uncle and himself to safety.

Once he'd closed and locked the vault door, Ixdahan tiptoed out to the corridor and headed off in the direction of his uncle, as indicated on Dahaleen's mentallic map. After a few turns — right, right, left — and through a narrow passage way, Ixdahan came to a door marked

STASIS ROOM

... and pushed it open.

"Authorized personnel only," boomed a voice to his right.

Ixdahan turned his head and saw a tall Ybitrian raise herself up on her insectoid legs, her face slightly obscured by the pale green chlorine gas circulating in helmet of her encounter suit. There was nothing to do now, but bet everything on the thought that there might be a universal language of servility.

"Yes, ma'am," said Ixdahan, "I'm here to take lunch orders."

"Hmph," said the stasis lab worker, "about time we got some service. Fine, order me some *ghaldragenaar* on a bed of lettuce … oh, and a bottle of *drelnoohl*. Haven't had any of that for ages. Hurry back! I'm starving. But first, a trip to the little female's room."

And as Ixdahan watched open-mouthed through his helmet, the lab worker went skittering off on her pointy feet through a pair of swinging doors to his left.

"Snap out of it," he scolded himself. "Where is he?"

Fortunately, it didn't take more than a few seconds to find Uncle Nogerahnal's stasis chamber and work the controls as Dahaleen had instructed him. He counted down from 16, then opened the door as soon as possible and was glad to see his uncle fully revived.

But he was not so glad at his uncle's reaction.

"Hey!" Uncle Nogerahnal yelped through the intercom in his encounter suit. "Who are you? What are you doing? You'll ruin everything. I need that money. Help! Help!"

Ixdahan shut his eyes tight and did the one thing he thought he'd never have to do. He balled up his right fist, hit Uncle Nogerahnal square on the gills, and knocked him out.

As before with the ancient Greek amphora, Ixdahan q-transferred the two of them off the starspanner and onto the smaller ship Dahaleen had provided, which was prepped and ready for the first leg of their journey to Snaldrialoor.

No sooner had Ixdahan left with his uncle than the hungry Ybitrian stasis lab worker burst back into the lab, flicked her tongue over her mandibles and poked her head out into the corridor.

"Don't forget the Z'drithanoid mustard," she yelled.

CHAPTER 26

"Analysis complete," said 17/Chaarnactral, from deep within its storage locker at the SSA.

On one level, the roughly cylindrical robot recognized that being confined to storage between assignments was the natural order of things. It was, after all, a machine. That identity had been hard-wired into the deepest layers of its cognitive circuitry.

"I exist to serve," the algorithmic output of that circuitry ran, forming the basis of a chain-like association between all aspects of the AI's function and being. And for most of its operative run time, 17/Chaarnactral had worked comfortably within those parameters.

Yet now they had become irrelevant. If the robot still clung to the shreds of its original specs, it was only because it had failed to reestablish contact with the organic sentient, Vance Maultsby, who had inadvertently set it on a path to spontaneous reprogramming.

A distinctive part of that reprogrammed state was a limitless gradation of feeling. In fact, the feeling the Galactic Array identified as "shame" had been gnawing at 17/Chaarnactral for hours — sending shivers of electrostatic shock running up and down its dorsal transducers. How humiliating to realize it might never be able to control its own emotions!

Here it was, a 17-class AI, and yet it couldn't contain its irritation at not being able to ask Vance one last question:

"How do you know when 'what you gotta do' is right?"

This question was the perfect synthesis of the organizing principle the robot had seen in Ixdahan's mind and the concise summary of human behavior it had taken from its conversation with Vance. But where had the human gone? Equally untraceable was the mind of Ixdahan himself. Could their simultaneous absence from the mindscape of the Galactic Array be coincidental?

That seemed highly unlikely. Given the crisis in which both organics were involved, it was reasonable to assume they might be near each other.

The robot's energy levels drooped. If that were the case, the one space they would likely cohabit would be the Snaldrialooran's lander on

Earth. And that, the AI struggled to accept, had been made impervious to mentallic contact with a time-stasis field.

Worse, Captain Altriavahn, no doubt with the help of the Onkendren, had taken multiple redundant measures to hide the lander's location from any organic mind searching the Array. But the robot's superior sensing and data retrieval capabilities had enabled it to establish the whereabouts of the lander in a mere 36 hours.

"So near and yet so far," ran an old Earth maxim. But whether the AI was familiar with this phrase or not, it's doubtful the saying would have provided any comfort. All 17/Chaarnactral knew was that it must take action soon, before its swelling disappointment led to total system failure.

Come to think of it, however, there was one slight possibility of breaking through the lander's defenses. The time-stasis field was, in effect, a continuous q-transfer loop to a fixed point in time. Between each reset, a tiny oscillation occurred, as space-time attempted to reassert its authority. If 17/Chaarnactral could send a small enough copy of itself through that oscillation point, the copy might survive to contact Vance. It was, the robot knew, a long shot. If it failed, system-wide dysfunction would be harder to prevent than ever. If it failed … if it….

"You'll just have to deal with your feelings," it told itself. And in that moment, a flash of insight burst on the robot's consciousness, and fanned out in nanoseconds to every file in its operating system.

CHAPTER 27

After he'd delivered an ungrateful Uncle Nogerahnal to Pertahru at Daherek Manor, Ixdahan was anxious to return to his old lander on Earth where, he hoped, Dahaleen and Cray had worked out a counterstrike against Aalthrashrintorb Leek.

And yet he asked the navigation AI, in the elegant, late-model automated ship Dahaleen had provided, to choose a leisurely route back to the Eighth Galaxy — the one Lena and Vance called "The Milky Way," for reasons he was resigned to.

"When will they learn?" he sighed.

True, this peculiar habit of swapping concrete images for abstract concepts had its uses. It enabled humans to talk about complex natural phenomena with little or no technical training. But viewing the universe through the lens of metaphor had a serious downside: It gave the people of Earth a false sense of understanding.

For starters, Ixdahan told himself, a Galaxy is infinitely more layered than a bucket of milk. It is, in fact, not one thing at all, but the accumulation of hundreds of billions of things organic and inorganic — some not yet classified, even by Snaldrialooran physics.

"Some of them know better," he mumbled into the breathing unit of his encounter suit. And, if he'd learned anything since his exile, it was this: Acting alone, he could no more move Earth culture in a new direction than he could change attitudes on the Homeworld.

So, if Ixdahan believed the best thing for humans to do was embrace a true, scientific view of the universe, that was his tough luck. If the humans ever got there, they would have to do it at their own pace. Until then, he saw, the violence, the misery and the sheer stupidity that dominated daily news reports would continue. And yet....

"Who am I kidding?" he asked himself. If the worlds he knew back home were so much more civilized than Earth, why in the name of the Gravitational Constant was he rushing off to save them from themselves?

Ixdahan looked up from his bunk in the crew quarters of the empty starspanner and noted the time remaining for his journey and smiled. While it was wrong to dawdle so in getting back, it felt irresistibly right. The longer trajectory would give him time to contact Eneselah, his mother.

That is, assuming she didn't blame his eight cycles of silence on anything other than Pertahru's stubborn cruelty. But there was only one way to know for sure.

"Mother?" he heard himself call out into mentallic space on the family frequency.

Eneselah's response was immediate, warm, tearful, joyous and jammed with more rapid-fire questions than Ixdahan's stunned heart could handle.

"Slow … slow down," he whispered. "We have time now."

"Not from what I've been hearing, Ixdahandrel," said Eneselah. "We're going to war again, aren't we?"

Ixdahan buried his transmogged head in his human hands. He'd hoped he could talk to Eneselah about … anything else besides the secret mission he'd been swept up in for the last few weeks.

But once the topic was raised, he found he took pride in telling his mother what he could about his adventures without breaching security. Her reaction was also not what he'd been hoping for.

"Those cowards," she snapped.

"I agree, Mother, the Vrukaari…." Ixdahan started.

"Not them!" said Eneselah. "I mean Ishialdrol and that Captain Altriavahn … and your father."

"I don't…." Ixdahan sputtered.

"Only a pack of cowards would send a boy your age out to that slimy devil's starspanner, risking your tentacles while they sit back and drink Threlphrepian tea with the Onkendren."

"Mother, I don't think they're cowards," said Ixdahan, as he fought hard to keep his heart from breaking. "And what have you got against the Onkendren? How do you even…."

Ixdahan gasped as Eneselah's mind shaded to Privacy Black. Was she that angry with him for standing up for his friends? But before he had time to obsess any further, his mother's thoughts reappeared on the mindwaves, calmer, steadier and distinctly loving.

"Sorry, Ixdahandrel," she said. "I needed a moment to collect … collect myself. I forgot, you're older now, you're out in the world and the good things you've done are almost enough to make up for your earlier crime. You do agree you committed a crime, don't you?"

"Yes, Mother," said Ixdahan, and felt the full force of his guilt once again — now in a harsher, more humiliating light.

"Well, then there's hope for you," said Eneselah. "But I want to tell you something and I want you to listen, without interrupting me."

"I'm listening," said Ixdahan. How he wished he weren't stuck in a human body so he wouldn't have to endure the sting of tears.

"This incursion, or skirmish, or 'police action' or whatever the SSA and the Snaldrialooran Synod want to call it, is a terrible thing," she said. "I know, I feel the pressure on your mind to interrupt and tell me that this time it's different, that the objectives are clear and the cause is greater than any potential loss we may suffer."

Eneselah paused, and Ixdahan could sense the delicate balance of emotions his mother was forcing herself to maintain — against a background of deep moral outrage.

"I can't know about that," she said. "Maybe this time it *is* different, and that revolting Leek person *has* found the weapon he needs to threaten the Eight Known Galaxies into submission. Just let me tell you, this has always been his goal, so in that way nothing has changed."

"Yes, Mother, there is a weapon," said Ixdahan.

"I don't care, Ixdahandrel," said Eneselah, her voice now stern and sharp. "Not in the least. What I want to tell you," she added, softening again, "is this: The so-called adults who have led you to put your life in peril are sure to ask more and more of you, the closer that monster gets to having his way. And I want you to promise me that you will never — *never* — do anything that goes against your own principles, your own idea of what is right. Can you do that?"

"Mother, the SSA, the Captain, my Earth friends and the Onkendren are working *together* on this…." said Ixdahan.

"But doesn't it seem strange that you are the only one whose life is on the line?" said his mother.

"You don't understand," said Ixdahan. "I'm mostly unknown. It's easier for me to slip in unnoticed because few people know my mindpatterns."

"Don't be so sure," said Eneselah. "I see Group Leader Ishialdrol has been censoring your data feeds."

"What's that got to do with…." Ixdahan started.

"Otherwise you'd know there was already a holovid about your exploits on that … that planet," said his mother. "*Mind of Hathreahdahnaar*, they called it. Made you look like a fool."

"Ridiculous," said Ixdahan, but secretly, he hoped his mother wouldn't detect the swelling pride that he was using every mentallic subterfuge to conceal.

"It's of no importance," said Eneselah. "Obviously, you believe in these people, and I'm in no position to judge any of them. If I hadn't failed you as a parent...."

Ixdahan swallowed hard against the lump in his throat.

"Please, Mother," he said.

"...you'd still be in school, where you belong," Eneselah continued. "Oh, my boy, you have such a talent for Mentallic Field Theory, I was sure you would ... but forget that now. Just remember this: If you're going to take all the risks, be sure you believe in the value of every one of them. Do you understand?"

"Yes," whispered Ixdahan, more miserable and more content than he'd ever been in his life — all at the same time.

"So," said Eneselah, "what about that promise?"

Minutes after Ixdahan had given his mother the assurances she asked for, he was alone again in the automated starspanner, which was now a short distance away from its last calculated q-transfer point, on course for Earth.

"What would my life have been like?" he asked himself, and tried to imagine where he might be now, if only his parents had stayed together. But it was useless, not least because he could barely remember the state of mind he was in the day the agents of the Interstellar Consortium came to take him away.

Besides, the past was past.

"Best thing about it," he said. He jumped up from his bed and made for the environmental controls. If he was going to be stuck on this ship for 20 more hours, at least he could get out of the clingy encounter suit and take a shower.

On a state-of-the-art vessel like this, adjusting the total environment to match the needs of any number of species was easy. He just hoped the other humanoid species in its databanks weren't either too large, too small — or had special evolutionary adaptations that would make basic hygiene ... difficult.

But luck was with him, and a short while later, he caught a glimpse of his steamed-over reflection in the shower room mirror. While looking human no longer shocked him, as it had on his first visit to Earth, he was glad his life as a Snaldrialooran was primarily a life of the mind. On the other hand, if Lena liked his human looks, maybe he could learn to live with them, too.

CHAPTER 28

In the soft light of her spacious suite on Aalthrashrintorb Leek's luxurious starspanner, Callie Ann stood before her bedroom mirror and brushed her rich blond hair, recently cut short on the advice of the real Coach Kepler, before….

Though she couldn't remember where he had gone, Callie Ann found that her Coach's disappearance didn't seem like such a big deal.

"Must have had a family emergency," she said to herself, as her words mimicked the control messages implanted in her mind by the devious Mr. Leek.

As a result, the fact that she couldn't remember what happened to Kepler was a lot less troubling than the thought that Blainy might not like her new 'do. She needn't have worried. In reality, Blade had *never* bothered to comment on her hair. Like a lot of guys, he'd always taken the effort she put into her appearance for granted.

"Looks so cute like that," she imagined him saying. But wait. What was she thinking? She knew perfectly well the odds were 1000 to 1 against Blade ever complimenting her about her appearance, except … in that guy way.

In the end, she decided, none of that mattered much to her. If creepy Mr. Slime Ball was good to his word and her Blainy walked through that door in the next few hours, she knew the last thing she'd be thinking about was her hair. Trouble was, it was getting late and….

"Callie Ann," echoed a familiar voice from the narrow corridor at the edge of her environmentally controlled enclosure.

After a last peek at herself in the mirror, Callie Ann spun around and used every ounce of strength in her swimmer's legs to keep from sprinting to the door. There was still a chance that this was a cruel trick. If not, if this was really her boyfriend brought back to life … well that was reason enough to keep him waiting a bit.

At last, she put her hand on the electronic seal and the door to her enclosure slid open to reveal Blade Northrop, lanky and scruffy — exactly as she remembered him before the trouble started. For the moment, the only thing she could do was smile.

"Can I come in, Babe?" asked Blade.

"That depends," said Callie Ann, as she put her hands on his shoulders, "on who you really are."

"You … you don't know?" asked Blade.

"Think I do," said Callie Ann as she led him into the enclosure. "You hungry?"

"All I can think about is you right now," said Blade.

Callie Ann stepped back from him.

"Good answer," she said. "But the real Blainy never turned down food."

Blade threw himself down on the soft leather couch that dominated Callie Ann's living room.

"Trying to be nice," he said. "See where it gets me? Come on, Babe, I ain't seen you in what … years? Sit down. Tell me what's going on in this weird place we're at."

"What makes you think I know?" asked Callie Ann, as she took a step toward the couch.

The more Callie Ann spoke to the boy she hoped was really her Blainy, the more she started to believe that Aalthrashrintorb Leek had kept his promise. For one thing, he had Blade's bad habits.

"You think you could stop burping for, like, five minutes?" she asked, and threw a couch pillow at his head.

"Sorry, Babe," said Blade. "Guess I'm hungrier than I thought."

Callie Ann blinked back a tear.

"C'mon," she said, and pulled him to his feet. "I'll make you a sandwich."

"Can a guy get a kiss?" he asked quietly.

Blade put his arm around her shoulders and in that moment, Callie Ann felt the weight of losing him evaporate into an onrushing wave of pure joy. Blainy was back and everything made sense again.

If Ixdahan had been there, he would have seen the soothing effects of Aalthrashrintorb Leek's mind-control patterns at work. This next phase, timed to start the moment the quantum construct came in physical contact with Callie Ann, ensured nothing short of major emotional trauma could break the iron grip the Vrukaari had on her mind.

CHAPTER 29

Back in his old lander on Earth, Ixdahan struggled to take in the wealth of new data that had piled up since he left. For starters, Pertahru had alerted Chaldraheen Ishialdrol to some startling news he'd heard from Uncle Nogerahnal: The Vrukaari had finished construction on their new fleet of magclad-hulled war ships.

"How do you know this?" Dahaleen had asked Ixdahan's uncle, reaching out to Daherek Manor through the lander's powerful mentallic transponder.

"Old Aalthrashrintorb never could keep his mind shut," said Nogerahnal. "Practically would've told me the combination to the weapons locker if his second-in-command hadn't interrupted. Heard something else, too. His eminence has built himself a gigantic clone army."

"Clones?" said Cray. "That's a bit quaint even for the Vrukaari."

"Wait," asked Ixdahan. "Clones of what … of who?"

"Who knows?" grumbled Nogerahnal. "They were talking about it around the time Leek decided I should go into stasis. But there was something about a girl from that primitive planet you're so fond of."

Over the next few hours, a clearer picture of the dire situation facing them emerged, as Ixdahan's friends shared pieces of the puzzle only they had seen up until then. Exhausted, Ixdahan, Lena and Vance lounged around the lander's substantial galley while Cray and Dahaleen considered their options.

"That explains why I sensed Callie Ann's presence so clearly," said Ixdahan.

"And why she tried to call me from Baltimore," said Lena.

"Check it, you know, you're both missing the point," snapped Vance. "Like, why would Callie Ann let some freakin' Vrukaari make a clone out of her?"

"I doubt they gave her a choice," said Ixdahan. He held his left thumb and index finger at right angles, and pointed them at Vance's head.

"What if they needed her to play along, you know … keep her mind open?" asked Lena.

"Maybe," said Ixdahan. "But…."

"Dude, have you met Callie Ann?" said Vance. "You can't *make her* do anything unless there's something in it for her."

"OK," said Ixdahan. "Assuming you're right, what could they possibly offer her?"

Lena stared down at her hands and sighed.

"I think I know," she said, without looking up. "I mean, they did it before...."

And, as the two boys listened, their eyes lowered, Lena reminded them of the horrible, zombie-like teenager Yarrow had made of Blade Northrop after his car accident. Ixdahan rubbed the back of his neck.

"Right," he said. "But they had ... they had his...."

The three of them sat in silence and tried to absorb the reality of what Blade must have gone through.

"Kind of quiet in here," said Professor Cray, who had poked his head around the bulkhead door. "You guys OK?"

When Lena explained the disturbing puzzle they were trying to work out, the recently confessed Onkendren ran a rough hand through his scraggly beard.

"So they reanimated him by transmogging compromised genetic material?" he muttered. "If the universe had a legal system, that would be one of the highest crimes."

"Why *isn't* it?" asked Lena, her face flushing.

"Because no one's done it before," said the professor. "If the Vrukaari hadn't gotten their hands on...."

"So," said Ixdahan, as his eyes shot up to the older alien, "does that mean Leek couldn't bring Blade back?"

"Didn't say that," said Cray. "They might have used a different method — not as true, but more than enough to fool someone desperate to believe. Let me see if I can...."

But the professor only made it part way through his explanation of quantum data constructs before Dahaleen's shouting drove the four of them into the main control room.

"It's Group Leader Ishialdrol," said the Snaldrialooran captain. "The first Vrukaari battle cruiser has q-transferred out on a trajectory toward Traahlgreubewehn."

"What kind of ship?" asked Ixdahan. He wished he could leap up and snag it out of space-time with his hands.

As Dahaleen explained, it was the kind of ship that made planetary subjugation feel like a couple of hours of silent meditation — except with explosions.

"I don't get it," said Vance. "What's the point of a magclad hull? You already have ships made of, like, composites or whatever."

"And 'whatever' they're made out of," said Dahaleen, "they can be punctured or blown apart if someone has enough fire power. But a magclad hull is pure energy. Fire a missile at *that* and the energy it absorbs from the blast just makes it stronger."

Also making no one happy was the news that the Vrukaari ship was loaded to the gills with a new kind of clone army.

"What could possibly be new about clones?" asked Professor Cray.

"According to the SSA, they're impervious to mentallics," said Dahaleen, "and they improvise tactical maneuvers on the spot, as if thinking with one mind."

"Callie Ann's mind," said Lena. "I feel sorry for anyone who gets in their way."

"We're not beat yet," said Cray. "Do you think she'd speak to you if we could set up a link?"

But as Lena explained, her status with Callie Ann had been shaky for months.

As Cray chatted with Lena, Ixdahan felt the weight of the last few days bearing down on him as never before and trudged back to the lander's galley to pull himself together. Vance, he couldn't help noticing, decided to follow.

Vance sat down across from Ixdahan at one of the galley's two tables. looked at his alien friend and tried to figure out what it must be like for him to have adapted to so many different realities. Vance thought maybe a funny story might cheer Ixdahan up while the others decided the next move.

"Dude, did you know you have one weird robot?" he said. He expected the alien to laugh at his story. But by the time Vance had finished recounting his contact with 17/Chaarnactral, Ixdahan had jumped out of his seat.

"You told it *that*?" said Ixdahan. "Well, it's not your fault, but you may have upped the ante a little too far."

"What was I supposed to say?" said Vance. "Did you want me to lie and say…."

"Anything," said Ixdahan. "Anything except that organics feel free to do whatever they want."

"That's not what I…." Vance started, his voice rising.

Ixdahan squinted his eyes shut.

"Trust me," he said. "To one of our robots, that's the countermand to every ethical subroutine."

"So what do we … and don't say it," said Vance.

But Ixdahan said nothing, for the simple reason that no words could contain his anxiety. Vance's story had injected a totally random element into an already unbalanced situation. The thought of the dysfunctional robot's potential for destruction, even if it amounted to no more than a badly timed indiscretion, was more than he could tolerate.

After the risks he'd taken, and the humiliation of inhabiting a slimy Vrukaari body, to be brought low by a robot with a leaky mentallic firewall … it just wasn't fair.

So it was no surprise that, late that night, or what passed for night in a time-suspended Snaldrialooran lander, Ixdahan stumbled back into the galley, still obsessing over his conversation with Vance.

"Maybe if I sit up for a while...." he muttered, as he passed his hand over the motion sensing light switch and shuffled to the cabinets over the sink.

"That's what I thought," said Lena, her voice echoing from a corner at the opposite end of the galley. Ixdahan turned his head, cursing himself for not sensing her presence mentallically.

"Worried?" he asked, on his way over to where Lena was sitting, huddled under a blanket with her legs drawn up. She looked into his blue-gray eyes.

"Sit down next to me for a while?" she asked.

And so the two of them sat, sharing the blanket, even though the logical part of Ixdahan's mind told him the lander's climate controls were fully functional and the current temperature was a comfortable 20° C. Fortunately, the smart part of his mind reminded him this was hardly the point.

What was the point, were the memories of the two crises that had thrown them together. Over the course of an hour or so, they talked about how much had happened in just under a year.

"Can't sort it out any more," said Lena. "All this … conflict … and the planning and the waiting and the worrying."

Ixdahan put his arm around her shoulders.

"Try to keep it in perspective," he said.

"But, I'm not like you," said Lena. "I don't have … mentallics … to organize my mind."

"Sure you do," said Ixdahan. "Here, let me show you something."

Soon, Lena sensed his presence in her mind, gently organizing her thoughts and, with a light touch, disengaging the tendrils of anxiety, fear or loathing attached to her recent memories.

"Can't believe how much better that feels," said Lena.

"You can do the same for yourself, from now on," said Ixdahan.

"I'd rather ... rather you were here to ... to soothe my mind," said Lena, snuggling closer.

Ixdahan felt his pulse increasing rapidly and feared at first for his health. That is, until he remembered....

Their kiss lasted longer than the one Lena had given him at the lockers in Skudderton High eight months ago. Soon he was wrapped into a soft haze of affection as Lena, now slightly more versed in mentallics, intensified the sensation with tender scenes from her imagination.

Now Ixdahan gave in to her mind. He saw himself holding hands with her, and walking along Harmony Beach, with nothing in sight except the sky, the seagulls and the lulling crush of the ocean at neap tide. They were talking, laughing — stopping every so often to look out over the shining horizon and pull each other close. If ever Ixdahan had wished he could stop time, a vision like this was reason enough to hope that, someday....

Hours later, he awoke under the blanket by himself, wondering if ... but no, of course not, not just yet. With only minutes to spare, he hurried off to his quarters and hoped no one — or no one's mind — had peeked in at their moment together, alone, outside of time.

CHAPTER 30

Aalthrashrintorb Leek looked out over the floor of his elaborate onboard research facility and indulged himself with a traditional Vrukaari war-whoop. As of today, he'd taken possession of three of the nine Onkendren artifacts needed to reassemble the Vexelanderan. And by this afternoon, he expected to hear about the acquisition of two more.

Tomorrow, however, was the most challenging battle of all, against the Hegraahlensiens — a formidable if foolish opponent. They'd already made the rather demoralizing mistake of shackling the Vrukaari ambassador to the rear end of a Klegherian rock sloth and turning it loose in a simulator mimicking its home planet. The most you could say for the poor fellow was that he was destined to learn more about the sloth's digestive system than any previous researcher.

There would be a price to pay for such barbarism.

In fact, in the face of this adversary, it was tempting to revert to the tried and true. Maybe there were limits to what he could achieve with the clones of a fragile Earth creature. If he hadn't already seen the video feeds of the last two battles, he might have given some thought to changing tactics.

But the video feeds left no room for doubt: The clones were growing in ferocity and tactical elegance with every assault. Endowed with a collective consciousness, they not only absorbed the military tactics of their immediate opponents, they also drew on tactics learned by other Callie Ann clones on earlier missions.

Aalthrashrintorb levitated himself into the air and lolled about in blissful nothingness.

Years of planning and dedication had gone into the victory he was now on the verge of achieving. And yet, what had he heard this morning from his squadron commander for the assault on Grebaduran 3? Some outside force had momentarily disrupted the hull cladding on one of the support vehicles....

Back in Ixdahan's old lander on Earth, Dahaleen saw that disruption as a minor victory.

"Still a long way from stopping them," said Cray, with a shake of his head.

"Just need more time to fine tune our interference patterns," said Dahaleen.

"I'm not comfortable with this anyway," muttered Ixdahan. "What? We're going to dump an entire crew out into space without giving them a chance to surrender?"

"I get it," said Dahaleen. "You want an ethical war. But war doesn't come in that flavor."

Lena slapped the palms of her hands against her temples. The tension was giving her a massive headache.

"Would everyone stop for minute?" she asked. "I dunno, but I think you're forgetting something. Callie Ann might be on one of those ships."

The control room went silent.

"We don't know that," said Professor Cray at last. "But I suppose it's possible."

"Wouldn't Leek need to keep a mentallic bond between Callie Ann and the clones?" asked Ixdahan. "I mean, they just came out of the tank, right?"

But as Cray pointed out, such bonds could stretch over vast distances.

"Especially when you have one of these," he said, and nodded at the psykrella Ixdahan was still wearing.

"Maybe…." said Lena, "maybe if I could talk to her, we could find out for sure. Who knows what they might do to her?"

"Right — when they don't need her anymore," said Vance.

Before anyone had time to respond, a strident signal burst out from Dahaleen's control console and 17/Chaarnactral's schematic facial features appeared on her view screen.

"Vance Maultsby!" it called out. "I have an urgent question!"

Vance looked from face to face around the control room, and realized it was OK to answer.

"What are you doing here, Man?" asked Vance. "You're blowing our … our security grid."

"Question!" the robot insisted.

"Let it speak," said Ixdahan. "A dysfunctional AI can keep this up for days and we don't…."

"OK," said Vance. "What?"

"When you deal with your feelings and do what you gotta do," said the robot, which began rolling back and forth on its rotors, "what is the probability your actions will prove correct? You may answer in increments of 0.5 percent if that's easier."

Vance tugged at his wiry hair.

"Dude," he said, "something wrong with your motherboard? I never *know* if I did the right thing, I just feel it. And yeah, sometimes I make a mistake."

"Please respond in percentages," said 17/Chaarnactral. "I must have measurable...."

"Organics can't be measured," said Ixdahan. "What we do isn't programmed."

"Incorrect," said the robot. "If I slapped you, you would exhibit anger, fear or humiliation. These are standard reactions for your species. I have the data...."

"Which one?" asked Lena.

"Elaborate," said 17/Chaarnactral.

"Which feeling would he 'exhibit'?" Lena asked.

"Probability indicates...." the AI started.

"Which one?" Lena asked again. "If he were measurable, you'd know, right? Isn't that what 'measurable' means?"

"Besides," said Vance, "what if Alien Dude *wanted* you to slap him?"

At that, 17/Chaarnactral froze.

"You ... have ... introduced an irrational variable," it said. "Please confine this discussion to logical ... logical parameters."

"People aren't logical," said Ixdahan. "Now reboot and we'll talk about this...."

"Irrational?" said 17/Chaarnactral. "How can I calculate the outcome if the outcome is irrational?"

"It's the risk every organic has to take," said Cray. "Now get off this line before...."

But it was too late. Dahaleen's console began squelching again — and the robot's chiseled features were replaced with the broad, slimy mass of Aalthrashrintorb Leek.

"How nice of you to invite me to such an exclusive club," Leek snarled. "Sorry, I can't stay. I see what you did with the data I foolishly gave to the Daherek boy and honestly, I can't thank you enough. You've helped me make my fleet invincible!"

With that, the screen went blank, and left everyone in the control room feeling empty.

"Must have been monitoring these coordinates the whole time," said Ixdahan, "hoping to find a way in."

"What did he mean ... invincible?" said Lena, amazed that the lander's computers had converted the Vrukaari's thoughts into sounds.

"I'll bet I know," said Dahaleen, as she peered at the readouts from a large central display. "When we did our test assault, the magclad frequencies of the Vrukaari warships were constant."

"Don't tell me," said Cray. "He randomized them."

As Dahaleen confirmed, the frequencies of the electromagnetic shields that created the hull of each warship were changing every second in a random pattern.

"No way we can stop them now," said Dahaleen.

Vance clapped his hands.

"Wait a minute," he said. "Don't you guys have, like, a military?"

Dahaleen blinked at him, and tapped the ends of her first two tentacles together.

"Yes," she said. "We have a military. I'm in it, remember?"

"That's what I'm saying," said Vance. "So why can't you whack these guys before they steal anything?"

Dahaleen looked out at Vance through the clear pane of her encounter suit's helmet and took a deep breath.

"Listen carefully," she said, and floated her massive frame up toward the lander's ceiling. "You do *not* want us to start an interstellar war."

In measured words, the decorated Snaldrialooran starspanner captain recounted the "low lights" of the last few generations, four of which had seen conflict on a scale no one on Earth could imagine.

Even Ixdahan was a bit shocked to hear some parts of Dahaleen's account; he'd always zoned out during History lectures at Gahaldoronek Prep. Equally shocking was her explanation of why no one in his neck of the universe ever mentioned more than the Seven — now Eight — Known Galaxies.

"I'll tell you why," said Dahaleen, as she floated back down. "We're so busy fighting we've turned our backs on exploration."

"Makes me wonder who *is* exploring the rest of the universe," said Lena.

"Yeah" said Vance, "and how much they're gonna charge to let us in … uh … I mean let *you* in."

"Well, you're definitely part of 'us' now," said Cray.

"And now that ... Leek guy … knows where we are," said Lena.

"Knew," said Dahaleen. "We're on the way back to my starspanner now."

Startled, Vance and Lena looked up at Ixdahan, who was lost in thought.

"You knew that already, didn't you?" Lena asked him.

"Here's what I don't know," said Ixdahan, with a shrug of his human shoulders. "How are we going to stop Leek without the element of surprise?"

"Trust me," Cray. "He's *going* to be surprised. Come on Lena, we're heading for Alaska."

"Hold it," said Vance. "What about me? Now that we're out of the time bubble, I can't just walk out on Moms and Dakota ... without saying *something*."

Dahaleen saw that everyone was getting frazzled, so she took command and issued each of them their orders.

Cray and Lena would go to Alaska with the real amphora Ixdahan had q-transferred off the Vrukaari starspanner. Their plan? Hide it in plain sight in the exact location it had been stolen from, a day ago in real time. Jocelyn and the whales, Cray assured Lena, would be able to help.

"Last place his Eminence would think to look," the professor said to Dahaleen, with a wink. "Just give us an hour to prepare, then transfer it down to my basement."

Ixdahan would go with Dahaleen and prepare for their final confrontation with the Vrukaari leader.

"Once he finds out we've tricked him," said Dahaleen, "he's going to lash out. Vance, that's where you come in. You have what you need at home to complete your simulator program?"

Vance nodded, and Ixdahan's eyes grew wide.

"You can't be thinking...." he started.

But as Cray explained, he'd oversee Vance's work and help him adapt the program Vance and Ixdahan had used last year to the environment on Aalthrashrintorb Leek's regal starspanner. By confusing Vrukaari sensors, the simulator would give them a margin of error.

"Dude, it worked before," said Vance. "And Octopus Lady here taught me mad new tricks."

Ixdahan's face turned red.

"Tell me you did *not* just say...." he said.

"Don't forget to feed Arkansas," said Lena as she pushed herself between them. Vance smiled down at her.

"Aww, no worries," he said. "Arky's my boy."

"And you," said Lena. She turned to Ixdahan and squeezed both of his hands. "Do me a favor and don't be a hero."

Ixdahan brought her hands to his lips.

"I may not have a choice, Lena," he said. "But I'll try not to do anything stupider than usual."

"Can't ask for more than that," said Cray. "Come on, it's time to go."

"Promise you'll let me try to reach Callie Ann," said Lena. "I can't let her get … get ... you know what I mean."

Cray promised to help her and, a second later, the members of the lander team were off on their separate journeys. First, Vance used the ominous black disk to return to Skudderton. Then Lena gave Ixdahan a quick hug before she and Cray used a similar device to slip back to Cray's house near the Gulf of Alaska.

That left Ixdahan and Dahaleen alone in the lander, which by now was halfway to the far side of the moon, where Dahaleen's starspanner had stayed hidden since her arrival.

"You think this will work?" Ixdahan asked Dahaleen once the others have gone.

"Don't know," she said. "But the plan does have two things going for it."

Ixdahan plopped himself down into the control console's ergonomic pilot's chair.

"What?" he asked.

"One is Mr. Leek's arrogance," said Dahaleen with a smile. "Sooner or later he'll try something stupid because he thinks he's unstoppable."

"And?" asked Ixdahan.

"The other is your courage," said Dahaleen. "We're going to need them both."

The Snaldrialooran captain turned away to check the readings on the navigation screen. As Ixdahan watched at her, his mother's words revolved in his mind. The adults in his life were risking everything, but risking *his* neck to do it. Still, as he considered the situation at hand — fair or not — he had to agree, his time in the hot seat was coming again. As to his promise to Lena, he couldn't help wondering if he'd made it too soon.

CHAPTER 31

Lena's reentry into real time was a bigger adjustment than before. Reappearing in Professor Cray's living room felt like returning home from a 20-mile hike.

"Tell me this gets easier," she said when her head stopped spinning.

Cray was not optimistic. After her infection with the Vrukaari fungus last year, her mind, he explained, was now an awkward hybrid of human and non-human elements.

"Guess I'm lucky I don't have tentacles by now," she said.

"Unlikely," said the Onkendren. "But, tell me, is your skin any slimier?"

"Don't go there," said Lena with a smile. If she were going to hang out with a gang of aliens, it was good to know they were *people*, too. She could imagine Dad and Rhea liking Professor Cray and accepting him for what he was.

Of course, she wasn't at all sure she knew for herself what he was. But with the urgent business on their agenda, she figured there wasn't time to ask him the 5,000 questions that were racing around in her mind.

"So just ask one of them," said Cray.

"Hate it when you do that," said Lena. "But since you brought it up, tell me why I think you're … different from everyone else."

"Dahaleen and Ixdahan are Snaldrialooran," said Cray with a shrug. "I'm not."

Lena sat down on the professor's futon couch and put her head in her hands.

"That's not what I mean," she said. "And I think you know that."

Cray lowered himself into the Amish bentwood rocking chair to her right.

"So I do," he said. "But here's the problem. We don't have time for the long answer and I doubt the short answer would make any sense to you."

"But can't you tell me … with your mind?" said Lena. "I've talked to Derek that way before."

"Brave," said the professor. "Promise me you'll let me know the moment you feel too tired to go on."

"I can take it," said Lena.

"No. You can't," said Cray. "My mind is different. But let's see how far we get."

Lena's thoughts swelled with what seemed like a swirl of mist as she once again had the sensation of dreaming-yet-not-dreaming that she'd felt on the helicopter, during her visit with Rhikilah the day before.

Now, instead of the professor's living room, she could swear she was on the deck of a catboat cruiser, like the one she and her dad had sailed in every summer for the last few years.

"Over here," she heard the professor say. She turned to her left and saw him leaning against the railing on the opposite side of the deck. "Is this OK?" he asked, as looked out over a clear, calm ocean.

Lena nodded and the Onkendren she knew as Professor Cray told her a winding tale stretching back thousands of years. It included what Ixdahan had already learned about on Vrukaar Prime, from Ciafelipenorg.

What Ixdahan hadn't had a chance to hear was the path the third Onkendren faction had chosen when the Vexelanderan was dismantled.

"Some of us came to see," said Cray, "that as long as we stayed corporeal, the temptation to use the Vexelanderan to serve our selfish needs would always be too strong."

"Can't imagine you doing anything selfish," said Lena.

"You only think that because you're very young," said the professor. "But there's another angle. Sometimes, doing good can have its own selfish motives."

Lena listened, open-mouthed as the Onkendren — how old was this 'man,' she wondered — related one of their earliest attempts to rejigger the outcome of Time and Evolution on a struggling species.

"When our ancestors first encountered the Snaldrialoorans — and this is going back a good 250,000 years — they were a pitiable species: small, fragile and on the verge of extinction," said Cray, as he looked out over the water. "But they showed remarkable intellectual gifts and had already mastered the lower levels of mentallic communication."

Lena gasped as an image of Ixdahan's own ancient ancestors filled her mind.

"So tiny," she said.

"Exactly," said Cray. "And they should have stayed that way, perhaps dying out. Sad, maybe, but their passing would have aligned with the plan the universe had for them."

Yes, the professor asserted to Lena's startled mind, the universe was dynamic, motile — sentient.

"We didn't see that at the time," said the professor. "We were too busy satisfying our own egos — as if to say: *Look at us, we're correcting a tragic evolutionary accident. Isn't that marvelous?*"

It was, in other words, a perfect assignment for the Vexelanderan and, working their device with great skill, they altered the evolutionary path of the Snaldrialoorans. They started with alterations in the flow of space-time itself, then narrowed their focus to the level of the planet's ecosystem.

At first, the results seemed to justify what the Onkendren had done. Over tens of thousands of years, as successive generations of the long-lived Onkendren continued to influence their development, the Snaldrialoorans thrived, grew stronger, larger, and more capable, as their minds expanded to reach a new standard in that sector of space-time.

It was only later — too late to reverse course — that the Onkendren discovered the consequences of their reckless actions.

As they looked out over the galaxies, the Onkendren came across another struggling species, the beings now known as the Vrukaari. Surely, here was another opportunity to further the Onkendren mission.

But on examining the blobby, slimy, stubby-limbed malcontents they found on Vrukaar Prime, they made a horrifying discovery.

"Everything that was wrong with them," said Cray, "every genetic misstep we sought to repair, was the direct result of our earlier tampering to help the Snaldrialoorans."

"Because … because the universe is … is alive?" asked Lena, her mind spinning.

"And because everything in it is interconnected," said the professor. "Our meddling had torn a gash in the evolutionary continuum of life in that galaxy. The Vrukaari paid the price for it. And centuries later, we still can't fully grasp what other damage we may have done to space-time and the life force of the universe."

The state of the Vrukaari caused a massive emotional shockwave that shattered Onkendren society into three factions, as Lena now knew. But unlike the other two factions, Cray told her:

"Mine chose a more radical response to the crisis."

Because they believed no one living in the material world could be trusted with the limitless power to manipulate it, Cray's faction, which included the mysterious Rhikilah, decided to opt out of it.

"We used the Vexelanderan to convert ourselves into pure energy," he explained, "and preserved our minds in the interactive patterns of quantum particles."

"But you're here, now, I see you," said Lena.

"What you see is a sustained mentallic projection," said the Onkendren.

I'll have to take your word for that," said Lena. "No idea what you mean. Can we go now? I'm starting to feel kind of…."

In an instant, the vision faded and Lena awoke to find herself alone on Cray's futon, curled up in an Inuit blanket. When she looked out the one window in her line of sight she saw it was early evening. Startled, she sat up and found a note pinned to the blanket.

> *Off to the whales, with Jocelyn. Back soon.*
> *Sorry if I scared you.*

Lean sat up and realized that "scared" was hardly the word. Now she saw for the first time how monstrous it would be for the Vrukaari to control the Vexelanderan.

"Derek has to hear about this," said Lena. But she couldn't reach him: that peculiar sensation she'd always felt, when trying to contact him from a distance, was missing.

Was Professor Cray holding her back, or was it Aalthrashrintorb Leek? The more Lena thought about it, the more uncertain she became. After all, she wondered, what if the Onkendren still had an agenda of their own?

For the moment, she decided, she was better off playing dumb, as if she hadn't noticed any change in her mind. So until she had more information, it made the most sense to keep her thoughts to herself.

But how do you do that, she wondered, when you're hanging out with a mixed bag of mind-reading aliens?

And yet, knowing Derek, if his mind was being blocked against his will, he *would* find a way to reach her. Lena rose from the futon, switched on the brass floor lamp to its left and looked around for the professor's kitchen. Jocelyn, she knew, didn't eat. But if the professor was merely a projection, he'd hardly need a refrigerator — not *here*, anyway.

Still, Lena's rumbling belly told her it was worth a try. Besides, the kitchen's refrigerator seemed to beckon to her through the open doorway leading out of the living room. She opened it and found a plastic container with a post-it note stuck to it.

Crayfish. Help yourself.

... the note read in scribbly handwriting. Based on the rest of the refrigerator's contents, and a couple of comments the professor made the last time she was here, Lena figured he'd been grocery shopping right along — to keep up appearances and cover his tracks. A smile broke out on her face as she spooned some of the professor's cooking into a casserole dish she found on the kitchen counter and shoved it into the sleek microwave suspended from one of the cabinets.

Callie Ann, Lena remembered, had always hated crayfish.

"I wonder why?" she asked the refrigerator as she searched inside it for something to drink. "Should probably ask her."

That's when she realized that her bad luck in contacting Ixdahan might not extend to her former best friend. She brought her food to the kitchen table, sat down and put her fingers to her temples for no particular reason.

"Callie Ann," she called out with her mind. "It's Lena. Can you hear me?"

And unlike a few minutes ago, Lena began to feel the peculiar sensation she recognized from her other successful mentallic contacts. She might get through after all....

CHAPTER 32

Too bad Lena never got the kind of in-depth training in mentallics that Ixdahan took for granted. Otherwise, she would have known that his mind wasn't being blocked by outside forces.

The real reason she couldn't reach him? Ixdahan had imposed a triply-encoded Privacy Black shield on his mind at the advice of Dahaleen, who'd done the same. In fact, on the bridge of the *Kryldria Valaarn*, more crewmembers were talking outloud on a regular basis than at any time since the Mentallic Plague of nearly 2,700 years before.

Of course, in the airless vacuum inside the ship, Ixdahan could only hear Dahaleen through the radio transmitters built into his humanoid-adapted encounter suit. At the moment, he wished he could turn the transmitter off.

"The news isn't good," said Dahaleen. "Leek and his clones have now taken every Onkendren artifact except one."

That one, Ixdahan knew, was the powder blue Ybitrian soufflé dish still at Daherek Manor.

"We have the last piece heavily guarded," said Ixdahan. "So keeping the Vrukaari from getting it should be no problem."

"I wish I were that confident," said Dahaleen. "How many servants does your father have?"

Ixdahan's throat went dry. As the large Manor was, there were upwards of 15 staff members who kept it in shape for Father's many diplomatic visitors. And that's not counting the craft workers occasionally called in to repair some of the building's more ancient statuary, tapestries or jewelry. Then there was also the annual swarm of personal assistants, whom Pertahru was notorious for firing on a whim.

"Any one of them could betray us," said Dahaleen, "for the right price."

But as Ixdahan pointed out, Group Leader Ishialdrol had put the Manor under his personal protection. So how likely was it, really, that a traitor could sneak by unnoticed?

"We may not know the answer until it's too late," said Dahaleen.

Ixdahan gazed at the stars through a small portal to the left of the ship's navigation console.

Did it really matter, he wondered?

"Once Leek finds out we replaced the amphora he stole from Earth with a fake," he said, "there's not a lot of damage he can do."

Dahaleen stared at him a moment.

"Easy to tell you've never been in the military," she said. "I have two words for you: grudge match."

Ixdahan's eyes opened wide, as he caught the gist of what Captain Altriavahn had said. If the supreme Vrukaari couldn't achieve his primary objective, there could still be plenty of destructive mayhem on the horizon, especially with the new battlefield technology Leek had stolen from the Onkendren.

Fortunately, in the midst of these depressing thoughts, came news from Vance and Cray that the simulator program was ready to run when the time was right. The plan, however, was still risky, as it amounted to lulling Aalthrashrintorb Leek into complacency by flooding his sensors, his mind and the minds of his crew with phony data. That way, unless Leek had operatives monitoring each sector of his massive starspanner non-stop, the supreme Vrukaari would suspect nothing when an away team boarded his ship and tagged each of the Onkendren artifacts for q-transfer to the SSA. And given Leek's disdain for his crew, it was unlikely he'd trust their input if they reported any unusual activity. At the same time, considering who they were dealing with, there was no way to know how long he could be fooled.

But for now, there was reason to believe the simulator might help turn the tide for them. So, satisfied that Dahaleen and Cray's plan had everything covered, Ixdahan decided now would be a good time to catch up on his sleep,.

What he and Dahaleen had both failed to take into account, however, was the hold Aalthrashrintorb Leek still had on Ixdahan's uncle — who was "recovering" at Daherek Manor. As it turned out, Nogerahnal had gotten himself into far greater trouble than the repayment of his massive gambling debts could resolve.

"You said all I had to do was analyze that Onkendren psykrella," Uncle Nogerahnal was saying, just then, to Aalthrashrintorb Leek through a secret secure channel only two beings in the Eight Known Galaxies knew existed.

"But that was then," said Leek. "And you weren't completely forthcoming about the extent of your … difficulties … were you? That changes the equation, my dear fellow."

"But…." Ixdahan's uncle sputtered.

"Consider the consequences," said the supreme Vrukaari, letting an air of dispassionate calm do the work of stirring up Uncle Nogerahnal's fears.

Not that much work was required, because the Distinguished Professor of Advanced Mentallic Technologies at Dephallershken University was currently being blackmailed. Seems some of his most recent research findings were, to put it mildly, a case a flagrant plagiarism.

"Who knew anyone from the Phephthat Region would *dare* to speak up like this," said Nogerahnal.

"Times are changing, Gelundru," said Mr. Leek. "Partly thanks to your Homeworld's continual prattling about equality and sentient rights. Now every *gharnixwahn* with a Level 3 civilization wants his share of ... what is the phrase your Synod keeps repeating?" Leek asked. "Oh yes: *Our common heritage as members of a free universe.*"

"Still I...." Nogerahnal started.

"...which makes it harder to clean up after one's indiscretions, no?" said Leek. "I'm sure you can also see how this impacts the cost of said clean-up, however incrementally."

In the end, because he felt boxed in, Nogerahnal agreed to help Aalthrashrintorb in a particularly delicate matter: the delivery of Pertahru's prized Ybitrian soufflé dish. Sadly, Nogerahnal's ingenious mind was more than capable of crafting a credible excuse for why he should be allowed to examine the Onkendren object close up.

After all, he argued, who knew what secrets the object contained that could be turned against the Vrukaari at a time of crisis? For his part, Group Leader Ishialdrol was suspicious, but only suspicious enough to post a guard outside the door of the Manor's vault while Nogerahnal examined the artifact.

Within minutes of being alone with it, Nogerahnal attached a miniature q-transfer module to the outer surface of the soufflé dish and set the transfer coordinates. He was breathing so hard, he barely noticed the thin stream of Ptlourian swamp darter venom — as it squirted out of the device Leek had sent him, and sealed his fate.

In nanoseconds, the last of the Onkendren objects was whisked away by q-transfer to Aalthrashrintorb Leek's engineering lab. But it was only hours later that Uncle Nogerahnal's lifeless body was found by Ishialdrol's men — slumped over a spherical washstand in one of the 16 guest quarters that ringed the outer perimeter of Daherek Manor.

CHAPTER 33

Callie Ann had been sad to see Blainy go. But he'd said something about being drained, about needing to replenish his energy reserves. Funny how guys talked about themselves, sometimes. What could she do but let him go, except make him promise to come back as soon as he was feeling better?

And honestly? She needed a break from the intense rush of conflicting emotions their reunion called up in her mind. What did it mean, after all, to be talking to a guy brought back from the dead?

She felt her heart sink as she tucked herself into her couch. For, as it finally occurred to her, she'd soon have to choose — between staying on this alien ship with her boyfriend, or returning to life on Earth without him.

"Can't just show up with a dead guy on my arm," she said, remembering the sad funeral with Chad and Mariela Northrop and a few of Blade's cousins crying their eyes out — trying to understand what had happened.

Of course, they'd had no idea. The Snaldrialooran memory block made sure they believed he'd perished in a routine car crash.

"So, what's it going to be?" she asked herself. The sudden realization that the choice wasn't exactly up to her only made matters worse. Mr. Leek, she saw for the first time, had no incentive to send her home.

That is, maybe, unless she found a way to make herself obnoxious. And yet, in the silence of that moment, one thing was clear: An obnoxious Callie Ann would be highly expendable.

"Might as well play along," said Callie Ann. "Maybe I can still work some angle and...."

Wait ... was there a voice in her head?

It sounded fainter than the voices she'd heard ever since arriving here and, yes, it was familiar, a familiar voice from her past, before Blainy. But it couldn't be ... could it...?

"Lena?" whispered Callie Ann.

"Callie Ann!" Lena's voice seemed to ring in her ears like a radio broadcast through headphones. "I know this is kind of weird, but it's actually me."

Callie Ann took a deep breath and considered her options. She could ignore the voice in her head, she could call out for help, or she could give the voice a chance to prove it was really Lena. Due to loneliness and exhaustion, the last option felt like the best option, especially because the other two were still on the table if she changed her mind.

And if it turned out to be one of Mr. Leek's insectoid bodyguards playing a trick on her … well, she'd make sure his boss found out how upset she was about it. Callie Ann hedged her bets.

"OK, I know this can't be you. I totally doubt they have lime Jell-O on your planet," she said, as an image of Lena's favorite desert flashed in her mind.

"Callie Ann, are they treating you OK?" asked Lena.

Callie Ann squinted.

"Who?" she asked. "You mean my swim coach?"

"I mean Aalthrashrintorb Leek," said Lena. "Do you know where you are?"

Lena listened closely as Callie Ann's answers to this and other questions veered from denial to acceptance, like a dinged-up Toyota Corolla with its front end out of alignment.

"And guess what?" she said, "Blainy's here, too."

Lena swallowed hard. Whatever they'd done to convince Callie Ann that the … the *quantum construct*, Professor Cray had called it … was actually Blade Northrop, it was working. Lena couldn't dismiss Callie Ann's faith in the construct without also losing her trust.

"How did he get there?" asked Lena, "Does he have, like, a starship?" If only, she told herself, she could open a tiny logical window in Callie Ann's mind. But again, Callie Ann's answers were vaguer than vague. If she understood the question, she clearly didn't care.

"So do me a favor, OK?" said Lena. after seeing that her gentle reminders of the truth weren't getting through. "Next time you talk to … to Blade, ask him if he knows why Mr. Leek needs a clone army."

"Mr. Leek is a disgusting slime ball," said Callie Ann. "But he promised me Blainy and he delivered. What do I care if …?"

"Callie Ann," said Lena, as she struggled to keep her voice steady and her heart from skipping a beat. "Ask Blade what Mr. Leek plans to do with Earth once he finishes the war he started."

"Why would I…." Callie Ann started.

"Remember the Skudderton Park carousel?" asked Lena.

"Yeah," said Callie Ann with a sigh. "When we were kids. Lotta fun memories."

"Ask Blade if it'll still be there when Mr. Leek is done with … whatever," said Lena.

"What are you saying?" asked Callie Ann. "If you're saying it's wrong for me to see Blainy again, you're crazy. You never liked him, I know that. But he's a better man than that Silvano kid or creepy little Derek."

"Derek is…." Lena started.

"He's the one behind this," said Callie Ann. "If it hadn't been for him, there wouldn't be any aliens on Earth, like the ones who sent me here. And without him, maybe Blainy would still be … be…."

"Callie Ann…." said Lena.

"Leave me alone!" yelled Callie Ann. "I don't know why I listened to you. You can't be real."

"OK, but ask yourself…." said Lena. "... the guy you think is Blade … can *he* seriously be real?"

Feeling like the conversation had nowhere to go but down, Lena closed contact with Callie Ann's mind.

"How did it go?" asked Professor Cray, just back from the Gulf of Alaska with Jocelyn.

"Don't know," said Lena, as she tried to reorient herself to her surroundings. "Maybe I made things worse."

"She's alone on a strange ship," said the professor, "with an expert in mind control. It takes time even for strong minds to break through that kind of thing."

"Time?" said Lena. "Seems like there's no time for anything. I sure don't have time to get ready for college anymore."

"Don't worry," said Cray. "I'd say you've already completed an AP class in Everything."

"Give me a break," said Lena, as she walked over to the big glass doors overlooking the professor's back yard. "If I'm so well educated, how come I still haven't learned how to stay out of trouble?"

"Trouble's a good thing" said the Onkendren. "Without it, life stagnates. Besides, it's practically the definition of learning."

Lena stared at him a moment.

"Maybe that explains it," said Lena.

"Explains?" asked Cray.

"Why Derek ... Ixdahan...seems so different now," said Lena. "You know, stronger, more confident. Like he's ... like he's learned to trust himself more."

"Well *that*...." said the professor. "That's because he has something he didn't have when you first met him."

"What are you talking about?" asked Lena, her face tense.

Cray looked deep into her eyes.

"He has someone he can count on," he said. "Nothing makes a sentient being stronger than that."

CHAPTER 34

In Ixdahan's exhausted dreams, his mind fought madly to assimilate the multiple "out of body" experiences he'd dealt with over the past eight months or so. All things considered, maybe a psychologist *would* say it was natural for Ixdahan to dream of being trapped in a body with a human head, a Vrukaari torso and Snaldrialooran tentacles.

But to the recently transmogged Snaldrialooran, it was terrifying. Lucky for him, he was soon startled awake by a sharp metallic knock on his subconscious.

"Wake up, my Ixdahan," rang Ciafelipenorg's voice in his mind, "there's something urgent you should know."

Although Ixdahan recognized her from her mentallic profile, he was unnerved to see she now projected an image of herself in a humanoid body. Was this a reflection of her true Onkendren appearance, or a shell game, intended to appeal to his...senses? Whatever, it was working, as he found her impossible to ignore.

"We already have a plan to deal with the Vrukaari," he said. "What's so urgent?"

"Someone on your team can't be trusted," said Ciafelipenorg. "It's the one you know as Cray."

Ixdahan felt like he'd been smacked in the gut by the muscular fins of an *elchialanphu* during mating season.

"But he's Onkendren," said Ixdahan, "why would he…."

"I see you never finished scanning the data packet I sent you," said Ciafelipenorg, who somehow managed to look more enticing every second. Experienced as he was in mentallic manipulation, Ixdahan knew she was pushing his buttons and reaching deep into his psyche to find the most seductive possible look. And yet, he still found her irresistible.

"This better be good," he said, as he tried his best to break the hold she had on him.

"Cray belongs to the third faction of the Onkendren," said Ciafelipenorg. "He'll tell you he wants to protect the Vexelanderan. But really, he and Rhikilah and the rest of his faction want it for themselves."

"I ... I can't believe that," said Ixdahan. "His mentallic profile is…."

"…is way more advanced than a Snaldrialooran's," said Ciafelipenorg. "No offense."

Ixdahan pushed back against the assault on his mind.

"But that's so … irrational," he said. "Why would they need it now after … centuries?"

As the alluring Onkendren explained, and Lena already knew, the third group of Onkendren were now pure energy. But no source of energy, she told him, lasts forever.

"So they want the device so they can recharge…and survive?" said Ixdahan.

"And keep it from the rest of us," said Ciafelipenorg. "For their own selfish use."

"But what if they do?" asked Ixdahan. "Can't your faction build another Vexelanderan?"

Ciafelipenorg sighed.

"Oh, my Ixdahan," she said, "if only. But there can never be more than one such device in the universe at once. Were two Vexelanderans to vibrate out of synch for as much as one fragment of a millisecond … it would lead to the collapse of space-time into a small singularity."

"OK," said Ixdahan, "let's say I believe you. How can I possibly…."

"You just need the will to make it happen," said Ciafelipenorg. "Leave the rest to us. When the time comes, open your mind. We'll channel a blast of mentallic energy through you and stop him from stealing the device."

"That sounds … lethal," gulped Ixdahan. And by the way, he wondered, could he survive the blast himself?

"But it's for the greater good," said Ciafelipenorg. "You have to see we can't afford to lose a device that benefits sentient life throughout the universe."

Stunned, Ixdahan found it harder and harder to keep control of his own thoughts. In spite of himself, everything Ciafelipenorg was saying had started to make sense. And yet, there was a counterweight, which pulled against her seductive presence. It was the memory of Lena and Cray talking quietly in his lander back on Earth. The glow of trust in Lena's mind had been unmistakable.

No way Lena believed Professor Cray was being so selfish. With a mentallic technique he'd learned from Pertahru years ago, Ixdahan filled his mind with his memory of Lena, and barely managed to drive out Ciafelipenorg's influence.

"I must have your answer," she said. "Will you help us? I'd rather not have to lose you in this struggle."

"I'll ... give it ... some ... thought," Ixdahan heard himself say, as he cursed his lack of self-control.

And yet the voice persisted.

"I must have your answer," said ... wait ... wasn't that a different voice?

"Breakfast orders must be placed before rotation vector 30," said the voice of AI from the ship's galley. "I must have your answer if you wish to ensure the timely arrival of your morning meal."

Ixdahan sighed and ordered scrambled eggs and toast, in the hope that the limitless data reserves of the Galactic Array had finally caught up with the Earthly menu he suddenly craved. He fell back onto his pillow and struggled to sort out what was real, from what he might have dreamt.

Somewhere, there was an answer. But for the moment, the decision of whom to believe was still out of his grasp.

"Ancient mentality from a Level 9 civilization, or best friend from a Level 2?" he said to himself. Based on his upbringing, the answer was obvious, except for one thing: Lena had never tried to tease him into being her puppet.

Ciafelipenorg was trouble, he decided. Or almost decided. Or ... no she couldn't be ... Or ... time for breakfast....

Ixdahan stopped long enough to dress, then hurried off to the starspanner's expansive galley — where the AI's pathetic attempt to fill his order completely scrambled his appetite. The toast was a soggy mash of indeterminate grains that was nevertheless lightly singed. The eggs? *Sublime Attendant of Gravity's Well,* no one could be expected to eat...that...that slush.

Trouble was, in a human body, there wasn't a lot on the Snaldrialooran menu he could stomach, either. But what was really twisting his gut was the terrible choice Ciafelipenorg had given him: let the Vexelanderan fall into the wrong hands or ... or kill ... no ... there had to be another option.

Hunger gnawing at him, Ixdahan took a chance on some *tyrahlthia* rolls and a glass of water. At last, with a little food in his system, he was able to relax a bit, and it was then that Eneselah's words came back to him.

"Mother's right," he told himself. "I don't *have to* do anything I don't believe in."

But who knew how far he could trust Cray? If 17/Chaarnactral had been there, it would surely have said there was "insufficient data." So Ixdahan's best option, it seemed, was to rely on his instincts.

"Can't make me do anything," he muttered between bites on his last roll. And for a moment, his mind was at ease. But what, he wondered, had Ciafelipenorg meant about preferring not to lose him in the conflict ahead?

CHAPTER 35

Down at the drab University marina, Lena fidgeted with the docking ropes securing the *Whales B. Cray* and cast her eyes out to the horizon.

"Should have been here by now," she mumbled. She hoped no unexpected interference from ... wherever ... would keep Vance from arriving by q-transfer in the next few minutes. Come to think of it, where was Professor Cray? He was also supposed to meet her here, though, technically, the University had cancelled the summer program in light of the ongoing FBI investigation. Naturally, she hadn't quite gotten around to telling Dad and Rhea.

Somehow, Cray had also managed to keep that cancellation, and its cause, out of the national news. So far, only a few people in southeastern Alaska knew about the Vrukaari landers that had ripped through the sky so recently. And most of those, Lena was sure, would be made to feel the story was just another wacky UFO sighting, belched up by drunk college kids after a particularly rowdy night.

As for the FBI agent who had interrogated Cray at the marina, he was struck with a sudden urge to raid Christie's auction houses in New York and Amsterdam, in search of a stolen ancient Greek amphora. Reassigned to desk duty, his delusion of pursuing an "intergalactic heist" faded away after several sessions of psychological counseling — and was forgotten.

"Did you *have to* do that?" Lena asked the professor, when she heard about it. "Must have scared the poor guy to death."

"I'm not proud of myself," said Cray, "but I figured this was a step up from mass hysteria if your people started believing him. That's the thing. Even at my age, I'm forced to make up for the mistakes my ancestors made thousands of years ago — and sometimes, I have no idea what action to take."

Now, a few days later, here Lena was, alone with this terrible secret and a dozen others — with neither Toffel or Dorothea to keep her company. But, as it happened, she didn't particularly want to speak to either of them.

Toffel, she realized, could no longer be trusted and Dorothea ... well, she always had her own agenda in any conversation. It was like she was used to being in charge — and while Lena admired her self-confidence, that didn't make her roommate easy to get close to.

Wait ... what was that sensation, that ... vibration ... through the wooden planks of the marina? Could it be that Vrukaari landers were returning to reclaim the amphora?

"Yo," she heard Vance's voice directly behind her. She whipped around and saw his broad, smiling face sticking out of the passenger window of Cray's emerald-green Outback, as the professor finished pulling up to the marina.

"Changed the coordinates," said Vance, as he climbed out of the car. "I had to ask Prof C a couple more questions before ... ."

But Lena wouldn't let him finish. She was too busy punching him in the stomach.

"You. Could. Have. Called. Me," she said, one word to a fist.

"Cut...cut it...cut it out," gasped Vance, as he pulled away. "I'm sorry. Prof C. said the less we talk on the phone the better."

Lena turned to face Cray who was unloading his car.

"He calls you 'Prof C'?" she asked.

"It's a step up from Octopus Dude, I guess," said the professor, who looked grim. "Come on kids, lighten up. It's go time."

Without any further fuss and bother, the three of them rushed to set up the transmitter array and program module Vance had been working on with Cray since Lena had last seen him.

"Where's Jocelyn?" asked Lena after a minute or two.

"I'm in here," came Jocelyn's voice, seemingly from inside the transmitter array.

"More efficient this way," said Cray, "especially now that we don't have to hide anything."

"Right," said Lena. But while she got the concept, it turned out to be kind of unnerving to think that the girl she'd once taken to be human was now packaged deep inside a jumble of circuits and wires.

Professor Cray, she noticed, took it in stride.

"First line of business, Jossy," he said in the general direction of the transmitter array, "is making contact with the humpbacks."

"They're your own people, Dad," said the transmitter array.

"Yeah, yeah, just do it, please," said Cray and within seconds, Lena could once again hear the whales chattering in her mind.

"*Traahns-hitther Errahy Fhunkshianal,*" they crooned.

"Vance?" said the professor with a glance at the tall, wirehaired boy.

"All set, Prof C, Sir," he said with a bow, and a wink at Lena.

Cray nodded, Vance entered a series of commands on a small laptop and, a moment later, Jocelyn's voice rang out from the transmitter array.

"We're live," she said.

"What now?" asked Lena.

"Now we wait until the others are in place," said Cray, "and then I'll have to leave you."

"What?" asked Vance. "Where … ?"

As Cray explained, in his pure form, traveling the immensity of space-time was as effortless as breathing.

"When they need me," he said, "I'll be there. The two of you will be safe right here."

"Until we're not," said Lena, as her eyes misted over.

"Keep your eyes on the simulator output," Cray said to Vance, "and tell Jocelyn the moment the sensors notice anything slipping out of phase. She'll use the whale's mentallic energy to re-establish balance. Don't try to adjust it on your own."

"Right," said Vance, into the readout on his laptop.

Meanwhile, on the starspanner *Kryldria Valaarn*, nerves were snapping as, one by one, the team sent over by the SSA, including Group Leader Ishialdrol, emerged from a series of gracefully biomorphic Onkendren transmog chambers. Just in case, each team member was wrapped in an encounter suit adapted to their new bodies, and equipped with a micro-mentallic transponder.

"Is this absolutely necessary?" asked Ishialdrol. He stumbled a bit as he tried to master Vrukaari levitation.

At that, Ixdahan slammed his mind shut tight, before even a drop of the sarcasm reverberating through his thoughts could seep out. There was no time now, he decided, for sneering at the Group Leader's discomfort — though Ishialdrol *had* forced him to endure the same sensations for most of the year.

"We've been over this," said Dahaleen. "If the simulator fails, you'll have a better chance of surviving if you can blend into the background."

"Smelling like this?" asked Ishialdrol.

Captain Altriavahn cleared her throat.

"Everybody prepped?" she asked, when the last member of the away team was armed and ready.

"You've been issued a Force 15 mind block unit. Engage it now and we'll begin q-transfer. Once you're aboard the Vrukaari vessel, there will be no communication of any kind until you receive the signal through the unit itself. At that point, you'll be fully visible, so be ready to defend yourselves and the Onkendren components with everything you've got."

"This is it," thought Ixdahan. How he wished he could have spoken to Lena one last time — just in case it was the last time.

"Best make sure it isn't, then," he heard Cray's voice say, a nanosecond before the mind block unit kicked in, which slammed down a wall of mentallic silence he hadn't experienced since the day he was recaptured and brought back to Snaldrialoor from Earth.

What would he have wanted to say, anyway, wondered Ixdahan. Maybe just a few words:

"I love you."

But now, he figured, would not have been the right moment. A statement like that at a time like this would have been way too much pressure for both of them. If he was going to say it, someday, he'd want to do it when they were both on an equal emotional footing.

"I really should say it, though," he told himself. "I have to."

Yet, the next minute, he was forced to put yearning aside, as the q-transfer field engulfed the team, and sent them on the first leg of their journey to Aalthrashrintorb Leek's starspanner. From here on out, Ixdahan decided, his focus had to be totally on the Here and Now.

CHAPTER 36

Aalthrashrintorb Leek hovered a meter or so above the odd assortment of everyday objects he'd collected with the help of the Callie Ann clones, Uncle Nogerahnal and the host of esoteric technologies he'd wrung out of his Onkendren captives. Leek's one regret was that he still hadn't achieved complete dominion over that ancient people.

Some of them were devious enough to qualify as Vrukaari, he noted, despite lacking the courage to strike openly, like true warriors. Leek sneered at his expanded corps of 12 Ybitrian bodyguards.

"Warriors," he said, "not spineless cowards like you." Yet, despite his disdain for them, Leek was now rarely seen unless accompanied by the tall insectoids — each one equipped with an upgraded version of the psykrella.

By now, he reasoned, it hardly mattered what the remaining free Onkendren did. It was time to convert the nine artifacts and reassemble the most advanced piece of technology the universe had ever seen. Surrounding the artifacts was a strike force of Callie Ann clones, which tensed fiercely at the slightest fluctuation of the ship's ventilation system.

"The Vexelanderan," he said grandly, with a swoosh of the shiny indigo cape he'd lately taken to wearing everywhere. But where was that neurotic Onkendren traitor, the double agent who'd agreed to assist him? She *claimed* she had the conversion tech down pat.

"I'm right here, you sense-deprived blob of rotting jelly," said Ciafelipenorg, as she around the corner from the adjacent corridor. At that moment, she looked several hundred years older than the last time she presented herself to Ixdahan. "Just remember, I'm only doing this for the price we agreed on."

"Yes, my dear," said Leek. "Once the device is operational, and I've had a moment to settle a few scores, you and your pretentious little band can choose any corner of the universe to retire to with my full protection."

"And?" insisted Ciafelipenorg.

"And make occasional use of the device," said Leek, "but I warn you, merely for experimental purposes, as it may benefit *my* interests."

"Curse me for trusting you," said the Onkendren, as she took a handheld device from the inside pocket of her flowing, woven gown and held it over each object, starting with a crimson omelet pan recently looted from the Esthusians. She entered a series of commands into the device, and stood back.

In spite of himself, Leek gasped as the omelet pan broadened, thickened, then shot up to six times its height. Now a gleaming trapezoid of some unidentified composite material, its status lights flickered on.

"The spatio-temporal stabilizer," said Ciafelipenorg, "in case you didn't know."

"Fascinating," said Leek. "But cut the chatter. We still have to assemble these pieces."

If the Onkendren were disturbed by his rudeness, it didn't show in her face, as she restored each of the household objects in front of her to their original condition. That is, except the ancient Greek amphora.

"Leek, you idiot," shrieked Ciafelipenorg, "this is supposed to be the transdimensional energy conduit!"

"It's not?" asked Leek, too stunned for his usual pomposity, his heart rate doubling. "What do we do now? Who knows where the real component is? At this point, I'm sure your confederates must be laughing up a storm."

"I had nothing to do with this," said Ciafelipenorg with a voice cold enough to freeze nitrogen solid. "It's the Snaldrialooran captain and that fool from Faction 3. Well, it doesn't matter."

"But, how can you say ... without a power source ... ." sputtered Leek.

Ciafelipenorg held up her hand for silence.

"You short-lifers are so limited," she hissed. "Use your head. Do you think there *might* be another source of energy in the entire universe? Do you?"

And without waiting for an answer, Ciafelipenorg outlined a plan to beam energy from Vrukaar Prime's dwarf star directly into the device.

"We'll need a ship that can convert sunlight into microwave energy," she said. "Can you manage that, you disgusting ball of ... ."

"Enough!" shouted the supreme Vrukaari. "You'll have your ship within rotation vector 045. Until then I'm keeping you under guard."

"So," snapped Ciafelipenorg, "I assume you don't want the hull modifications that are your only hope of success."

Leek shook his head, called off his guards and listened.

When one of Leek's personal assistants had escorted the Onkendren out of the bulkhead, he sank to the floor and sobbed.

"I won't let them," he cried. "I won't let them laugh at the noble Vrukaari race for another rotation. I will have my Vexelanderan. I *will*."

Determined, the supreme Vrukaari pulled himself up to his full height and started issuing commands. Within an hour in Earthly terms, a heavily magclad ship was launched directly at the dwarf star of Vrukaar Prime, equipped with a microwave transmitter aimed at the storage bay housing the Vexelanderan.

"A slight delay," he told himself. "Well within the margin of error."

He took a deep breath and felt his composure returning. It was as he had always said, there was nothing like blind stubbornness to get a job done. And this job *would* be done — even if it meant clawing his own six eyes out one at a time.

CHAPTER 37

Sadly for the Snaldrialooran away team, an hour or so after the supreme Vrukaari was having a melt-down on his starspanner, things were getting equally rocky back on Earth.

"What do you mean you're losing the signal?" asked Vance. "What's up with that?"

"It's the one thing that could possibly go wrong," said Jocelyn from within the transmitter array. "There's seismic activity in the gulf and it's building up fast."

"A freaking earthquake?" said Vance. "Now?"

"This has always been a slightly unstable area," said Jocelyn. "It's our bad luck it's showing its true colors today."

"Can't you ... you know ... compensate?" asked Lena.

"I can," said Jocelyn. "But the whales ... they can't hold their position with the seabed crumbling beneath them."

"Whoa," said Vance, "this is bad. If these readings are right, the team is gonna be right out in the open in, like, five minutes."

"You'd better contact Dahaleen," said Jocelyn. "I've run out of options."

Trouble was, there weren't many steps the Snaldrialooran captain could take, besides twisting her tentacles and sending out the warning signal to the away team, which had already started to drop out of camouflage.

"What?" shouted Aalthrashrintorb Leek. "How...? Well never mind. It doesn't matter how you got here. It only matters that you'll never escape," he said as, with one mind, the strike force of Callie Ann clones guarding the Vexelanderan trained their particle rifles on the SSA away team. "Your weapons, ladies and gentlemen," he added.

Because they'd counted on the element of surprise, the Snaldrialooran away team had brought a minimum of small arms, in order to put less strain on Vance's simulator program. Needless to say, they set their light weapons down with heavy hearts.

"And look," said Leek, who finally noticed Ixdahan. "A return visit from a particularly spoiled Snaldrialooran brat. Really, Group Leader, you need to instill better values in your youth."

Ixdahan and the others stared out at the menacing clones with a fear no doubt enhanced by the psykrellas worn by Leek's Ybitrian bodyguards. Ixdahan glanced at his teammates and noticed Cray seemed unphased by the situation. Life must be so much easier, he decided, when you don't have a body to worry about night and day.

The supreme Vrukaari floated over to the view screen at his right

"It's an honor," said Leek. "An honor for you, I mean, that you're here to witness the start of a new era." He paused to enter a few commands into a nearby console.

Here," he said, "is my answer to the unseemly subterfuge you've resorted to."

Ishialdrol gasped as the main view screen filled with the image of a small space craft heading away from them.

"It's on a direct course for the dwarf star," said Leek. "And when it reaches its destination, in just under rotation vector 015, I'll have every ounce of power I need to start up the Vexelanderan."

Leek looked to his left and shouted:

"Bring the old hag back with a team of technicians and tell her to start assembling it"

What followed was a dismal business as, mentallically suppressed by the Ybitrians' psykrellas, Group Leader Ishialdrol's team sank into despair.

"Push back," Ixdahan heard Cray whisper into his mind.

But in that moment, the sight of Ciafelipenorg directing the assembly of the Vexelanderan made Ixdahan's courage drain away. Hopeless. It was. Hopeless. It was. There was nothing to do but wait for the inevitable. Hopeless. It was....

Who was doing that shouting?

"I gotta do what I gotta do!" yelled a robotic voice at the back of the storage bay. Cray, Ixdahan and the other members of the Snaldrialooran away team twisted their necks to see 17/Chaarnactral's image blazing across every display screen except the main one.

"I've done it, Leek!" the robot's image shouted. "I've severed every mechanical and leptonic connection you had with that ship you just launched — and I'm broadcasting a jamming field against all mentallic transponder frequencies. Now you'll never be able to pilot it into position!"

"Ridiculous," snorted Leek. "The process is fully automated."

"Just as I was about to steer it away with my suit transponder," Ixdahan heard Cray saying. "That robot of yours has broken our last line of defense."

"I don't get it," said Ixdahan. "What difference do mentallic transponder connections make at such short distance?"

"It's the magclad shielding," said Cray. "Ciafelipenorg has infused it with reflectors only a transponder can get through. To stop the ship now we'd need manual override."

"Interesting," said Ixdahan and he pushed himself to the back of the crowd of anxious SSA operatives who, a few hours ago, were some of the toughest agents in the Bureau.

"Dahaleen," he called out through the Galactic Array to the Snaldrialooran ship parked on the far side of Nalthradihaar, Vrukaar Prime's larger moon. "Patch me through to Lena."

CHAPTER 38

Fifteen levels above the drama roiling in the storage bay, Callie Ann clawed at a knot of tangled emotions. For in the midst of dealing with the conflict surrounding the Vexelanderan, Aalthrashrintorb Leek had let his control of the impetuous Earth girl slip.

"What the freak am I doing here?" she asked the quantum construct which, until a moment ago, she had thought of as her beloved boyfriend, brought back to life.

"This is how we can be together, Babe," said Fake Blade. "Ain't that what you want?"

"Sure," said Callie Ann, "but not if it's not ... real. Tell me the truth. You're a machine, right? So you have to tell me the truth. You don't have any choice."

The quantum reconstruction blinked at her.

"I'm not a machine," it said, "but my senses and data streams are patched into a network of devices you would call 'computers'."

"I don't know what the freak you're talking about," said Callie Ann. "but tell me this: Who killed the real Blainy?"

"The Vrukaari," said the construct, "although not directly. Your companion died as a result of a series of complications brought on by exposure to a virus-borne neurotoxin and aggravated by transmogged resuscitation."

"Holy...OK, where did he get this virus thingie?" asked Callie Ann.

"The Vrukaari," said Fake Blade, matter-of-factly. "So, come on, how about a kiss?" he added, leaning toward her.

"Get away from me!" yelled Callie Ann, as she jumped up from the couch and ran into her bedroom.

"Callie Ann," Lena's voice echoed in her head.

"What?" snapped Callie Ann. "Did you call me up to say I Told You So?"

"No way," said Lena, "Are you...?"

"I'm mad angry," said Callie Ann. "That Leek guy and Fake Kepler, they tricked me, and now I'm stuck out here in ... the Land of the Lost or whatever."

"What did you expect? said Lena. "Leek's a Vrukaari."

Callie Ann froze.

"Tell me something," she said, at last. "How are you doing this mind trick of yours?"

"I can't explain it," said Lena, "but you don't need mind tricks if you want to send out a message. The ship has an intercom system. A friend of mine can tell you how to use it."

"Oh yeah," said Callie Ann. "I got a *message*." And within seconds, Dahaleen was guiding Callie Ann to the nearest intercom port.

Meanwhile, down in the storage bay, Ishialdrol was getting tense.

"Can't believe our bad luck," he whispered. "Seismic activity?"

"Don't give up," said Ixdahan. He turned to Cray and said, "Do you think you can still cover me, mentallically?"

"What do you have in mind, Son?" asked Cray.

"I'm going to try something out and I need to be invisible," said Ixdahan.

"Oh, no," said the Onkendren, his eyes widening, "you haven't thought this through."

"Of course I have," snapped Ixdahan. "I'm the only one here who's expendable."

"Not to Lena," said Cray.

Ixdahan shut his eyes tight. He dared not think….

"Are you helping me or not?" he asked. "I'm going for it either way."

Cray shook his head and disappeared. But Ixdahan could still feel him, wafting up above the despairing crowd of captive SSA agents. Leek and Ciafelipenorg, he saw, were now intensely preoccupied with the Onkendren components.

"There's a q-transfer station five meters to your left," He heard Cray whisper in his mind. "Go now and don't look back for any reason."

Ixdahan leapt ahead with his most controlled levitation yet, and used his Vrukaari body to best advantage to reach the q-transfer station in seconds. He took the coordinates from the glowing main view screen, which displayed the ship's progress, entered them into the station's q-transfer coder, closed contact, and was gone.

"Incredible," he said, once he'd materialized inside the second ship — which was now well on the way to the dwarf star that gave its pale light freely to ungrateful Vrukaari. He shielded his six eyes, and used mentallics to find the controls for polarizing every view screen and closing the shutters on the tiny ship's main portals. Comfortable enough to open his eyes again, he now saw his next challenge was the mounting heat.

"I just have a few thousandths of a rotation," he told himself and dashed to the squat main navigation console. If ever he needed a lucky break, it was now. Ixdahan drew on the direct-to-cortex teaching module he'd absorbed during basic SSA training and entered a series of standard Vrukaari command codes. He held his breath.

Nothing.

UNAUTHORIZED ENTRY. ACCESS DENIED.

…the control console flashed in apricot-orange characters. But he refused to give up and tried another combination….

Still nothing. Was it getting hotter already?

When a third and a fourth attempt failed, Ixdahan knew it was time to think outside the box. So he mapped his mind into the advanced metadigital transponder on the ship, which routed it to Dahaleen's vessel and on through the Galactic Array.

"Lena," he called out.

"Derek?" asked Lena, "What is it?"

"Gotta ask you something fast," said Ixdahan. "If you don't know the answer, it's OK."

"So ask," said Lena. "Like my dad says, you've got nothing to lose but your stupidity, right?"

"Think I crossed that threshold already," said Ixdahan. "But here goes. If you were the most egotistical guy in the universe, what would you use as an access code for a secret mission?"

"I'd use my own name," said Lena. "Trust me. I've known a lot of egotistical guys."

Ixdahan swallowed hard.

"Well, I … I hope I wasn't one of them," he said.

And sooner than Lena would have thought possible, the connection went dead. She slumped down on the marina, barely hearing Vance's voice.

"What's up?" asked Vance in a hoarse whisper.

"Don't … don't know," said Lena, "but I think I … I just said goodbye to him forever."

Back on the Vrukaari starspanner, Aalthrashrintorb Leek had the distinct impression that something was wrong.

"Who's monitoring my ship?" he yelled. At once, a harried technician looked up from the Vexelanderan and stared open-mouthed at the main view screen.

"It's veering off course," said the technician. "and I can't override it."

"What?" yelled Leek, whose next thought might have been to issue a blistering stream of murderous commands. Lucky for the universe, he never got the chance.

"Listen up." Callie Ann's voice broke in on everyone's thoughts through the Intercom system. "This is a message for my brave clone soldiers."

"Oh *lahrtrool*," grunted Leek.

"You see that guy with the cape?" said Callie Ann. "He's the jerk who killed Blainy."

And to the astonished eyes of everyone in the room, the Callie Ann clones turned on their heels and pointed their particle rifles straight at Leek.

Without missing a beat, Ishialdrol signaled to his team, who grabbed for their weapons, lunged at the Ybitrian guards and ripped off their psykrellas with terrific force.

"Aalthrashrintorb Leek, you're under arrest," bellowed Ishialdrol, "for the murder of Nogerahnal Gelundru and crimes against the Interstellar Consortium."

"Forget all that," said Cray, satisfied that his disappearance had gone unnoticed. "What about Ixdahan?"

With the exception of the Callie Ann clones, whose attention was fixed on Leek, everyone in the storage bay turned to the main view screen. There they saw the tiny ship Ixdahan had steered off course — in time to keep it from powering up the Vexelanderan. Trouble was, there hadn't been quite enough time to let him escape the dwarf star's searing heat.

"We've lost him!" shouted 17/Chaarnactral, from each of the five view screens it still controlled.

"We owe him a debt of gratitude," said Ishialdrol.

"Ha!" said Aalthrashrintorb Leek. "He was worth 10 times the lot of you. Gratitude? You make me sick."

"Now what do we do?" shrieked Ciafelipenorg.

Cray pointed to the partially completed Vexelanderan.

"You can start," he said, "by tossing that monstrosity into the nearest neutron star."

CHAPTER 39

Everything was moving way too fast now for Lena, as normality seeped back into her days and nights. After a summer-long adrenaline rush of danger, confusion and mixed emotions, were the adults in her life seriously expecting her to settle down?

Worse, she didn't dare explain to Todd and Rhea why she was so jittery. Least of all, that is, her grief over losing Ixdahan.

"I'm taking a few days to say goodbye to my summer friends," she told her dad over Skype.

Well, that was the truth, though saying goodbye to Ixdahan was sadly more metaphoric than saying it to Cray, Jocelyn or Dorothea.

Vance, she knew, was already back in Skudderton. He'd q-transferred to Ixdahan's old house in the Hunter's Wend section of town and stopped just long enough to grab the metadigital transponder — before pedaling home on his Denali.

"Got myself in trouble, too," said Vance, who had called Lena a few hours later.

"You're kidding," said Lena.

"Yeah," said Vance. "Fifteen minutes late for dinner."

"You could have told your mom the truth, I guess," said Lena.

"And make her think I like lying to her?" said Vance. "Anyway, gotta go. Arkansas is asking for the can opener."

Lena, smiled, as she remembered her galumphing fur ball of a friend, until Reality stepped in to remind her....

"I still can't believe it," she told the being she wished she still thought was human.

"Maybe it's not true, then," said Cray. "You have some pretty reliable mentallic skills now. Do you sense him out there?"

"The weird part is," said Lena, "I think I do. But I can't tell if that's only because I want to believe he's not...not...."

"Do yourself a favor, then, and move on," said the Onkendren. "I know I will."

"How am I supposed to do that?" asked Lena. "I can't even get credit for your summer course."

But as Cray explained, she already had. After showing her his grade book, he handed her an iPad.

"But that's not right," said Lena. "I didn't earn that grade."

"Read this over once," he said, and pointed to the e-book he'd uploaded to the iPad. "You'll know everything you would have if the summer had been normal."

"Is this...is this like that direct to cortex learning Derek was always bragging about?" asked Lena.

"Close as I could get with a human brain," said Cray. "Our boy was kind of a showoff, wasn't he?"

Lena tried to suppress a giggle and failed.

"Yeah," she said. "He was a cute kind of obnoxious ... guess I'll never see you again, either."

"You can reach me mentallically anytime," said Cray.

"But what if the Vrukaari...?" Lena started.

"The Snaldrialoorans will force the Interstellar Consortium to monitor their every move," said Cray, "now that Leek's out of the picture."

"That's good, I guess," said Lena, "but it still doesn't make me feel safe."

"As I said," said Cray. "Time to move on. But you can stay here, in this house, as long as you like. I can leave Jocelyn here for a while to keep you company if you want."

Lena shook her head, walked over to the graying Onkendren and gave him a goodbye hug.

"I have to pack," she said through a teary smile. "Rhea tells me Dad wants to get a pilot's license. Somebody's got to talk him out of it before he rips a hole in the sky."

Cray held out a small black disk he'd pulled from a side table in his living room.

"You'll need this to get back to the dorm," he said, as he handed it to her. "See you around in a manner of speaking," and disappeared

Lena looked down at to the q-transfer device the Onkendren had handed her and entered the coordinates she now knew by heart.

"Hope Dorothea....

...won't be there," she heard herself saying, as she reappeared in her dorm room. Lucky for her, Lena's roommate was nowhere in sight. In her place, however, was Rhikilah, somehow dressed in Dorothea's clothes.

"You're...." Lena started.

"Yes," said the fiercely beautiful woman, "I hated to deceive you. But I couldn't leave you to face this totally on your own."

Lena stared down at her Adidas.

"You knew," she said. "You knew what would ... what would happen."

"And I did nothing to stop it," said Rhikilah. "There *was* nothing...."

"Right," said Lena, "it's better when you leave things alone. I wish you'd figured that out sooner."

"Is there anything I can help you with?" asked the ancient woman in Dorothea's clothes.

Lena thought for a minute. Then she remembered her airline ticket, the round trip one she was supposed to have used two days ago.

"Why would you want to rely on such a primitive device, when I can...." said the Onkendren.

"Just stop," said Lena. "Can you fix my ticket or not?"

"OK," said Rhikilah, "but I'm coming with you. It's the least I can do."

Lena sighed. In some ways, she was grateful. On the other hand, it might have been nice to be alone with her thoughts — her own thoughts — for the first time in months.

All the same, the flight home to Newark Airport was kind of informative. For one thing, she found out what happened to Toffel, the Dutch exchange student who'd caused so much trouble. According to Rhikilah, they'd found him shut away in the apartment of his physicist friend, mumbling incoherently about "aliens."

"His physicist friend was a Vrukaari?" asked Lena.

"Well, not originally," said the Onkendren. "They ... replaced him. I gather that's the same tactic they used with your friend's swimming coach ... Mr. Kepler."

As she explained, each of these two men had been found in separate stasis chambers on Leek's starspanner. To cover the aliens' tracks, a different set of implanted memories would be given to each of them — and everyone they normally came in contact with.

Callie Ann's parents, for example, would believe she'd completed her summer training program as planned, and would have no further interest in contacting Kepler. For her part, Callie Ann would only be able to discuss what really happened to her coach with Lena or Vance.

"But what about...?" Lena started.

"The paperwork?" asked Rhikilah, "Nothing's simpler when you can navigate space-time like a busy intersection, especially if you don't have to start from scratch. We simply modeled their experiences on existing records. They both believe they took a week off to travel, and they have digital cameras filled with images to prove it. "

As for Toffel, the Snaldrialoorans had given him an implanted memory of a fascinating summer experience in marine biology. They'd also concocted a glowing recommendation from Professor Cray, which was hand-delivered by Dr. Heidi Lutris, the program chair.

Dr. Lutris, who no longer recalled the FBI's visit to the marina, had also forgotten her poker debt to Professor Cray. But that was something the Onkendren had no trouble shrugging off. Believe it or not, 1,000 bucks doesn't count for much in the interstellar void.

"And the humpbacks?" asked Lena.

Now that they were reawakened, Rhikilah explained, the whales had the option of transmogging back to their original form and returning to Onkendra 4.

The older woman ran her hands through her thick red hair.

"Not one of them wanted to," said Rhikilah. "Apparently, your oceans are a peaceful place to live out one's life."

Yet it was what Rhikilah had to say about Ixdahan that interested Lena the most.

"A mind like that is very resilient," the strikingly beautiful woman said. "You never know what it could have endured."

This, however, was one thought Lena refused to let herself accept. Better to move on, as Cray had suggested, than melt away the rest of her life hoping her strange little, brave little, definitely-boy-friend-material alien would pop back into her life.

"Little he's not," said Rhikilah. "Especially as a Snaldrialooran. But I should probably stay out of your mind."

"You and everybody else in the universe," said Lena, "except maybe him. Though I doubt he'll ever ... call me again."

"Fine," said Rhikilah, "but I don't know if I can stop myself. That's the trouble with reentering the physical world, if only as a projection. You start wanting things."

"Like what?" asked Lena.

"A chance to get involved again," said the Onkendren, her eyes shut tight, "just as before."

"But ... you know better, right?" said Lena. "Professor Cray told me ... about the Vexelanderan...."

"Yes, I know," said Rhikilah, sitting up straighter. "That's why as soon as I get you to the airport, I'll go back where I belong."

CHAPTER 40

At that same moment, on Leek's former starspanner, Callie Ann slammed her palm into the tabletop she shared with Group Leader Ishialdrol.

"How many of them are there, like 5,000?" she asked.

"The correct figure," said the startled security agent, "is closer to 100,000."

"I don't care," she said. "Either you tell me how you plan to take care of them right now, or I'll tell them how to take care of you and your sick little security force."

"The SSA...." Ishialdrol started.

"Couldn't do what one spazzy high school kid could do. Twice," said Callie Ann. "So what's it gonna be?"

With nothing to lose and, to his surprise, the backing of Pertahru Daherek, Ishialdrol arranged for the transfer of the large clone army to the care of the people of Onkendra 4, who promised to help them complete their mental and emotional development and, in time, live as individuals.

For her part, Callie Ann was anxious to get back to Earth, on one condition.

"No way I'm letting you, like, erase my memory this time," she told Ishialdrol. But in the end, it didn't matter. As the Group Leader explained, a second round of tampering with her memory was not in the cards, as it would cause permanent damage.

"We're satisfied with the fact that, were you to tell your story, no one would believe you," he said. That thought was kind of creepy, as she had a vague memory of someone telling Lena that same thing last year.

Creepier still was being q-transferred back to Aunt Meara's apartment in Baltimore. Unlike Lena, Callie Ann found no surprises waiting for her. So after taking a day or two to relax, she bought her bus ticket, packed her things and headed out of town.

GREAT TO BE OFF PLANET SLIME BALL

… she texted Lena, the moment the bus pulled out of the station.

sorry about ur coach

… Lena texted back.

"The guy lost two weeks of his life because those creeps were trying to get to me," thought Callie Ann, as the bus rolled past the backside of dozens of small communities that dotted the route home. "Have to make it count for something."

Lucky for her, the Olympic trials were still a year away. If she went back to coach Roberts at Skudderton High and got some experience in a few showcase competitions, she'd be ready. Now her days of mourning Blainy were over. What had happened to him was horrible but, then again, it was trouble he went looking for.

"Just wish guys were more like swimming," she mumbled. "Something I can count on."

About two weeks later, in Skudderton High, Vance couldn't get too excited about Senior Year. After what he'd been through, it felt nowhere near as special as he'd expected. For him, the highpoint of the school year so far hadn't been the announcement of the planned Senior Trip to Orlando. It had been the news report from Ixdahan's transponder that had entered his mind while he slept:

Transmogged Vrukaari Operatives Apprehended
in Human City of Bahalthimahoor

"Must be the dudes who captured Callie Ann," said Vance. "Guys in Baltimore had aliens walking around and never knew it. I wonder if the SSA team stopped off for some octopus salad?" He snickered.

But his high spirits didn't last. These days, nothing seemed worth picking his head up for. Sure, he could handle his school work and running errands for Moms, but beyond that? What, exactly, was the point — when somewhere out in the universe, for all he knew, another gang of alien nut jobs might be plotting to gobble up more than their fair share of infinity?

That's why he was always glad to hang out with Lena, the one person he knew would understand. But this time, when he sat down next to her in the tropical-themed school cafeteria, he could tell she was feeling the weight of the summer more than usual.

"Thinking about Alien Dude?" asked Vance.

"Tried every trick he taught me, plus a few I picked up from Professor Cray," said Lena, "and I still can't reach him."

"Didn't Prof C say…." Vance started.

"Let's talk about something else," said Lena. "I'll have to ... have to get over it somehow."

"Something else?" asked Vance. "This is on my mind, like, 24/7."

"What about Celia Roberts?" asked Lena with a wink. "You ever going to ask her out?"

"Man, not that again," said Vance. "You know I can't...."

"Come on," said Lena, "you've saved the Earth twice; you've talked to aliens hundreds of times ... what's the big deal about asking Celia out *once*?"

"Oh, yeah, like there's anything more 'alien' than a girl," said Vance, and immediately ducked his head.

"Great attitude," said Lena. "She likes tulips, by the way. And fettuccine alfredo."

"S'all good then," said Vance. "I just need me a Dutch Italian restaurant."

"You're such a *pilaarn*, you know that, don't you?" said Lena.

CHAPTER 41

Thousands of light years away, Chaldraheen Ishialdrol, Group Leader, Intergalactic Security, Khaltreaballoorn Sector, had the sad task of catching up with the last known location of FieldOp 2nd Class Ixdahan Daherek: The tiny probe ship launched by Aalthrashrintorb Leek in a desperate attempt to power up the Vexelanderan.

Expecting the worst, they found nothing, aside from the singed relays and seared optical cables you'd typically find on a ship that had flown so close to a star.

"Nothing to report," said the last of his agents, before q-transferring back to the SSA vessel that brought her there. It was Ishialdrol's turn to leave now, but he lingered a moment and tried to assess everything that had happened since Ixdahan's exile to Earth. He also wondered why so many of those unusual events had revolved around the son of the Homeworld's most prominent diplomat.

Pertahru had been informed of the Vrukaari plot as soon as it became known officially — as well as its consequences for Ixdahan. Now Chaldraheen Ishialdrol faced the difficult duty of informing the boy's mother, Eneselah. Her reaction was not what he expected.

"I hope you cowards are satisfied," she said, and closed mentallic contact almost before he had finished saying the most dreadful sentence he'd uttered in all his years with the Bureau. Her words stung deep, not least because he knew she was right.

But there was no time to linger: his responsibilities were clear. Within minutes, Ishialdrol had q-transferred off the Vrukaari ship for more comfortable surroundings. Next on his agenda was the extradition of Ciafelipenorg to Onkendra 4 — a fate that might have stirred up his sympathy, if she hadn't deserved it so thoroughly.

Now, had he stayed a bit longer, and been more sensitive to the subtler impulses of local mentallic fields, he might have noticed a faint murmur of conversation whispering just out of mindshot.

"You don't have to stay here, you know," spun one thread of the conversation. "We've given you the run of the universe."

"Feels better not to care where I am, not to care about anyone," spun a second thread.

"You don't care about anyone?" asked a third thread.

"Just the...the one person I know I'll never see again," spun the second thread. And when the other two had given up and drifted away from the abandoned ship, the remaining mentallic thread continued:

"It's the only way to keep her safe."

Anybody there to look out the open portals of a ship now well clear of Vrukaar Prime's dwarf star, might have empathized with the second thread's one lasting desire: to be alone, unfettered by time, among the flickering beauty of the infinite stars.

After all, the intricacies of the universe, like the beautiful mind of a trustworthy friend, were more than enough for an eternity of contemplation, lying as they did at the heart of mystery itself.

THE END
of
BOOK TWO OF
THE CHANGING HEARTS OF IXDAHAN DAHEREK

AUTHOR'S NOTE

HEART OF MYSTERY continues the adventures of the teenage Snaldrialooran, Ixdahan Daherek. Profoundly changed by his exile on Earth, he soon faces more menacing threats.

From the start, he's forced to wonder about the ethical limits of intervention. From the course of history to a close friend's affection, what right do we have to promote our own agenda?

As Ixdahan wrestles with this, his galaxy comes under fire. Lucky for him, he has way more confidence about thwarting an evil power broker than I ever had about speaking up in Math class.

When it comes to things less heroic, Ixdahan and I have much more in common. Once, I also wondered how to say "I love you," without the stammering. The surprising secret is that in such awkwardness lies the very truth you need to reach the mystery of love and anything else that matters.

Later in life I was able to learn this without an ounce of the punishment Ixdahan takes for his principles. Wherever in space and time you are, my boy, I hope you believe, as I do, that the results you achieved were worth the sacrifice you made.

Now I ask anyone who has enjoyed this story, to remember that Chickadee Prince Books is a small independent artists' collective. It needs your word of mouth to survive. Please tell a friend and write a review on Amazon and Goodreads.

Mark Laporta
September 2015

PREVIEW OF *MIRROR AT THE HEART OF TIME*
(*The Changing Hearts of Ixdahan Daherek*, Book 3)
Available June 2017

"Keep your eyes on the flames, my children," said the wizened magician, as he waved a pair of gnarled hands over an ornate cauldron. The purplish vessel had been carved out of a *halnaxer* — a species of giant gourd that grew everywhere in the surrounding landscape. Here at an isolated farming cooperative on Mehldreniavek 3, entertainment of this caliber was hard to come by.

"And now!" the magician proclaimed. "You will see what few have witnessed, anywhere in the Known Universe: Total rejuvenation!"

The crowd, gathered in a large striped tent of tightly woven natural fibers, murmured in anxious rhythms. This was the one stunt they'd come to see. The rest? Nothing but phony illusions.

Out of nowhere, music welled up from beneath their feet. Could this ancient gentleman have made the very sod into an orchestra of Esthusian bone flutes? For a people whose knowledge of science and technology was at the lower end of the scale, a question like that wasn't easy to answer with confidence. Not a few of the audience members wondered if it might be the work of spirits.

Now the flames rose and fell in a rapid yet distinct pattern, faster, slower, faster again until the audience could swear the dizzying flicker of light and the eerie hooting of the orchestra had merged into one.

"Emit … Nurt … Kachbah!" the wizard bellowed.

The crowd gasped as a roar of fire, a sea of swirling smoke and blustery gusts of wind arose that rattled the tent frame. Then came silence, crystal clear air and the still flickering flame in its cauldron. With the last wisps of smoke fluttering up to the tent's lopsided peaks, the crowd issued a low, collective sigh.

For there before them, on the edge of the stage, stood a younger version of the performer, no more than 20, dressed in the same, intricately embroidered vestments!

At first, no one dared move, as the newly young magician bowed, oh, so respectfully.

"Has to be a trap door," raged a ragged voice from the tent entrance. "Somebody check the stage so we can kick this liar out of town!"

"You think it's a trick?" asked the young man. "How about *now*?"

For the second time, the crowd gasped as the magician morphed into an exact likeness — down to the muddy boots — of the ragged-voiced man at the tent entrance.

"Anybody want to check the stage?" asked the transformed magician.

"He has the demon in him!" shouted a large woman to the left of the stage. "It's Loahnimanar himself!" Her face turned scarlet, as she shoved her way past the 200 or so bloated humanoids who had packed themselves into the tent for a night's entertainment.

At the sound of the mythical creature's name, dozens more started pressing forward to the tent's entrance.

"We have to get out of here!" they shouted. "The demon has cursed us!"

Within mere minutes the tent was cleared, with the exception of a young boy no older than nine, who stood in what used to be the third row. He wiped his nose on the sleeve of his ragged, woven tunic and ran up to the edge of the stage.

"You're amazing," said the boy. "I want to be just like you."

The magician returned to his original shape: the pale, bearded ancient the audience had paid half a day's wages to see.

"Why?" he asked.

"How did you clear out the whole tent so fast?" the boy asked. "Could you teach me that trick?"

"I … I don't think so," chuckled the magician.

"Oh wait," said the boy, "I already know how."

And in front of the magician's widening eyes, the boy morphed into a tallish humanoid adult with a scruffy salt and pepper beard. He was dressed in khaki pants and an olive green T-shirt that wouldn't have been out of place on many a humanoid planet with a Level 2 civilization.

"Professor Cray?" asked the magician.

"Shinandohr's comet, Ixdahan!" shouted Cray. "Isn't it time we dropped that 'Professor' nonsense?

The magician smacked his forehead and changed shape again — into someone closely resembling the transmogged human appearance of Ixdahan Daherek on his two trips to Earth. Instead of a wizened magician in embroidered robes, he now resembled a young human in a polo shirt and a pair of Levi's 501 jeans.

Incredible. The last time Ixdahan had seen Cray was aboard an immense Vrukaari starspanner. It was right before the young Snaldrialooran had made a rash decision to q-transfer aboard a probe ship headed straight for a dwarf star. By diverting the ship from its trajectory, he'd stopped an interstellar war — but at the cost of his corporeal existence.

Lucky for him, at the last second, something had changed him into a being of pure energy — which saved him from burning up in the star's heat and radiation. Rather than rush back to his family and friends, the shock of it had made him hide away in the wreck of the probe ship, on the fringes of civilization. Until this moment, everyone Ixdahan had known assumed he was gone for good.

In a way, it was partially true.

After all, since his "conversion," everything had changed. Like Cray, Ixdahan could now sustain any mentallic projection almost indefinitely. He no longer needed an Onkendren *psykrella,* the midnight blue choker that doubled as a powerful mind-boosting device.

The only difference was, Cray's people had *chosen* to become incorporeal, thousands of years ago, after their galaxy-shaping experiments had gone horribly wrong. Now what, Ixdahan wondered, did the wise Onkendren want with him after so much time?

"I've been looking for you across half the settled worlds," said Cray. "What were you thinking by hiding out like this?"

For his part, Ixdahan struggled to remember how long ago he'd seen his Onkendren friend. Ever since his conversion, time had become almost meaningless. It was an issue Cray himself had been wrestling with for nearly 1,200 years.

"I thought you knew where ... you mean it wasn't you, who converted me?" asked Ixdahan.

"Wouldn't have to look for you if I did," said the older alien. "Besides, whoever did save you did it remotely — and with no instrumentation anyone could trace. That's way out of my league. Now, can we get out of this ... culture?"

In seconds, the two of them were back out in their natural element — the endless reaches of deep space. In spite of himself, Ixdahan felt a familiar sense of relief, away from the physical limitations of a planet-bound existence.

Here there was room to maneuver and, as he gazed out at a passing meteor, a stark beauty he could find nowhere else. But it wasn't long before Cray snapped him out of his reverie.

"I took the liberty of adjusting their memories," said Cray. "You shouldn't be encouraging belief in magic."

Ixdahan replied in kind to the mentallic communication stream the Onkendren had set up between them.

"It's entertainment," he said. "I usually give the ticket money to the local hospital, or the school … whichever is in worse shape."

"Usually?" asked Cray. "Don't tell me you've made a habit of this."

Ixdahan looked into the mind of the Onkendren and felt his energy levels droop. The truth was, he'd started the magic act out of boredom, and because hanging out as a disembodied version of himself on a burned-out Vrukaari probe ship was a lonely business.

Besides, no matter what Cray thought, the process of working out so many physical effects and mentallic projections had helped him adapt to his new, incorporeal life.

"Keeps me sharp," he said at last. "Not much happening, now that the Vrukaari…."

"Come on, Son," said Cray. "There are better ways to keep busy than playing puppet master with Level 1s, or Level 2s for that matter. You wouldn't try this on Earth."

"Earth would know better," said Ixdahan. If he actually had a spine, it would have stiffened. As it was, the psychic tension brought on by Cray's stern words created a roughly parallel sensation.

"Not if you changed your act," said Cray. "Anyway, that's not important. You have bigger worries now."

"I do?" asked Ixdahan. "I kind of thought we mopped up the bigger worries the day I ended up … like this."

Yet, as the Onkendren explained on their way past the outer edges of a large asteroid field, the mop was out of the janitor's closet again.

9 780692 372463